UNDERSTANDING DESIRE

CLUB DESIRES #2

QUINN WARD

Copyright © 2021 by Quinn Ward

Cover Design by Cover Me, Darling LLC

Edits by AGEdits

All rights reserved.

No part of this book may be reproduced in any form or by any electronic or mechanical means, including information storage and retrieval systems, without written permission from the author, except for the use of brief quotations in a book review.

WELCOME TO ANNANDALE!
FIVE SERIES SET IN ONE KINKY TOWN

These series do have overlap, but can be read in any order.

Marino's - The Marino brothers explore their kinks and sexuality, learning what unconditional love is along the way.

Club 83 - These daddies and boys will work their way into your kinky little heart.

The Lodge - Daddies and their boys find a home away from home at The Lodge.

Talbert Hall - Welcome to the kinkiest residence hall on campus.

Club DeSires - Things are heating up as the back of The Lodge reopens!

1

TANNER

My phone buzzed for, at least, the tenth time since I got out of the shower. I didn't bother checking it to see who was texting me. It would either be Haley, making sure I wasn't running behind, or one of my friends trying to convince me to stay home rather than ring in the new year with my family.

I wished they'd get the hint and quit sending me invites to all the best parties. As much as I dreaded the next three days, I'd be a petty bitch to miss my best friend's wedding just so I could get shitfaced and possibly laid for the first time in too damn long.

It sucked ass that the groom-to-be also happened to be my older, judgmental as hell, brother. I'd never understand what she saw in him, but it was impossible to deny they were totally in fucking love.

Gag.

I mean, good for them and shit, but oh my god, I couldn't think of much worse than standing around listening to everyone say how perfect they were for one another. Deegan and Haley were like royalty, the ones who were going to carry on the family name and give my mother grandchildren.

Knowing my family, they'd then turn to me with their snooty glares, silently judging every damn thing about me. It was their love language or something.

I tried to keep my hand steady while applying my eyeliner. Deegan was going to have a conniption about me wearing makeup, but I didn't give a shit at this point. I wasn't about to change for him, and sometimes makeup felt like war paint when I had to deal with my family.

When I was a teenager, I'd hidden my bag at the bottom of my backpack so I could do my face on the way to school. That hadn't gone over well the day Mom had to pick me up because I'd puked all over the hall when I couldn't make it to the bathroom. After that, she inspected my bag and strictly forbade me from wearing anything that wasn't appropriate for a young man.

So, I hid it until I moved out of their house, and then managed to find a group of friends who accepted me the way I was. I spent as little time as possible with those I shared a genetic bond with, hating the way they made me feel.

Fuck all of them. Seriously. If they didn't like it, I could come home in time to ring in the new year with friends.

Next came mascara that made my lashes look a mile long, and a pop of lip gloss. Nothing too dramatic, just a subtle hint of color that would undoubtedly make my family squirm. This was a daytime look, after all.

If I thought Deegan wouldn't drag me back inside and scrub my face with steel wool, I might have gone a bit further. This little bit should be minimal enough he wouldn't notice until we were on the road.

My roommate stepped into the bathroom as I carefully styled my hair, a steaming cup of coffee outstretched.

"Have I told you lately how much I love you?" I didn't even care that I'd have to reapply my gloss. I cradled the mug, inhaling deeply before taking that first blessed sip. "Let's say screw this whole wedding and run away to Vegas."

He laughed, assuming I was joking. Okay, so I was. Mostly. But not because I didn't love Maverick. It was a damn shame that we were two peas in a pod, and we would never make it as a couple.

"Honey, you couldn't handle me," he quipped. He tipped his glasses down and looked at me over the top of the frames. They were a recent involuntary addition to his wardrobe, and Mav was making the most of it. "You know I'm right."

"Fair enough," I responded. "If only you weren't such a messy little diva. I swear, I had to organize all your shit just so I had room to work in here this morning."

I started tossing makeup into my bag with one hand as I continued guzzling the coffee. It burned my throat on the way down, but I still had to finish my hair, get dressed, and be outside waiting when my brother and the bride-to-be arrived. No way was I subjecting any of us to a Haley and Maverick showdown this early.

He pressed a hand to his chest in mock offense. "As if. Does that mean you're the pot or the kettle? Most of the shit in here is yours. I'm not sure what I'm going to do when I don't have to wrestle you for bathroom time this weekend."

"You're going to miss me, and you know it. But hey, on the bright side, you won't have to compete with all this fabulousness when you're out partying. You should be thanking me for bowing out on one of the biggest nights of the year." I pulled him into a mostly platonic hug, closing my eyes as I thought about how much I wished he would have agreed to go to this damn thing with me.

He'd refused because he knew it would make Haley uncomfortable. I wasn't sure what the deal was between the two of them, and I hadn't asked because I didn't want to be forced to choose between my two besties.

My phone buzzed yet again. "Can you check that while I get dressed? Haley's been chill so far, but I don't want her to turn into a bridezilla right before a three-hour drive." I tossed him my phone and headed to the closet.

"Oh shit," Maverick mumbled.

"What's wrong?" I called back.

"Haley said you need to be ready to go in about fifteen minutes," he warned me as he stepped into my bedroom, phone outstretched and facing me as if I could see the screen.

As tempting as it was to rant to him about what a self-centered piece of shit my brother was, I held back. Mostly. He didn't understand why I wasn't bailing on the wedding since everyone but Haley and her family made me miserable. Given their beef, he didn't think they were enough of a reason for me to put myself through this torture.

And maybe he was right, but when you added on the guilt trip that would follow me into the next two lifetimes from my mother, I truly didn't have a choice. But that didn't mean I was going to rush myself to meet their tightened timeline.

"Screw that. They told me they'd be here at nine o'clock." This had Deegan written all over it. He was the uptight one of that couple, and he probably wanted to get on the road early just in case there was an accident or a freak snowstorm or some shit. Never mind that it was almost January, and we hadn't seen the first snowfall yet. "If they get here before I'm ready to go, they'll just have to wait."

I spun around and the moment I caught a glimpse of Maverick's face, I knew something was wrong. My heart raced, wondering what in the hell was in those messages that had his face looking like he was wearing foundation three shades too light. His anxiety made my gut churn to the point I regretted the little bit of coffee I'd consumed so far.

"What the hell's going on?" I snatched the phone out of his hands. As soon as I read the messages from my brother, my chest tightened.

I scrolled back to the start of the messages. The first two were from Haley, even though it was Deegan's phone number. I could tell by the lack of shitty snark.

6:07am: Hey Tanner. I hate to do this, but do you think you could be ready to go early? We need to get up to the resort.

6:20am: I just tried calling and you didn't answer. I really need you to call me back.

7:00am: *Of course you're not up yet. We have to be on the road by 7:30. If you want to ride with us, let me know.*

And there it was. Funny how he made it sound like I had a choice in the matter. There was a reason I lived in the city. I could get everywhere I needed on public transportation or using a ride-sharing service. And as much as I hated having to do things on Deegan's timeline, carpooling with them was better than having to ride with my—

Oh hell no. If the next message was telling me Mom and Dad were picking me up, I wasn't going. They were the last two people I wanted to be trapped with. Haley would understand. She'd hate me for the rest of her life if her makeup and hair looked like shit in her wedding pictures, but she knew I couldn't be trapped for that long without any way to escape.

8:02am: *You're lucky I got ahold of Ryan. He's going to pick you up. I already texted him your address. He'll be there as soon as his flight lands and he gets his rental.*

Scratch that. This was far worse than listening to my parents nitpick every decision I'd made in my life. I flopped onto the bed, draping an arm over my eyes.

"Does Deegan know what happened?" I shook my head. No one but Maverick knew why I suddenly wished it was my parents picking me up. He was the only person who knew about the single biggest regret of my life.

Well, and Ryan, too, but if he'd told Deegan I couldn't ride with him, it would have raised even more suspicions. And no way in hell would Ryan sully his gleaming reputation by letting anyone know what he'd allowed to happen when he was nearly blackout drunk one night... I wasn't naive enough to believe his silence had been for my benefit.

"If you want, I can drive you up there after work," Maverick offered.

"No, it's fine," I reassured him, even though I wanted to take him up on the offer. "We all knew this would happen eventually. Better to face the music now. It might be better that we'll be stuck in the car for three hours with nothing to do other than ignore one another or address the elephant in the room. Maybe this way things won't be so awkward by the time we get there."

Maverick scoffed. "Yeah. Or maybe you'll get yourself so worked up you won't be able to leave your hotel room the entire weekend. Seriously. You don't have to do this. I know you want to be there for Haley, but you could always text Deegan and tell him you're sick. They couldn't be upset with you for missing the wedding if you woke up this morning puking and with a fever. 'Tis the season, after all."

"No. I'm not willing to subject myself to a lifetime of guilt trips just so I don't have to face him." Ryan had been my brother's best friend since elementary school. The wedding was just the start of having to interact with him for the rest of my life. Down the road, there were bound to be baptisms, birthday parties, and god knew what else.

It was time to grow up and face the mistakes of my past, otherwise Haley would eventually figure out something was going on and she'd slap me for being so stupid. Or for not telling her sooner, but by the time I fucked up, she was head over heels for Deegan and I hadn't wanted to put her in the middle of my drama.

"Okay. But remember what I told you," he conceded, obviously convinced I was an idiot. "If you get up there and the shit gets too deep, you can call me, and I'll come get you. I don't care how late it is, I'm not going to let you suffer alone. That's a shitty way to start the new year."

Maverick sat down next to me, lacing his fingers through mine. Neither of us said anything for a while. He was giving me time to process what was about to happen. The memories of the kid I had been begged me to stay home. The independent, zero-fucks-given man I'd become said it was time to show them all that I wasn't hurt by their shitty opinions.

I leaned my head on Mav's shoulder and he wrapped me in a warm hug. I closed my eyes, remembering that this was what love felt like. It might not be romantic love, but that didn't make it any less valid.

If only things were different. If only there was a way to be with someone as sweet as Mav. But, no, I had to be terminally infatuated with toxic closet cases who'd never be brave enough to give in to their needs. And no one could convince me that wasn't what was going on.

He knew who he was in bed with, and he'd definitely been into it...right up until he woke up the next morning, sober and overcome with regrets. And I'd stupidly allowed myself to believe the sweet things he'd slurred in the middle of the night with his arm holding me captive against his body.

"Okay, babe. As much as I know you don't want to, you need to finish getting dressed if you're going to have any chance of being ready on time." A chill shot down my spine when

Maverick stood. I already missed his warmth and knew it had nothing to do with the temperature in the room. "I'll go downstairs and make you something you can take with you for breakfast if you want."

"Thanks, but no. I'm pretty sure I wouldn't be able to eat anyway." If it wasn't because of the lump in my throat, it would be the churning stomach that left me unable to eat. "I'm going to go over my list again, to make sure everything's packed. You know damn well they're not going to have shit up there if I forget anything, and no way in hell am I using hotel soap and shampoo."

Maverick narrowed his eyes on me. "Don't do anything stupid."

I gave him my best innocent smile as I fluttered my lashes. "Who, me? I would never do anything to purposely make my family as uncomfortable as possible."

He let out an audible sigh. "That's exactly what I'm afraid of." He hugged me again but didn't release me as he stepped back, looking directly into my eyes. "Look, I know you want to prove a point to them but remember that you love Haley. You don't want to do anything to ruin her special day."

"I won't do anything on their wedding day," I promised, making an *X* over my heart. "But the rest of this weekend, I'm going to be me. If they have a problem with it, that's on them."

Maverick released me, shaking his head as he retreated from the bedroom. Once I was alone, I did a quick job repacking. I also tossed aside the comfy jeans and sweatshirts I'd been planning on wearing for the trip into the mountains. It was time for me to show Ryan that I wasn't the pathetic teen who'd cried himself to sleep after making the biggest mistake of my life.

Maybe I could convince myself along with him.

2

RYAN

My mouth went dry the moment I turned the corner and saw Tanner standing at the curb waiting for me. It didn't matter how long it had been since we'd seen one another or how his formerly gangly body had filled out, I'd know that frame anywhere. If part of the familiarity was because I'd stalked him on social media, always zooming in on his face in any pictures Deegan shared, I would never admit it.

He was stunning, his eyes always bright with laughter as he hugged and kissed his friends when they were out dancing. More than a few times, I'd jerked off to images of him wearing skinny jeans and heels, with flowing tops I wanted to feel beneath my fingers.

Deegan always complained about Tanner flaunting his sexuality, but I didn't think that was his plan at all. He was simply trying to be comfortable in his own skin and it showed. I envied him that confidence.

I was proud of him for standing up no matter what his family threw at him, but there was no way I could say that to him without it sounding condescending as fuck. Hell, I'd been the chicken who'd avoided spending time with their family when I knew he'd be there, so I didn't have to face him. I was the one who'd lied to him, letting him think what happened had been one-sided.

And now, I was ten feet away from him and he did *not* look happy to see me.

Not that I could blame him. I'd tried to come up with a plausible excuse for why I couldn't have him riding to the resort with me, but Deegan sounded desperate. Things were a wreck with the accommodations, and Haley insisted on being the one to sort things out. So, I'd sucked it up and lied to my best friend, telling him I'd be happy to pick up his younger brother.

This was going to be the longest drive ever.

I couldn't even count how many times I had considered reaching out to apologize over the last six years. I'd panicked, not because his advances were unwelcome, but because giving in to what he offered would have ruined everything. He had still been a kid, and I'd been jealous of him.

I wished I could've had the same fuck-the-world attitude that he had when it came to my sexuality. But I hadn't then, and, even now, that was a piece of me I left on the other side of the country.

I was fully aware what a coward that made me. And now I had to face my greatest regret. I put the car in park and turned on my hazards because I couldn't pull up to the curb.

Tanner waved me off when I rounded the back of the car to heft his bags into the trunk. He kept his body turned away from me, an obvious *fuck you* move. Rather than fight him, I let him do it himself, closing the trunk as he walked to the passenger side of the car.

"I thought we'd stop for coffee before we get on the road," I told him as I pulled into the flow of traffic.

He shrugged, twisting to look out the window. I supposed I deserved the silent treatment. I'd give him time to throw his tantrum, but I wanted to talk things out before we got to the resort. It was going to be a long weekend if the air between us was icier than the winds blowing down from the mountain tops.

The air inside the car was laced with the strangest combination of woods and vanilla I'd ever smelled. It should be almost sickly sweet, but knowing the scent belonged to him had my body thrumming with low-level arousal every time I caught a whiff. I watched him out of the corner of my eye, wondering who he was so busy texting instead of talking to me. I hated them for getting the attention I wanted.

As we approached the interstate, I pulled into a small, locally owned coffee shop. I wouldn't admit to having looked up places while I waited in line at the car rental counter. Unless something had changed, Tanner despised the large chains, accusing them of trying to undercut small businesses to the point they couldn't survive. It may have been a whim from when he was younger and more idealistic, but I didn't want to do anything that could wind up with me digging an even deeper hole in his eyes.

"Do you want something?" I asked as I pulled up to the drive thru menu.

He blinked a few times, and I caught the smile he quickly schooled. It didn't even bother me that his attention was back on his phone as he said, "I'd take a mocha with an extra shot. Thanks."

"You've got it." I didn't know what most of the drinks on the menu were, so I opted for a large coffee. I hadn't slept last night because, even before Deegan called to ask me to give Tanner a lift to the resort, I'd been trying to figure out how to put the past behind us. Seeing him was an inevitability, but I hadn't been prepared for an extended time alone with him. "Do you want a pastry, too?"

Tanner shrugged. "Yeah, maybe a muffin or something."

I pulled into a parking stall once I had our drinks. Before handing Tanner his muffin, I unwrapped it and placed it on a napkin, ignoring the curious look he gave me. This weekend was going to be one fucking challenge after another. I couldn't coddle Tanner as if he was my boy. He wasn't, no matter how many times I'd wondered if that would be something he was into. But there were certain things I'd learned about myself that weren't easy to turn off.

"Thank you." He made eye contact and his cheeks brightened slightly when our fingers brushed as he took the muffin from me. Food wasn't an instant cure for the tension, but I did feel more relaxed as I watched him pick at his breakfast.

I considered using the time to apologize, but I wanted to savor the peace a bit longer. Plus, it wouldn't earn me any points from Deegan if Tanner stormed off and called his roommate for a ride home before we got outside of city limits.

I watched as Tanner neatly rolled his napkin after he finished eating. I held out my hand for his garbage, leaning closer so I could reach the bag I'd placed behind his seat for trash. He sucked in a quick breath and shivered. "Are you cold?"

Before he had a chance to answer, I grabbed the blanket I'd brought for the flight off the back seat. I'd regretted bringing it because I hadn't used it while I was traveling, but now my more possessive side was glad to give him something that smelled like me.

I draped it over his body, preening a bit when he drew the edge up to his nose. He might be trying to stay pissed off at me, but a guy didn't go around sniffing blankets if they were repulsed by the person it belonged to.

"Why don't you recline your seat and try to take a nap?" I suggested. He looked as tired as I felt, and his family was draining on the best of days. If he was sleep-deprived when we got there, he was bound to snap on someone. "I'll wake you when we stop for lunch."

"Shouldn't we drive straight through? I'm sure there will be a place to grab lunch once we get to the resort." Tanner looked so damn small when he curled up on the seat next to me. I considered it another minor victory that he turned to face me instead of looking at the side of the car.

"I'm not as young as I used to be. I'm going to need to stretch at some point and I thought it would be nice to catch up before we're both pulled in different directions," I explained. Even though I knew a lot about what he'd been up to, I wanted to know more. And by the time we stopped, he'd be rested and I could figure out what I wanted to say to him so he'd understand why I had to leave that morning.

When Tanner rested his hand on the console, it took everything in me to not curl my fingers around his. If I gave into the urge now, I would be setting myself up for rejection. Better to exercise restraint until he consented.

Tanner fell asleep within minutes. Every time he made a soft noise or moved around trying to get comfortable, my attention slipped to him. When his hand reached out and landed on my thigh, I held as still as possible, not wanting him to wake up and freak out.

He was sleeping so soundly that he didn't notice when we pulled into the parking lot of a little diner along a deserted strip of the highway. I turned off the ignition and watched him until I felt the bite of cold air seeping in past the windows.

I shouldn't have, but I couldn't stop myself from combing my fingers through his dark brown hair. It was longer than he'd kept it as a teen. He scrunched his nose when my fingers caught in whatever gel or product he'd used to style it. I leaned in closer. "Time to wake up, sleepyhead."

"No," Tanner mumbled as he tucked the blanket tighter under his chin.

"You're going to get cold if you stay out here," I warned him as I slipped my hand under the blanket and released his seat belt. "Come on, sweetheart."

I cringed as Tanner's eyes shot open. That was a line I shouldn't have fucking crossed. I held my breath, waiting for him to unleash a tirade of expletives that were well-deserved. What I hadn't expected was the look of utter confusion before his expression fell. "Fine. Let's go in and eat."

Fuck. We'd been so close to the right track, and then I'd let my heart and dick take the lead.

3

TANNER

How in the hell could he call me sweetheart as if it was the most normal thing in the world?

I didn't wait around for him to apologize or tell me it had been a mistake. I'd heard that one too many times in my life already. Sue me if I wanted to hold onto the fairy tale that he'd meant what he'd said.

I slammed the car door shut behind me and stormed toward the diner without waiting to see if he was behind me. Unfortunately, I wasn't paying attention and, in my haste to flip the proverbial bird to Ryan and everybody else who told me I needed to tone it down, I hadn't picked the most sensible footwear for winter.

I felt my foot kick out from under me and flailed my arms, praying I didn't break something when I landed. But my ass never reached the ground. Warm arms grabbed me, yanking me upright. I spun around, throwing my arms around Ryan's waist, burying my face in his chest as I tried to catch my breath.

"Look at me, Tanner." Because I also hadn't thought to wear a winter coat since I had no intention of spending any time outside, the heat of Ryan's hands gently rubbing my back seeped through my thin sweater.

Despite the freezing temperatures, my face flushed hot. I shook my head, not wanting to see his amusement with my near accident. I let out a small sob.

"Tanner, are you okay? Look at me, sweetheart." My traitorous heart melted hearing him use the term of endearment again. I was still scared about dredging up the past, but it was hard to stay mad when he was being nothing but kind.

Enough time had passed since the night I'd snuck into his bed that perhaps he had forgiven me for taking advantage of him. Now, it was my turn to forgive him for the way he'd reacted. Looking at it through older, more mature eyes, I could understand how that night might have thrown him for a loop.

I hadn't considered whether the attraction between us was mutual or if he wanted me the way I wanted him. I had been a horny teenager who'd seen a hot guy jerking off and seized the moment. Everything had been amazing for a few hours.

I'd never slept as soundly as I did with his arms wrapped around me. But eventually, the sun came up. The moment I'd felt him tense next to me, I'd known he was about to shatter my world.

It took every bit of energy I had to roll over and face him. I hadn't stuck around long enough to hear anything beyond "last night was a mistake" before I was running away from him as fast as I could. He'd turned me away, and I'd assumed it had been because he was repulsed.

Now, I wasn't so sure.

What if *I* was the one who'd fucked up? What if sticking around to hear why he felt the way he did would have changed everything?

What if he'd been missing me as much as I'd missed him in the six years that had passed?

Ryan hooked a finger under my chin, tipping my head back. "Say something, Tanner. You're starting to freak me out a bit."

"I'm sorry," I whispered. I was sorry for everything. For what I did back then and for the way I treated him this morning. For acting like a spoiled little brat when he was trying to be nice. For almost destroying his friendship with Deegan because I couldn't control my own impulses. For jumping into bed with him without knowing for certain it was what he wanted. For trusting that a drunk man's tongue spoke the truth he couldn't admit to.

Ryan didn't respond right away. He also didn't let go of me as he guided me to the entrance. When I slipped again, his hand was steady at the small of my back, holding me upright. We didn't talk while we waited to be seated.

The waitress rattled off the lunch specials, and Ryan ordered for both of us. That was only mildly irritating, even though I would've snapped if anyone else had dared assume they knew what I wanted. With Ryan, it only made me more curious.

All morning, it felt like he'd been going out of his way to do little things to take care of me. The nicer he was, the shittier I felt. I didn't deserve a man like him.

Ryan waited until the waitress returned with our drinks and left before clearing his throat. "What were you apologizing for earlier?"

I swallowed hard, trying to figure out how many of my transgressions I wanted to lay bare.

"Is it about that night?" he prodded when I didn't answer quick enough. I nodded, sucking my bottom lip between my teeth. The bubblegum lip gloss had long since worn off. I jumped when I felt Ryan's hand on top of mine. "I'm the one who should be apologizing to you. I was heartless and a bit cruel that morning."

"Because you were surprised," I offered. "Most guys would be when they go to bed drunk and wake up with someone's hand on their cock. Part of me knew you weren't all there when I walked in and saw you jerking off, but then you looked right at me, and I let myself believe you wanted me with you. I know that what I did was wrong. I took advantage of you and you have every right to hate me."

"Oh, Tanner," he sighed. His Adam's apple bobbed as he swallowed. "I could never hate you. Was it fucked up? Yes, but you were young, I was drunk, and that's a recipe for bad decisions."

"But you should," I insisted, a bit too loudly. "You didn't ask for it. You didn't tell me you wanted to be with me. Do you know what that means?"

Ryan let out a low growl. Then he spoke, his voice deep and gravelly. "Don't you even say it, Tanner. I hate that you would've thought that for even a second."

"But it's the truth," I argued. Why and how was he letting me off the hook this easily? If the roles were reversed and anyone had climbed into my bed while I was sleeping, Deegan and Ryan would have castrated them. But all of a sudden, because it was the pathetic, lovestruck younger brother, it was okay? Fuck that. "If I had it to do all over again, I wouldn't have touched you."

"Is that because you think it was a mistake or because you didn't enjoy it?" He shifted in his seat and I didn't miss the way he quickly adjusted himself. He was turned on talking about this?

I had to have slipped and hit my head, and I was now in some alternate reality. This couldn't be real life.

My mouth fell open and I gaped at him. He leaned forward, pressing my mouth closed with one finger. I shivered when the back of his finger ghosted across my jaw. "Tell me, Tanner. If not for the way things happened, would you have regrets?"

I nearly blurted out that I would regret that night as long as I lived but I couldn't. Not with the anxious, sad, pleading eyes blinking slowly across the table. If he'd invited me into his bed with more than an unfocused, drunken look, I could have died a happy man. He was the first person I ever fell in love with, even though he'd never even kissed me.

"I'm going to let you in on a little secret," Ryan said as he swirled his spoon around in his coffee mug. He didn't look up as he spoke the words that shattered everything I thought I knew about my life up until this point. "When I woke up and you were next to me, the first thing I felt was happy. It felt like I had to still be dreaming because there was no way that you were actually in the bed next to me. I hated that the night before was hazy because I wasn't sure what was real and what I'd imagined while trying to get off so I could go to sleep. But then I panicked. We were in your parents' basement and you were still a kid—"

"I was seventeen," I corrected him. "That's hardly a kid. And it was less than a month before my eighteenth birthday."

"It doesn't change the fact that you weren't an adult," he insisted. "I wanted to flip you over and bury myself inside of you, but all I could imagine was the look of horror on your brother's face if he walked out and caught us. To this day, I've never even told him I'm gay."

"Because of me?" I rolled my eyes and wished I could slide under the table to get away after making such a stupid comment. I knew better than to think one sloppy, middle of the night blow job could make a guy gay.

"No, sweetheart. As pretty as you are, even you couldn't have made me gay if I was straight." He took a sip of his coffee. The spoon clattered against the edge of the mug when he set it down. "I don't even know why I've kept it a secret this long. I'm not in the closet back east, but whenever I come home, I neatly pack that part of myself in a box and put it on a shelf high in the closet. And it's not even like there's any reason for it other than not wanting to answer questions about why I waited so long to come out. It's easier to pretend to be the guy everybody here thinks they know."

"Why did you wait?" What I really wanted to ask was why I couldn't have been special enough for him to tell. Even if he didn't say anything to Deegan, he knew I was gay. He could have told me. I would have understood, and he wouldn't have had to feel so alone.

Now it was Ryan's turn to blush. He kept his chin tucked against his chest as he glanced up at me through his lashes. "Well, that *is* because of you."

"How in the hell is this my fault?" I'd definitely fallen and hit my head. He wasn't making any sense now.

"You were always so open and honest about who you were. I envied that about you," he admitted. "It wasn't long after you came out that I understood why I didn't react the same way the rest of the guys did when a pretty girl gave them attention. You were the person who made me feel those butterflies in my stomach. I had to be careful whenever you were home so you wouldn't see how hard I got whenever you walked into the room."

My head spun and it was hard to breathe. Ryan Schmidt was sitting across the table from me, telling me that I was the person who made him realize that he was gay.

"The problem was you were still a kid."

"I was seventeen," I repeated, a bit more curtly this time. But I was starting to understand that, from his perspective, my age was a problem to be avoided at all costs.

"Wrong. You were only fifteen the first time I noticed you, and I was nineteen," he corrected me. My mouth fell open and I blinked a few times as I processed what he'd just said. "That was before you started exploring your style and sneaking Haley's makeup when you thought no one was home. You were wearing an oversized red t-shirt and jeans, but I couldn't stop looking at your ass every time you bent down to get something out of the fridge. Do you understand what a mind fuck that is? I could've fucking gone to jail if I'd given in to all the things I wanted to do to you."

We were so engrossed in our conversation, neither of us noticed when the waitress appeared with our lunch. She let out a squeak of surprise. Ryan buried his face in his hands, muttering under his breath about how I was trouble.

"Sorry about that," I apologized to the shocked waitress. "I promise, there's nothing hinky going on here. We're old friends, catching up after not seeing one another for a long time. We're actually on our way to my brother's wedding. He thought it would be a good idea to get married up in the mountains, so now we have to drive all day to get there, and I don't have a car, so Ryan offered to drive me."

I didn't stop rambling until Ryan squeezed my hand. When I looked at him, he winked, and I pursed my lips. He narrowed his eyes and his nostrils flared as he sucked in a sharp breath. That should not have made my dick hard, but he was my Ryan, and simply being close to him and knowing I hadn't destroyed everything turned me on.

"No need to apologize to me, sugar," she reassured me. "You wouldn't believe some of the things I hear around here."

She gave me a wink before quickly leaving us alone.

"So where do we go from here?" I asked in between bites of the chicken club sandwich Ryan ordered for me. It wasn't something I would've ordered on my own, but it was damn tasty.

"I'm not sure there's anywhere to go," he responded sadly. "I'm only in town until the first, and then I'm headed back east."

"Then it sounds to me like we need to make the best of the time we do have," I responded confidently. I was certain he'd wake up and realize this was a horrible idea, but he needed to know I was game for a bit of holiday cheer if he was.

4
RYAN

I WAS ABOUT TO MAKE THE BIGGEST MISTAKE OF MY LIFE. A stronger man would tell Tanner that his brother's wedding —my best friend's wedding— was the wrong place and time for a fling. I'd spent enough time stalking Tanner over the years to know I was a weak, weak man when it came to him.

The last half of our drive to the resort wasn't nearly as painful as the first. I expected Tanner to push for us to have a no-strings-attached fling, but he seemed content to avoid the subject. We caught up the way any old friends would after a prolonged absence.

He asked me what I'd been up to out east and told me about his string of jobs. He claimed he was trying to find himself, but the longer he talked, the more it seemed like he was doing everything possible to shock and annoy his family more than follow his own dreams. I wondered if he ever slowed down long enough to know what he wanted out of life. I may have called him out on that if our time together wasn't limited.

Sleeping with him would be one of the biggest mistakes of my life, and yet, the only thing I feared more was getting on that plane without knowing how his lips tasted when they glistened with lip gloss or what he sounded like as he came.

I didn't want the confused, hazy memory of the way he looked when he first woke up, I wanted that picture to be crystal clear. I wanted to know how he smelled when his body was warm and sweaty from sleeping curled in my arms. Tanner Fincham was an obsession and being near him only made my body twitch with need.

But there was a lot Tanner didn't know about me. No one here knew about the piece of my life that was something I wasn't sure I could turn my back on, not even for a fling. If he was repulsed, I'd deprive myself because Tanner had always been my one who got away. A chance with him would be worth trying to live a vanilla life.

My secret was something I never had to bring up with previous partners. I tended to meet guys at the club whose tastes were similar to mine. And then, when there was a connection, we explored it beyond the boundaries of a single scene.

None of them had ever lasted long and I tried not to read too much into why that was. On the outside, they were all perfect. I gravitated toward men who were tall and slender with dark hair and dark eyes. Their outward appearance might be right but there was always something missing.

Now that I was so close to Tanner again, I knew there wasn't actually one particular thing that was missing, it was everything that made him special. They all shared traits with him, but they were nothing more than crude stand-ins for the man I knew I shouldn't be with.

Tanner's family got on his case for being flighty, but in reality, he was always paying attention, even when you thought he was a million miles away. His insecurity came out in the slump of his shoulders and the dullness in his eyes. Around them, he smiled, but it was as painted on as his makeup when he went out clubbing. He wore cockiness like a layer of protective armor, and it was enough to convince most people.

But when you dug deeper, you could see desperation and longing. He was my weakness, and I could only hope giving in wouldn't bring my world crashing to a halt. I didn't necessarily want to talk to Tanner about this, especially if we were only going to have a couple of days together but, at the same time, I wanted to know if it was something he'd be willing to indulge and explore.

I reached across the console, lacing my fingers with his. When he smiled at me, I lifted his hand to my mouth, kissing each of his fingers before placing our joined hands on my lap.

"I want to tell you something, but I need you to keep an open mind." I held my breath, glancing at him out of the corner of my eyes as I tried to focus on the road in front of me. He nodded, but that wasn't enough. Not for something this important. God, I couldn't remember the last time I'd felt so vulnerable. "I need you to promise you won't judge me."

"If you're about to tell me where you have a pile of bodies buried, please don't," he teased. "I don't want to be complicit in a crime."

He smiled—complete with shimmering eyes—and the tension between us crumbled away. He'd always had a way of doing that. It was hard to be stressed out when Tanner was being a goofball. "I'm sorry. I shouldn't joke if you're trying to be serious."

"No worries," I assured him. "You always were the joker, weren't you? Your brother was so damn serious all the time. You balanced one another out well, even if you drove each other crazy."

Tanner groaned. "Could we not talk about him right now? I was just starting to stop stressing about dealing with my family all weekend."

"We aren't going to be able to completely avoid the subject, but sure, we can hold off if that would make it easier on you," I agreed. It wasn't as easy for me to pretend we were just two guys taking off for a weekend vacation, but I didn't want Tanner upset.

"Not easier, so much as whenever you mention him, I keep waiting for you to tell me we can't do this," he admitted, his voice cracking with ill-disguised anxiety.

"We shouldn't," I pointed out. "But I'm pretty sure that ship already sailed. Don't you think?"

Tanner glanced down at my jeans, which had been tighter than usual ever since he suggested a fling. His tongue peeked out between his plump lips, licking from one corner to the other. The way he shivered when I groaned made me wonder if he was as innocent as I had imagined.

Seeing his reaction bolstered my confidence. "When I'm at home, I'm not the guy everyone here thinks I am."

"I'm going to kick your ass if you tell me you've kept a wife and kids stashed away from us. I'm not that type of boy," he quipped. If I hadn't known he was a master of deflection, I would have been offended by the accusation that really wasn't.

I narrowed my eyes and shook my head. If that was my big secret, people would be upset with me for not introducing them, but it wouldn't create nearly the level of drama I worried about. I was supposed to be straight. Hell, I'd tried to be what was expected of me, but once I was away from the judgmental eyes of everyone who knew me, it was impossible to ignore any longer, and I wasn't only talking about the fact I was gay.

I released his hand long enough to brush my fingers over his cheek. Now that it wasn't forbidden, I never wanted to stop touching him. "No, sweetheart. There's no wife and kids back east. No boyfriend, either," I added before he could make another smart ass comment. "I am pathetically single lately, it seems."

"Saying I'm happy about that would probably make me a dick, wouldn't it?"

I chuckled. "Perhaps, but if you are, then so am I for being relieved you're not with anyone. I always wondered how it would feel when I eventually heard that you'd found a boyfriend. You deserve someone who will take care of you."

His scowl quickly softened but I could tell he was trying to keep his walls up. "Who says I need to be taken care of? I'm more than capable of keeping myself alive."

"I know that," I reassured him, hoping to stave off his tantrum. If there was one thing Tanner hated, it had always been anyone treating him like he was fragile or incompetent. "That doesn't mean you don't deserve someone who will treat you like a prince. You need someone who will encourage you to figure out what you want most out of life and cheer you on as you achieve your dreams."

"If it wasn't for the complications, would you be that guy for me?" Fuck, I was right; this was a mistake. If I hadn't opened Pandora's box, he wouldn't sound so hopeful and sad at the same time.

"Would you want me to be?" The air between us grew heavy and I felt a weight dropping onto my chest with every second he didn't respond. Stupid. I couldn't not know what he was thinking, even if it was going to lead to heartbreak.

"I'm not sure I can answer that without more information." I wanted to praise him, tell him what a good boy he was for not giving me the answer he thought I wanted to hear, but I still needed to be careful until he knew what he'd be agreeing to with me. "After all, you're being cagey and secretive. So why don't you spit it out and we'll see what happens?"

There was no easy way of saying this, so I started rambling, hoping I wasn't making too much of a fool of myself. Maybe a bit more about college and what I'd been up to since moving out east would help him understand more.

"Part of what scared me about that morning was how right everything felt with you," I admitted. "And there were things that I wanted that I knew you wouldn't be ready for."

"You could have asked for my input," he interrupted. I narrowed my eyes and pursed my lips. He folded his hands neatly in his lap. "Sorry. Go ahead."

"Thank you. And I know making that decision for you was upsetting, but I can't lie and tell you I would have done anything differently if I had it to do over again. If you knew the type of things I'm into, you'd understand more why the age difference was such a dealbreaker for me then.

"The year leading up to that day had been life changing for me. I know that sounds cliché, but I mean it." The GPS interrupted with the next series of directions. I glanced at the screen, irritated that I'd waited until we were only fifteen minutes away from the resort to have this conversation.

Even the full drive from the curb outside Tanner's apartment to the resort wouldn't have been enough time to cover everything. "I'll explain more to you later if you want, but I'd really like to get this out while it's just the two of us. Do you think you can let me talk and save your questions and objections until the end?"

"Have you met me?" Tanner scoffed. I shot him a playful glare. "Fine. Is it enough if I say I'll try?"

"That's all I ask." I squeezed his hand before pulling it back to my thigh. There was something comforting about the idea of being connected to him as I went through the short version of the story.

"Your brother and I drifted a bit that school year. He knew that I had been hanging out with a different group of people and he didn't approve, to say the least." I chuckled as I thought about all the shit he said to me when he walked into the apartment we shared and found me spanking my flavor of the week, as he so eloquently put it. "That year, I had still been trying to convince myself I was straight, and for a while, I thought I'd found what was missing. I could never get hard when I was making out with a girl, but the first time one of my new friends took me to a club, I thought I'd found my missing link."

"You really aren't doing anything to help the situation here," Tanner pointed out. He pointed at the GPS. "You're wasting time. That means you're worried about what I'm going to say to whatever this huge revelation is. Just spit it out. I've probably done more than whatever you're worried is going to shock me."

"I sure as hell hope not." Just the thought of Tanner letting anyone blister his pretty ass was enough to make me see red. I had no right, but that was something I wanted to share with him. But who I was went far deeper than that. And there was no delicate way to put a bit of slap and tickle. "Fine. I was the one who said details later, so I'll stick to that. But if you have any questions, I want to hear them before you tell me what a disgusting creep I am."

"Oh sweetie, didn't you know disgusting creeps are my favorite creeps?" he teased.

"I'm being serious here, Tanner," I growled.

"So am I. Just spit it out already," he responded impatiently.

"Fine. Do you know what a Daddy Dom is?" It was hard to keep my eyes on the road rather than drifting to him.

Again, he didn't answer right away, but then Tanner let out a bark of sardonic laughter. "Seriously, that's your big secret? As if anyone who knows you wouldn't be able to figure that out?"

"It's a fair question," I insisted defensively. People who weren't into kink tended to freak out the moment they heard the word *Daddy*, as if it was something filthy and disgusting.

"Let's just say I am far from the innocent boy you walked out on years ago," he informed me. "Why do you think I crushed on you so hard? From the first time I fell down the gay porn rabbit hole, I wanted to find me a hot, brooding guy who'd tell me what to do. The cuddles and other stuff are nice, but there's something about knowing someone cares enough to put you in your place when you screw up. You radiate Daddy vibes, Ryan."

"I didn't walk out," I protested, trying to ignore the rest of what he'd said. "I thought I was doing what was best for both of us. You were seventeen. If I had tried to start that type of relationship with you, it would've just made things even worse."

"Worse for who? Because the way I see it, the only people who matter are the people who are in the relationship, unless you plan on having a 24/7 thing, and even then, I know you well enough to know you'd never do anything outside of consensual spaces. You wouldn't make someone call you Daddy or sit on your lap when you were in public, and you would wait until you got home to punish bad behavior. It's not your nature." Fuck. He really did get it. My stomach flipped and I white-knuckled the steering wheel as I wondered where he'd learned so much. He pressed the palm of his free hand against his groin and licked his lips. His eyelids drooped, and I wanted to ask him what he was thinking about.

"You're right," I conceded. "But I wasn't as clear-headed about things as you seem to be."

"Yeah, well, when you have nothing but time and an active imagination, you learn stuff," he stated flatly.

"Have you ever...been in that type of relationship before?" Just asking the question filled me with bitterness. I didn't want the answer, but I needed to know what I was dealing with.

Tanner tucked his chin to his chest and shook his head, almost as if he was embarrassed by the fact he hadn't. I bit back my pleased retort. "As it turns out, I have issues trusting people, and I'm not stupid enough to think there wouldn't have to be some massive trust happening to give myself to someone like that. So, no, it's stayed firmly in fantasy territory."

I almost made a comment about how he could explore it with someone safe—me—if it was anything more than jerk-off fodder so he'd know what to look for in a Daddy to take care of him, but I couldn't bring myself to say the words. It was painful to even think about Tanner being with someone who wasn't me.

"It's something I don't really let myself think about too much anymore," he continued, pinching his bottom lip as he stared out the window. "It sucks wanting things you can't have."

Somehow, I didn't think he was only talking about someone to look after him. And dammit, I couldn't stop myself.

"I know this isn't ideal, but if you'd like, I could be that for you while I'm here," I offered, hating that there was an expiration date on this thing. "Just to give you a taste."

I counted the passing mile markers as I waited for Tanner's response. Deegan often liked to complain about how impulsive his brother was, but I didn't see it. If anything, Tanner was one of the most cautious, thoughtful people I knew. A lot of guys his age would have agreed to anything as long as it meant getting a dick filling them.

"But it would just be for the weekend, right?" He sniffled, and I realized we were both screwed.

Sadly, it could only be for a few days. For me, it didn't matter how much time we were able to spend together; it would never be enough. We were going to spend the weekend telling ourselves that a few days would be enough, and then we'd have to clean up the wreckage later.

"I fly home the afternoon of the first," I reminded him. I couldn't break my own heart and verbally agree to only having him for a little while. I'd done that in the past, and when I felt myself getting attached, it was this physical ache in my chest. With Tanner, I didn't need time to feel connected to him; he'd always had a special place in my heart.

"And you promise you won't make me do anything freaky when we're in public? I am all for calling you Daddy and whatever else you want to do when we're in private, but if you try ordering my food or cutting it up for me, people might start asking questions."

I jerked the wheel to the right, catching the exit for a small rest area at the last second. I wasn't ready to face people just yet. Once we pulled up in front of the resort, both of us would be busy with our duties for the wedding. I needed a little while longer to ground both of us, to tide us over until we could find a way to be alone.

5

RYAN

"What are you doing? Couldn't hold it a few more minutes?" Tanner teased as I pulled into a parking stall and turned off the car.

I turned in my seat to face him. "Are you serious about wanting to do this? Even though I'm leaving, are you willing to let me take care of you for a few days?"

He nodded, wringing his hands in his lap. I held my breath, giving him time to speak but he seemed unable to form words. He just looked at me with those huge eyes, framed with long lashes, blinking slowly.

"Tell me, Tanner," I insisted. "Do you want me to show you what it's like to have a Daddy?"

His eyes grew wide, his pupils blown. When he reached down to adjust himself, I swatted his hand away. His tongue peeked between his lips. If he were already mine, I'd have to punish him for teasing me.

"I'm waiting, Tanner," I reminded him.

His chest rose and fell with ragged, shallow breaths. "Yes, please. I don't really know what I'm doing. You might have to teach me."

I combed my fingers into the hair at the base of his neck, twisting and yanking him over the console. "There is nothing I like more than showing a beautiful boy how good life can be with a Daddy to take care of him. It's going to be tricky because both of us have obligations once we get to the resort, but maybe it'll be easier for you knowing that you can come to me when it all gets to be too much. Daddy's going to take good care of you."

Tanner whimpered. He fumbled with the buckle on his seatbelt, finally freeing himself before trying to crawl over the console. I cradled the back of his head when he buried his face in the crook of my neck. His body shook, and I wasn't sure if it was from nerves or emotions. I pressed my lips to his hair, closing my eyes and inhaling deeply. He giggled, which got me going.

"Come on, my silly boy. Let's take a walk and talk about a few things." As much as it pained me to do, I pushed him back to his side of the car. He glared at me, his bottom lip sticking out adorably as I opened the door.

He seemed upset that I wouldn't let him kiss me, but I didn't want to be rushed. We'd kiss, but if he wanted me to be in charge, he would have to wait until I was ready to taste him. Or, at least, until I was ready to *admit* how badly I wanted to memorize the flavor of him. I'd wanted it for years now, but he'd been my forbidden fruit.

I quickly got out of the car, shaking out my legs as I rounded to his door. I pulled it open and held out a hand to him. He immediately shivered as a blast of cold air hit him.

"You should have brought a coat with you," I scolded him.

"I didn't think I was going to be spending any time outside," he explained. "I *hate* the cold. Why couldn't they have gotten married on a beach somewhere?"

"Because this is the wedding Haley wanted," I reminded him. I booped the tip of his nose and he giggled again. "When you get married, you can do it wherever you choose, but Haley's probably been planning this since she was a little girl. That means you should have planned better and packed appropriate clothing. You need to take care of yourself."

"I thought that was your job," he quipped. I couldn't bring myself to scold him for being sassy. The idea of caring for him made me feel alive in a way I hadn't felt in a long time. I quickly stripped out of my sweatshirt and handed it to him. He pulled it over his head, gathering the neckline and pulling it up to his nose, inhaling deeply. "It's warm and smells like you."

As soon as he said the words, he pulled the sweatshirt up over his face. I pulled it down, laughing at his adorable blush. "You like being wrapped in something that smells like me?"

He nodded.

"Good. Because I like seeing you in my clothes. Now, let's walk." I slid my hand into his, expecting him to follow my lead, but his feet seemed rooted to the ground.

"What about you? Don't you need a jacket?" He had a valid point. I couldn't chastise him for not taking care of himself and then wind up freezing my ass off.

I grabbed my wool pea coat out of the trunk of the rental car and slipped it on. "Better?"

"Much." He nodded, then grabbed the lapels of my coat, straightening them as he pressed his body to mine. I curled my fingers around his wrists, prying him off me.

I was dying to taste him but once we got started, I couldn't be sure I'd stop. That meant we needed to talk first. I guided him to a path leading toward the woods that had been cleared of this morning's snowfall.

He slid his hand into mine and I gave his fingers a squeeze. He leaned closer, and I sighed, loving how it felt like the tumblers of my heart were falling into place. He was going to unlock what I tried to keep protected, and there wasn't a damn thing I could do about it.

We weren't going to be able to go as far as I would have liked. His choice of footwear was sexy but not the least bit practical. I brushed the snow off a picnic table and sat down, pulling him onto my lap.

He wasn't going to like what I had to say, but it needed to be said. It felt like every time I opened my mouth, I was driving Tanner further away from me. I took a deep breath, needing to get this out, no matter the consequences. "I want you, Tanner. You need to trust me when I say that."

"Why do I feel like there's a but coming here? If you were going to turn me down after all of that, we could have stayed in the car. No reason for both of us to freeze," he grumbled. I could almost see his walls going up. If I screwed up this time, he wouldn't give me a third chance.

"You're right, but I am hoping that both of us are mature enough now to talk things out like adults instead of running. Can you hear me out?" I didn't care how desperate I sounded. I didn't want him giving up on us, even if it was only a temporary thing.

He nodded. I tried to tamp down my frustration when he leaned away from me. "Go ahead."

"This is your brother and Haley's special weekend," I explained to him. "As much as I want you, whatever we do can't take away from them."

"So, you're saying it has to be our dirty little secret?" His lip curled and I felt his fingertips dig into my shoulders through my coat. "I sucked at sneaking around when I was a kid, and it's something I swore I would never do again."

"I get that. And that's why I wanted to talk to you about this before we got to the resort," I told him. His body was stiff, even as he leaned against my chest. It was like cuddling a concrete block. "Again, it feels like I'm saying we have to keep this a secret, but that's not how I see it at all. What I want to do to you, and with you, would never be something that would take place in public. All I'm saying is we need to be cautious."

"And you thought I was going to throw a tantrum about that?" He bristled, turning to face me and scrunching his nose. He always had hated being underestimated.

"No, sweetheart. And honestly, I think it's something I needed to say as much for myself even more than I needed you to hear it," I admitted. I wrapped my arms around his waist, wanting to feel him close to me. "I thought about you so many times over the years, but you were always unattainable. First, because of the age difference, and then because we live on opposite sides of the country. And to top it all off, I know myself well enough to understand I can't turn off my Daddy side. It's who I am."

"And you didn't think I'd want that," he added when I didn't say it. "See, if you'd just talked to me about it, I could have jumped into your arms years ago and we wouldn't be freezing out here."

"Having you in my arms feels even more right than I could've imagined," I admitted, ignoring the jab about the past. He probably wouldn't ever understand how impossible that would have been back then. "Relationships like this can be intense. Because of the level of trust required, things tend to burn fast and hot."

I wouldn't freak him out by telling him how quickly I'd seen friends go from strangers to committed and living together. And in some ways, Tanner and I were completely different from them. Yes, we were just now starting to explore our desires but, on some level, it felt like we'd been dancing closer to this moment since puberty.

He wiggled around on my lap, pressing his ass against my hard erection. "It sucks that you're only going to be here for a few days. I like it fast and hot."

I held him tighter, and he rested his chin on the top of my head. I breathed him in, wishing I could hate the way he made me feel. It wasn't a matter of getting attached, he was already stuck to me, and it was going to hurt like a bitch to rip that apart. "Believe me, sweetheart, I know. And that's one of my biggest reservations about being open to what's between us. I don't want to hurt you because I can't stick around. You deserve so much more than that."

If this had been even a year ago, I would have made statements about how we'd find a way to be together, even if it meant leaving everything I'd built up out east in order to be with him. But now I was settled.

After working jobs I dreaded going to after the honeymoon phase wore off, I was in the final phase of buying into a business I believed in. I was confident enough that I'd found my roots that I'd bought a house. I had everything there... except this beautiful man I never believed I'd have in my arms.

"We'll figure things out as we go," I promised. He didn't need to know I wasn't talking about the next seventy-two hours.

"Is that all you brought me out here for?" He shivered, and I knew it was time to get back to the car. Soon. But there was something else I wanted first...

I lifted Tanner and moved him in front of me, so he was straddling my legs, then pulled down so he sat on my lap facing me. "No, my sweet boy. I had this long speech planned, but you were silly and didn't dress for the weather, so some of it will have to wait until later."

"Leave it to me to mess up plans I didn't know we had." His self-deprecation was one thing I'd love to spank out of him, but that was a job that would take every hour we had together and then some.

"Like you said, you didn't know," I pointed out. I bit my lip as my gaze traveled over his body. "And any other time, I would have loved seeing you dressed like this. I didn't realize it before, but I might have a thing for pretty boys in makeup and sexy shoes."

"I'll have to keep that in mind," he teased. I relaxed knowing he wasn't beating himself up. "So, what else?"

"Under different circumstances, people wouldn't rush into something like this. There would be time for building trust and exploring what each person expected, but we don't have time for that," I explained. "If you're not comfortable with it, you don't have to, but I would like it if, when we are alone, you tried calling me Daddy."

Tanner chewed on his bottom lip. "I... I think I'd like that, too. I want to try, for you... If this is the only chance I have, I might as well get the full experience, right?"

"Do it," I urged, sliding my hands to his shoulder blades and pulling him down so our foreheads pressed together. "Let me hear you say it, sweetheart. Tell me what you want."

Tanner swallowed hard and seemed to be having as difficult a time breathing as I was. He squirmed around, resting his knees on the bench on either side of my hips. He lifted his head and pressed his lips against my forehead. "I wanted to be mad when they told me you were picking me up today but I'm glad it was you now. I want you to show me what it feels like to have a Daddy."

Not quite what I wanted to hear, but we'd get there.

"You understand that means you'll have to follow Daddy's rules or there will be consequences, right?" My hands drifted down his back to his ass. "I know it's hard for you to be around your family, but you're going to be a good boy for me, aren't you?"

"Yes... Daddy," he responded breathlessly.

His entire body shook with need when I decided to push him further. "Remember, good boys get treats. I'd much rather give you rewards than have to punish you for being naughty."

Before he could say another word, I stood without letting him go. Tanner wrapped his legs around my waist, hooking his feet behind me, holding on for dear life as I closed the distance between us. I sealed my mouth over his, coaxing his lips apart with my tongue, sipping up every whimper he gave me. Next time, I wanted him wearing that shiny pink gloss he'd had on earlier, but for now, I savored his unique, undisguised flavor.

I reluctantly set him down and we walked back toward the car. If it had been warmer, I would have loved getting lost in the woods with him, kissing him against a tree, maybe finding a hidden clearing where I could push him to his knees. We'd still do those things, but it would be in the privacy of a warm hotel room. "I have a room of my own because I have a work meeting tomorrow before the wedding. Once we get settled in, come and see me. Bring everything you'll need to get ready for the rehearsal. We have a lot to discuss, and I don't want to rush anything. You'll only be going back to your room when I tell you to."

"Yes, Sir." Tanner gave me a mock salute and I smacked his ass. He startled and yelped, almost rolling his ankle before I caught him.

I held him tight, nipping at his neck before I whispered, "Not Sir. Daddy."

His knees buckled as I opened the door. How in the hell was I supposed to focus on being a good best man to my friend, when all I could think about was the noises his little brother was going to make tonight when I got him alone?

6

TANNER

The moment the resort came into view, I felt my stomach churning. Instead of thinking about what was about to happen, I clenched my eyes shut, desperate to hold on to the memory of Ryan's hands on my ass as he gave me a gift I'd been dreaming of for what felt like forever. I knew he'd be a good kisser, but so soon after he'd asked me to call him Daddy and called me his sweet boy, I was done for. No one could ever reach into my soul the way he did.

I startled when Ryan took my hand. "I've got you, sweetheart. Don't let anything they say get to you."

"Oh, they're going to have plenty to say." I waved a hand over my body. "I shouldn't have worn this today. They're going to give me shit for my makeup and the shoes. Deegan's going to think I did it just to piss him off."

And I had, but now I realized what a petty bitch I had been. Ryan—*Daddy*—was right. This was their weekend, and it was selfish of me to try to ruffle feathers. These were the times I needed someone to guide me. If he'd been my Daddy before now, he would have suggested I find a compromise that wouldn't start a fight.

Ryan pulled to the side of the snow-covered drive, putting the car in park before unbuckling and sliding closer to me. "No matter what they have to say, remember that you agreed to be my boy for the weekend. Daddy is always right, and I think you look beautiful. Unless you packed a whole other wardrobe, there's nothing you can do about what you're wearing at this point, so I don't want you sweating it. I'm here for you, boy."

Boy. It always sounded condescending before, but I shivered at the affection in that simple word. It was a reminder that I was his, if only for a few days. And dammit all if that didn't suck hairy balls.

I closed my eyes tighter, swallowing around the lump in my throat. Ryan had always been perfection in my mind, and I was glad I hadn't explored these desires with anyone else. When he said he was there for me, there were no words to describe the feeling that washed over me. To me, Daddy had always been something you called a guy in bed when they were manhandling you. The reality was different.

Ryan made me feel safe, like I didn't have to hide. I believed he wouldn't let them make me feel bad for being myself.

I didn't have to worry about saying or doing the wrong thing as long as I listened to what he told me to do. And bonus, he'd said good boys get rewards. I was down for a bit of positive reinforcement.

"What are you supposed to say?" Not giving a damn who might see us as they passed, Ryan nibbled my earlobe.

"Because you're new to this, I'll take it easy on you this time. The only correct answer is, thank you, Daddy."

"Thank you...Daddy." It seemed my dick was completely on board with thinking of him that way. I needed to calm down before we got out of the car, otherwise the entire family would have one more thing to hound me about, and I wasn't sure even Ryan could save me from their criticism over a poorly timed erection.

He rewarded me with another kiss, this time slipping a hand under the hem of the sweatshirt he'd loaned me. I didn't want to give it back. If anyone asked about me wearing something that was obviously his, I'd admit to poor planning and tell them he'd taken pity on me. Ryan's palm seared my stomach and had my dick ready to explode.

"Daddy, you have to stop that," I complained, lifting my ass off the seat, desperate to feel his hand around my cock. That was, regretfully, something I'd still never experienced, and I wasn't good about waiting, especially now that I knew I was his. "I don't think there's time for you to get me off before someone notices us sitting here."

"Oh, and you think I'd let you come already?" I shuddered at the gravelly warning in his voice. "You don't touch yourself until I give you permission. You're going to wait until we're alone and I can take my time with you. It's only fair since you already know what I look like."

No, it wasn't fair at all. I knew what he looked like when he was in college. His body had filled out since then, and I'd seen just enough to know his chest had more than a light smattering of hair. I wanted to run my fingers through that hair while I used his pecs as a pillow.

Fuck. I wasn't going to make it until tonight. Ryan pulled away and laughed.

"Stick close to me when we get to the lobby," he reminded me as he pulled up in front of the valet stand. "Once we get our keys from Haley, we'll plan the rest of the day."

"Didn't you make your own reservation?" Haley had taken care of my arrangements, but I figured that was because nobody trusted me to be responsible enough to fend for myself.

Ryan shook his head. "No. Deegan said Haley was taking care of everything for the wedding party and the family."

Must be rough having a nice fat bank account. I managed to keep that thought to myself, just barely. I loved Haley and knew she wasn't the type to flaunt the trust fund she'd never asked for, but sometimes I wondered what it would be like to have that type of cash to throw around.

"Oh. Okay cool. I just hope I'm not bunking with one of the single cousins. That would be torture," I grumbled. Ryan might have somehow gotten a room of his own, but there was no way Deegan would have agreed to the same for me. He thought I was being a drama queen when I said I needed space.

"I'm sure Haley wouldn't do that to you. Remember, she's not just the bride, the two of you have been friends almost as long as Deegan and I."

It was both heart-warming and sad that Ryan understood my issues better than my own brother did. And now I was getting emotional. I didn't have the time or the energy for that right now, so I tried to lighten the mood.

"Not possible. The two of you are old men." I was completely unprepared for the sharp crack of Ryan's palm against my thigh. "Ouch! That hurt, you ass!"

He just laughed as I rubbed the tender muscle. "What did I tell you the correct response was?"

Ryan quirked an eyebrow that made me squirm in my seat. When I didn't answer immediately, he slipped his hand under my sweatshirt again and pinched my nipple. Hard. I moaned, really hating him for teasing me like this.

Shit. He really was a kinky fucker. "Thank you, Daddy. I'm sorry for saying you're old."

He gave my knee a squeeze. "That's a good boy. Once we get some time alone, I'll be sure to reward you for having such good manners."

"Fuuuuck," I groaned as the valet opened my door.

We were whisked inside to where Haley and my mother were lying in wait. As soon as I caught my best friend's gaze, she rushed to my side, enveloping me in the biggest hug ever.

"I'm sorry we couldn't stick around to pick you up this morning. The hotel has everything all screwed up. They lost half the reservations, and I wasn't about to leave your mom alone with them." She gave me a meaningful look and I stifled a laugh.

"Worried they would've canceled your wedding?" I teased as she looped her arm with mine, her hand resting in the crook of my elbow. I caught a flash of the huge diamond solitaire engagement ring. I was one of the few people who knew she didn't like it. She loved my brother, but wished he understood that something so gaudy wasn't her style.

"You say that like it's a joke," she scoffed. "Come on, let's get a drink and you can tell me all about the drive." She wiggled her eyebrows, and I wondered if this had all been set up.

"Haley Jane—"

"Oh no. Don't you middle name me," she scolded. "Something's going on and it's long past time you come clean Tanner Patrick. See, I can do it, too. And before you ask, the hotel really did botch the reservations. But maybe that was the universe's way of stepping in to smack the two of you upside the head..."

How in the hell did she know? No, maybe I didn't want to know. Haley had always been a little scary about sniffing out gossip. Maybe I should have been surprised we kept that stupid night a secret for this long.

I'd have to think quick about what I could say to her that wouldn't create more questions than answers, because Ryan and I had agreed that the past was in the past and neither of us would ever bring it up again. If he forgave me and promised to help me forgive myself, that was all that mattered.

Haley flagged down the bartender and ordered each of us a drink. I glanced over my shoulder, feeling slightly guilty for leaving Ryan to deal with my mother on his own. I shouldn't have worried. He had always been the golden boy. Even though he wasn't her biological child, sometimes I think she forgot that. She had him wrapped in a warm hug, the type mothers should give their sons.

And yet, there was no doubt my mind that when she finally made her way over to say hello to me, it would be with little more than an air hug and criticism. Hell, she'd probably tell me I was turning into an alcoholic for having a drink before evening, even if it was Haley's idea. Haley stopped to say hello to a few people I didn't recognize as she led me to a corner booth.

"So, how was the ride? Did you and Ryan talk about anything interesting?" She slid into the booth and patted the cushion next to her. It was hard to believe she could look so relaxed the day before her wedding when she'd been dealing with last-minute issues. She scowled at me over the rim of her glass, then pouted. "Come on, tell me something good. I've been stuck with your family all week. It's a good thing I love Deegan as much as I do, or you might be an accomplice to a runaway bride at this point."

"There is still time," I pointed out. I doubted Ryan would help her getaway, but Maverick would be in his car before I could even tell him what was going on. Despite whatever had happened between the two of them, he'd be down for helping her escape a lifetime shackled to the more insane part of my family.

Haley elbowed me in the ribs just as I picked up my drink, sending a trail of red splotches down the front of Ryan's gray sweatshirt. "Shit! I'm sorry. Let me go get... Holy shit, Tanner! That's Ryan's. I'm going to get some soda to clean that up, but then you owe me one hell of an explanation."

"It's no big deal," I lied. Wearing anything of his was major, but she was seriously freaking the hell out about me wearing something of his.

"You don't know how much of a lie that is." Haley shook her head as she slid out the other side of the booth.

I buried my head in my hands while I waited for her to get back. Nothing about today was going the way it was supposed to. I hadn't had to suffer through a ride with my brother that would have left me numb to the rest of the family's insults. Ryan didn't hate me, he liked me and wanted to claim me as his boy for the weekend, and that was mind-blowing.

I had wanted to throw my fabulous femininity in everyone's faces, but now I wished I had a pair of comfy Chucks to go with my skinny jeans and Ryan's shirt. But I didn't, and no way could I strut around in a stained shirt.

Haley returned, while I struggled to keep my composure, and immediately started dabbing at the spill. "Deegan has a sweatshirt just like this. It's from some stupid club they were in together. Every time I've grabbed his because I wanted something warm and comfy, he swore there was some stupid ass rule about no one wearing these but the members."

"Why am I not surprised he's the one who took those ridiculous rules seriously?" I bumped into the table at the sound of Ryan's voice. This time, my drink toppled, glass shattering, but the pool of alcohol and juice spilling away from me. I hadn't even taken the first sip and I was already about to be cut off.

Ryan took the rag out of Haley's hand and started dabbing at the stains himself while an employee rushed over to take care of the bigger mess and the broken glass. His fingers grazed along my stomach, the thin sweater I'd worn doing nothing to shield my nerves from feeling every millimeter where our bodies touched. His eyes met mine, and I melted into a puddle at the tenderness in his gaze. It was like he was silently telling me everything was going to be okay.

I thought I'd been on edge before, but there was something dangerously erotic about having his hand drifting over my treasure trail while my best friend sat on the other side of me, pretending to be oblivious.

"Anyway..." she cut in, the way she did when she felt left out. I wasn't doing a great job of being her person-in-waiting, but technically it wasn't time for me to do my thing yet. "Ryan, I don't know if Lillian told you, but there was an issue with the reservations. We're short almost a dozen rooms that I know had been blocked off. I know you'd wanted a room of your own because of your meeting, but—"

"Yes, she told me," Ryan cut her off. His lips were pursed tight. He leaned past me so he could see Haley. "If it won't disrupt your plans too much, Tanner could bunk in with me."

My friend didn't miss a beat. She nearly bounced in her seat as she clapped her hands wildly. "I knew you'd say that. Lillian swore you wouldn't—anyway, that's great news. Housekeeping should have put the itinerary in the room already, and there's a few snacks and drinks in case the two of you get hungry. I know you probably want to get settled in and relax a bit before the rehearsal and dinner tonight."

"Haley, don't," I warned her. I believed her when she said Ryan giving me a ride was a matter of convenience, but this reeked of a set up. When I abruptly turned to her, Ryan rested his hand on my hip. He was the one who said we couldn't flaunt the fact we were more than casual friends, but if he didn't watch it he was going to be the one who outed us.

She batted her big blue eyes at me. "I have no idea what you're talking about, Tanner. I only meant I know you're probably ready for some downtime after the drive. That's all. I swear. And I *never* would assume Ryan's going to insist on you sharing that big bed with him instead of sleeping on the pull-out sofa."

"Mm-hmm." Obviously, Ryan wasn't buying it any more than I was. "It's cute how you still have time to meddle in our lives when your mother-in-law is over there berating the manager."

Haley gasped and I simply shook my head. Mom wouldn't be happy until everything was perfect, or someone ran off in tears. I just hoped she didn't upset Haley before the wedding. I liked to joke about her seeing the light before it was too late, but she'd be heartbroken without my brother. As she scooted out of the booth, I heard her mutter, "Deegan's lucky I love him. That woman could drive a saint to drink."

I laughed and Ryan pursed his lips before wrapping his arms around my waist. The same man who insisted we needed to keep things on the down-low was doing a shitty job keeping his hands to himself. I nearly protested, but whatever I was going to say escaped me when he started kissing the shell of my ear. "Well, that certainly worked out in our favor. I think it's our duty to listen to the bride and go up to the room to…relax. Don't you agree?"

"Uh-huh." My body melted against his as his fingers tickled their way along my stomach. If he suggested naptime, I was going to be one very cranky man.

7

RYAN

I didn't care what Haley said, it was obvious this had been carefully orchestrated once she saw an opening. I would be sure to thank her later because she'd truly gone above and beyond. Tanner's mouth gaped as he walked deeper into our room for the next two nights. Except, it wasn't any old room. It was a suite with a gorgeous view of snowcapped mountains and a gas fireplace beneath a big screen TV in the sitting area. Seeing the jacuzzi in the bathroom had my mind spinning with all the delightfully sinful things I could do to Tanner in there.

Although I didn't expect much time watching movies or anything like that, it would be fun to curl up with my sweet boy's head resting on my shoulder at some point. Maybe we could find a cheesy movie to watch so I could help him relax tonight before the true chaos kicked off in the morning. Rather than dwelling on the limited time we had together, I was committed to making the most of it and filing away those memories for the future.

"I can't believe Haley did this," Tanner remarked as he kicked off his high-heeled shoes. He sighed as he shook out his feet and curled his toes in the plush carpeting. I stepped behind him, wrapping my arms around his waist as I kissed his neck. I couldn't help myself. Now that I had permission to touch him, I didn't want to let go.

"Why do you wear them if they hurt your feet?" It was something I'd always wondered when I saw women suffering for beauty, and it irritated me that it was something expected of them. But for a guy, there wasn't the same societal norm at play.

Tanner spun around in my arms and gave me a devilish smirk. He kissed the corner of my mouth and leaned back. It seemed I wasn't the only one who liked my arms wrapped around him. "Because they make my ass look fabulous."

"That they do," I agreed, gripping his backside and pulling him closer. "But I don't think you need shoes for that. In fact, I'd be willing to bet your ass looks remarkable without you wearing a stitch of clothing."

Tanner barked out a laugh. "That might be one of the cheesiest pickup lines I've ever heard," he teased me. "If you want me naked, all you have to do is ask. Or, I suppose you could demand since you're Daddy and all."

"You make a good point." Without releasing him, I started walking him backward toward the bedroom. Tanner tensed with the first step. "Trust me, sweetheart. I'm not going to let anything happen to you."

I didn't bother turning on a light in the bedroom. I wanted to see him spread out, the light filtering in through the sheer curtains creating a contrast of highlights and shadows over his body. He fell back on the bed with a squeal. I stepped between his legs, flicking open the button on his jeans.

"One of my biggest regrets since the last time I saw you is not telling you how beautiful you are." As I lowered his zipper, I reached up to brush the hair away from his eyes. I peppered his high cheekbones with gentle kisses as my hand slipped inside his waistband. "I don't want to live in the past anymore. Nothing changes if you dwell on your mistakes."

Tanner arched his back, lifting his hips off the bed so I could slide his jeans down. They fell to the floor and I kicked them out of the way. He shivered as I ran my hands along the insides of his legs, carefully pulling down his briefs. They were tiny and purple, but I wondered if he'd be interested in wearing something prettier.

I made a mental note to check out the boutique I'd seen off the lobby, just in case he was up for giving me a sexy fashion show at some point. Hell, maybe I'd find something for him to wear under his clothes as a reminder that I was here for him, even when we weren't together. Tanner's body was even more exquisite than I'd imagined, and it was a shame for him to wrap it in boring cotton briefs, even if they were bikini style.

"I'm still annoyed that you let me go this whole time thinking you freaked out because you didn't want me. You should have talked to me. I know why you didn't, and maybe you're right and I was too young back then, but you should have trusted me. You've known me my whole damned life, Ryan." Tanner hooked his feet around my calves, pulling me closer to the bed until I fell on top of him. I braced myself so I didn't crush him, which left our mouths too close to resist.

While Tanner might be okay with giving up control sometimes, it was clear he'd never be completely submissive. This was a man who knew how to go after what he wanted. He tangled his fingers in my hair, yanking me down until my mouth crashed against his. There was no build up as his tongue forced its way into my mouth. I ground against him and he hissed at the rough fabric of my pants against his bare, tender dick.

"I'm sorry I couldn't tell you why I was so upset. It wasn't fair to you," I apologized as I broke the kiss. I stared into his rich brown eyes, thanking whatever forces in the universe aligned to make it possible for me to have a chance to make things right. "I had myself convinced that wanting you made me a creeper because I have known you for so long."

"You can make it up to me now," he responded breathlessly.

"Oh, I can, can I?" I slipped my hands under the hem of the sweatshirt I'd given him. It killed me to take my time, but Tanner was worth it. He scrunched up his nose, obviously irritated when I slid my body off of him. "I want to make this last."

"But, Ryan," Tanner whined as I flicked a finger over his nipple. "If you keep doing that, I'm going to come before you even touch my dick."

"Wrong," I barked out. I flipped him on to his stomach once he was completely bare and laid my body over his. "First, you don't set the pace. You'll hold back because you want to be good for me."

He whimpered when I bit the base of his neck.

"Second, what are you supposed to call me when it's just us?"

"I'm sorry, Daddy. Please, I'm dying here. You've had me hard all day," he rambled, writhing as I ground my dick against his crease. I hated staying clothed, but I knew as soon as I was naked, I'd want to be inside of him.

"We haven't even been together all day," I reminded him.

"Close enough," he complained. "I thought you said a Daddy's job is to take care of his boy."

"It is," I confirmed.

Tanner shoved a hand between his body and the mattress. "I have something I need you to take care of. It hurts."

"You're going to hurt a lot more if you keep pushing me," I warned him. "I thought I'd get a little payback, first."

"Payback?" His voice cracked and his muscles tensed.

"I don't think it's fair that you got to see and touch me, even though I was too out of it to reciprocate," I explained. I had another idea for helping absolve Tanner of any lingering guilt. If I'd known what he did that night had been eating away at him, I would've addressed it much sooner, no matter how uncomfortable it might have been. I trailed a finger down Tanner's spine. "But maybe I'm the lucky one. You were cute back then, but a little scrawny."

Tanner bucked his hips. "Gee, Daddy, you really know the way to a boy's heart."

I smacked him on the hip. "Come on, sweetheart, you complained all the time about how you couldn't put on any weight no matter how much you ate. But your body has filled out nicely."

I straddled Tanner's legs and scooted back as I began massaging his shoulders. His back arched as my fingers worked the tension out of his upper back. He was still slender, probably always would be, but he was toned. I could stare at his body all day, memorizing every inch of him.

"Please, Ryan," Tanner begged. As much as I wanted to hear him call me Daddy again, I wasn't going to force the issue. It was something new to him, and maybe it was wrong of me to push him into something we wouldn't have time to explore fully, especially when it came to sex. "I need you. Been waiting my whole life for this."

Me too, baby.

Fuck, but I had. He might be younger than me, but he was the person who opened my eyes to my own truth. He was the man every other was measured up to and found lacking. My dick pressed painfully against my zipper and I couldn't wait another second to strip for him. As fun as it would be to prolong things, the sooner we took the edge off, the sooner we could move on to round two. Because, whether it was right this fucking minute or an hour from now, the first time I sunk into his body, I wasn't going to last long.

I eased myself off the bed, dragging my fingers down his back to the swell of his ass. My thumbs dipped into his crease, spreading him, exposing his hole. Every time his muscles clenched, my dick spasmed, urging me ahead.

"Don't leave me," he whimpered, twisting to his side and curling his hand around my wrist. "I'm sorry I forgot. I'll do better."

"Oh baby, I'm not upset with you." His eyes fluttered closed as I cupped his cheek. I pressed a line of gentle kisses from his forehead to his nose, and finally to his mouth. I definitely needed him to put on some gloss for me later so I could finally taste the combination of him with an added layer of sweetness.

I grasped his chin tightly, forcing him to keep eye contact. "I know what I said, but I don't want you worrying about that right now. I want you to have fun. Nothing you do or say will be wrong. Do you understand?"

He nodded, sucking his bottom lip between his teeth. His eyes shone as if he was about to cry. "I want you to have fun, too. And you made it sound like being a Daddy is a huge part of your life. You shouldn't have to change for me."

"I'm not changing," I promised him. Tanner flipped onto his back and licked his lips as I shimmied out of my pants and kicked off my shoes. I debated leaving my shirt on just to tease him, but I wanted to feel his skin against mine. "This is all new for you, and even the best boys need time to get used to the dynamic. For now, we can keep that as something that's outside of bed if that makes things easier for you, okay?"

The words felt like a punch to the gut. Right now, was all we were guaranteed to have together.

"Don't look like that." Tanner slid his palm against mine, tangling our fingers and pulling me on top of him. "We can't change anything about the past or the future. Stay here with me in the present."

"Could you get any more perfect for me?" I kissed my way down his chest, pausing just long enough to flick my tongue over his nipples. Learning what made a new partner lose their mind was always fun, and with Tanner, it was even better. He couldn't hide anything from me. I'd seen every emotion possible cross his features throughout the years, and I could tell he was barely holding onto control. "I'm glad things worked out for me to be the one to give you a ride."

"I'd like a different ride now," Tanner teased. He dug his heels into my ass, holding me tight when I lost my balance and fell on top of him. Our precum combined to slick the way as his hips bucked off the bed, grinding our cocks together. I nearly scolded him until I realized this was how things were supposed to be for our first time. Both of us on even footing, with the promise of more later. "When I was younger, I wished it could be you. I thought about you when I jerked off. I knew that you wouldn't treat me like I was fragile, but you'd also make sure I was taken care of."

"I'll *always* protect you," I promised, even though I had no business making such declarations. I wiggled my way down his body again, kissing my way around the head of his cock without touching it. He whined as he threaded his fingers in my hair, trying to get my lips around his shaft.

"I'm not going to last long," he ground out. "Want you inside of me when I come."

"You'll have me." I hooked my arms behind Tanner's knees, spreading him wide for me. I stared down at him, committing the sight of his body spread out for me to memory. After this weekend, this was the image I'd recall when I got off. As I dropped to my knees and tugged him to the edge of the mattress, I kissed my way up his inner thighs. "But I know you did more than sneak into bed next to me that night, didn't you? I thought it was a dream at the time, but you touched me."

I dragged a finger along his hip, stopping short of where I knew he was desperate to feel me. Tanner clenched his eyes shut and nodded. I'd give him what he wanted, but first, I was going to play with him just a bit. An idea formed in my mind, but I still wasn't sure he'd be willing to go that far...

8

TANNER

"Tell me, Tanner," Ryan insisted. "I want to know exactly what you did to me."

Oh god, I couldn't admit to this. Goosebumps broke out across my entire body as Ryan kissed and licked and caressed every inch of my exposed skin.

"Did you climb into my bed that night wanting to seduce me?" he asked, his voice lower than I'd ever heard it before. He pressed his chest against my groin, glaring at me when I started grinding against him.

I couldn't help it. I'd been on the verge of coming in my pants since the first time he'd kissed me at the rest area, and now I had the worst case of blue balls ever. He kept getting me close and then backing off. This was his payback for that night, I just knew it.

"No," I insisted. "It wasn't going to be like that. All I wanted to do was lay next to you for a while. That probably sounds stupid, but it's the truth. I don't know why I couldn't stop myself that night. I climbed into bed next to you and watched you slowly stroking yourself. You passed out, and I told myself I'd only stay a couple of minutes. Then, you rolled over and started kissing my neck." At the time, I had tried easing my way out from under him, wanting to escape before he woke up and realized that it was me he was in bed with instead of some random hookup. "You wrapped me up in your arms and I couldn't go anywhere. I was scared to death because I knew you were going to wake up and you'd be mad at me."

"Oh, sweetheart." He kissed his way down the center of my chest again. I would have reminded him that was not the way to get me off, but I didn't want to do anything that might make him stop. Based on the little bits he'd told me about his experience in the kink community, I could see him thinking it would be fun to make me suffer through dinner with my family, if only so he could reward me if I was his good boy. "I'm sorry you felt that way."

"But I wasn't wrong, was I?" I pointed out. The next morning, he woke up and told me we couldn't let anyone know what had happened. He wanted to pretend like I'd never given him a middle of the night hand job that had him writhing in his drunken state, calling out my name. "I'll never forget the look on your face that morning. You were horrified when you found me in the bed. You couldn't get up and dressed fast enough."

"That's not because I was upset with you," he clarified. "No one knew I was gay back then. Hell, no one even suspected I might be bisexual. I couldn't let them find out like that. And I couldn't have you see how badly I wanted you. It was never a secret that you had a crush on me, and I'm sorry I made you feel like a fool because of it. There was never a time when I didn't want to be with you."

"Yeah, I'm kind of starting to understand that now," I scoffed. "But what was I supposed to think back then? Anyway... I thought we weren't talking about that right now."

I spread my legs wider, grabbing my legs behind my knees so I could hold myself open for him. He leaned in, burying his nose against my balls. Because he hadn't told me I couldn't touch myself, I curled my fingers loosely around my shaft and started stroking as I stared at him, silently daring him to make the next move.

"You smell so damn good." He leaned back never breaking eye contact as he fumbled around with something out of my line of sight.

Bile churned in my stomach when he held up a packet of lube and a condom between two fingers. I wasn't going to think too hard about where those came from or why he had them close at hand. It sure as shit couldn't have been because he planned on fucking his best friend's little brother when they were coincidently forced to share a hotel room.

No, he kept supplies handy for when he found a compliant, pretty boy at the bar and took him wherever someone like Ryan took his hookups. I pushed thoughts of any other boy out of my head. Today, there was only room for two of us in this suite. I grabbed one leg with the hand that wasn't in use and displayed myself wider for him, flexing my ass a couple times.

"Are you still trying to teach me a lesson or are you going to do something with those?" I teased. I let go of my dick, sucking two fingers into my mouth. He was transfixed as I circled my tongue around the digits, slicking them up. If he didn't put something in my ass pretty soon, I'd take care of it on my own. Maybe he'd wind up punishing me for getting off without his permission.

Finally, he yanked my hand away from my mouth. "You are such a brat. Maybe next time I'll have to find something to shove in your mouth to keep you quiet. It's obvious to me you have a bit of an oral fixation as it is. I bet you'd like being gagged."

I couldn't hide how much his suggestion turned me on. Maybe I could convince him to skip drinks after the rehearsal dinner and breakfast in the morning so we could fit in as many experiences as his kinky mind could come up with.

There weren't many men I could trust to provoke my ability to put a stop to things, but with Ryan, I knew he'd stop before he ever found my limits. I wanted him to gag me, bind me, and make me cry before holding me and telling me what a good boy I was for him.

Fuck, I needed more than a couple of days with him.

I gasped, my back arching so high I practically levitated off the bed when Ryan licked a stripe from my balls, back to my hole. He truly wasn't in any sort of rush. He spent what felt like an hour circling his tongue around my entrance, gently coaxing my muscles to relax with firm presses of his tongue.

After my hole was good and wet, he traced the tip of one finger around my entrance. I moaned, trying to decide if it tickled or felt good. When he said he didn't want to rush things, he wasn't lying. He worked the edge of my hole, dipping a finger inside and stretching me open, but he never even went as far as the first knuckle. I arched my back when he added the tip of a second finger, spreading my hole even wider.

"This is such a pretty little hole. I can't wait to be inside of you." I couldn't wait for that either. I tried to say as much, but my throat was clogged with emotions I'd been holding back for as long as I could remember. He took my ass in both hands, squeezing as he pressed his thumbs inside my body.

I bit down on my bottom lip, holding back a whimper as I writhed on the bed. He wasn't touching anywhere on my body that was supposed to make me come, but I'd been on knife's edge for so long, I wasn't sure how much longer I'd be able to hold back.

"Don't worry about holding back," reassured me. "I want to hear how good I make you feel."

I cried out as the drizzle of cold lube dripped down my crease and into my relaxed hole. "You could've warmed it up, you big meanie."

Ryan chuckled and I threw an arm over my eyes hoping to conceal some of my embarrassment. Calling someone childish taunts wasn't sexy in the least, but it didn't seem to turn Ryan off. He slid his finger through the trail of lube, coating his finger.

"Fuck, I can't remember the last time sex was fun," he mused. The more he laughed, the more I relaxed. I didn't have to worry about playing a role with him. With Ryan, I was free to be myself. "Look at me, sweetheart. I want you watching as I open you up."

I opened my eyes but didn't move.

"Get the pillows," he instructed me. "Prop them behind you so you can sit up."

It wasn't until he shifted to the side that I realized there was a floor length mirror behind him.

"Oh, shit," I moaned out. He had moved just enough that I was able to watch as his fingers breached my entrance. It wasn't that I was inexperienced, but it had been a while since I'd bottomed. The bar scene had gotten old, and I'd had other shit on my mind.

"Have you ever watched someone fucking you, sweetheart?" He slid a second finger next to the first, spreading them so my hole gaped. "You're still resisting. Relax and let me in, Tanner. I'm not going to fuck you until I know I won't hurt you."

Unless he planned on fisting me as part of foreplay, it was going to hurt. Ryan's wasn't the longest dick I'd ever had, but he was thick. My eyes fluttered closed as he curled his fingers, grazing along my prostate. While some guys loved that feeling, it hadn't ever been something I looked forward to. It was uncomfortable, but then right as I opened my mouth to protest, he pegged me just right and I saw literal stars dancing behind my eyes.

"Look at me," he demanded. "Your options are to watch yourself in the mirror or give me your attention. Don't hide away from me."

"I'm sorry, Daddy," I gasped. For all my internal bluster earlier about not waiting for his permission to come, now I found myself craving it. I wanted to hold out until he was inside of me. I wanted him to feel my ass clenching around his shaft.

My eyes shot back to the mirror. Somehow, that was safer than looking at him. He saw too much, knew too much. And if I focused on him, there was no way I'd be able to keep myself from falling in love with him. Or worse, admitting it, because I was sure I'd been in love with him forever.

"Yeah, you have a dirty streak, don't you?" he teased. He added more lube before stretching me with a third finger. "Someday, I'm going to Facetime you and make you do this to yourself for me. Daddy doesn't want to let you go now that he has you. He's going to call you every night to make sure you're taking care of yourself, and then he's going to help you get ready for bed. Since he can't give you goodnight kisses and tuck you in, he'll tell you all the filthy things he wants you to do with this hole. Would you like that?"

My head thrashed back and forth against the pillows. I wasn't sure I was capable of coherent thought at that point. Someday, as in after, as in not saying goodbye when he dropped me off at my apartment.

Daddy doesn't want to let you go.

Daddy's going to call you every night.

It had to be the lust talking. No way was he saying this didn't have to end when he went home.

"No? You wouldn't come for me? You wouldn't fuck yourself with the phone propped up at just the right angle so I could imagine it's your pretty hole I'm burying my cock inside of instead of my fist?" When he pouted, he looked ridiculous. It was exaggerated to the point of comical. "And here I thought you were the perfect boy for me."

"I am," I said in a rush. I'd do anything he asked of me, if only I could hold out hope a bit longer. "Or, I want to be. I'll do anything you ask me to."

"We might have to see how serious you are about that." He bent down, sucking one of my nuts into his mouth. He curled his tongue around it, tugging slightly, grazing the sensitive flesh with his teeth as he released me before giving the other side the same attention. He closed his hand over mine, guiding me as I stroked my cock. His hand stilled as he looked up the length of my body. "Would you go into the bathroom at work if Daddy was horny and needed to hear you getting off while I tell you how I want you to do it?"

"Yes, Daddy," I sighed. My dick twitched in my hand and my balls tingled.

He was more coordinated than I could ever hope to be. He flicked his tongue around the base of my cock and my balls while guiding my hand up and down my shaft and plunging two fingers from his other hand deep into my hole.

"Please, Ryan," I begged. "Don't make me wait. I'm going to come if you keep doing that." I was already leaking a steady stream of precum and I could feel my balls tightening, my shaft swelling. I was seconds away from coming with enough force the entire wing of the resort would know what we were up to.

"You've been waiting for this a long time, haven't you?" he asked as he sat back, resting his ass on his heels.

I nodded.

"One of those nights when I call you, I'm going to make you tell me what you wished you could have done to me that night you crawled into my bed," he warned me. I really hoped this wasn't just sexy pillow talk because I was already looking forward to hearing his voice on the other end of the line. It would be a shitty substitute for having him next to me, but it would be worth it to not have to let him go.

"And then I'll tell you everything I've thought about doing to you and you'll act it out for me," he continued as he suited up. Another pack of lube came out and he slicked himself up, his head falling back as he moaned. He stood, yanking me so my ass hung off the edge of the bed. He dragged the head of his cock through my crease as he said, "But I'm really curious what was going through that head of yours."

"It wasn't about what I wanted to do to you," I admitted.

"Oh? What were you thinking about then?" he asked. The head of his cock stretched my entrance. I bore down, waiting for that first uncomfortable thrust, but it never came. He pulled back and gave me nothing more than the tip over and over again. "Tell me, Tanner. Was there something you wished I'd do to you? Did you want me to wake up and take this pretty ass that morning? I could have punished you by burying myself inside your body without any prep. The lube on my condom would have to be enough. And I wouldn't have stopped until my hips were pressing against your ass."

"Yes!" I cried out as he filled me with a long, slow thrust. The languid cadence was frustrating and exhilarating at the same time. It wasn't enough, but the way the tendons in his neck stood out, I knew he was trying to stave off his own release. "I wanted you to be my first. No one had ever fucked me because I kept hoping it would be you."

"I'm sorry I couldn't give that to you." He bent down, curling a hand around the back of my neck. I could feel the slick sheen of sweat on his forehead as he pressed it to mine. "I hate that I wasn't your first, baby. If I had it to do all over—"

Before he could finish that thought, I twisted my fingers in his hair and forced his lips against mine. I could feel him smiling as my lips parted. He tasted like me now, and fuck if that wasn't the ultimate rush.

"This is our do over, Ryan," I promised him as he continued plunging in and out of my body. "Maybe this is the way it was always supposed to be. We're different people than we were then, and if you'd told me how you felt back then, it might not have worked out."

"I think you could be right." Ryan slid his hands between my body and the mattress, holding me as he fucked me. No, something had shifted, and this wasn't like any sex I'd ever had before.

I felt full, but not in the sexual way. It was this sense of peace and rightness that washed over me. I'd always been Ryan's, even when neither of us knew it. And now, it was up to us to figure out how to make things work when we lived on exact opposite sides of the country.

When my release finally came, it wasn't with an explosion and a scream, it was waves of pleasure, my ass squeezing

Ryan's cock until he let go. Ryan collapsed on top of me, holding me tightly as we both struggled to breathe.

"I meant everything I said, Tanner," he whispered as he kissed the shell of my ear. "I don't want this to be all there is for us. I know what I said earlier, but I can't do it."

"This is insane. I want to say I'm all in, but what if it doesn't work out?" I pursed my lips together to keep from saying anything else stupid while I could still feel his softening dick in my ass.

"Then at least we'll know we tried." Ryan pulled out and disposed of the condom. My eyes were already closed when he came back and gently cleaned me up. "Let's see if we can rest up before dinner. I don't want to spend a minute away from you unless it's unavoidable."

He pulled back the bedding and lifted me up, carefully placing me in the middle of the bed. Once he laid down, I curled up against him. I hoped the, *I love you,* as I drifted off to sleep had only been in my mind. Now that I had him, I didn't want to scare him away.

9

TANNER

I DIDN'T WANT TO GET OUT OF THE COCOON OF OUR BED. RYAN and I had spent as much time as necessary with the family, but we'd become masters at excusing ourselves—at different times, of course—so we could sneak back to the suite for a little fun. Or sometimes, we'd just cuddle. It turned out he was a sucker for cuddling me while we caught up on what we'd been doing since we'd last seen one another.

Last night, after the rehearsal dinner and cocktails we hadn't been able to skip, he'd asked if I would ever consider moving out east. I hadn't, but that was probably because there'd never been anything worth uprooting my entire life for, even if I was completely miserable here.

Now that he'd planted the seed, I was going out of my mind. Yes, we'd known one another since we were kids, but it was stupid to even think about that type of change when we'd barely had time to see if we worked as a couple beyond sexual chemistry. Granted, it wasn't like following him wherever he went would be giving up much, but that was beside the point.

But the thought of dropping him off at the airport sat in my gut like sour milk. That was the worst idea possible. Once he was home, he'd find someone more suitable, and he'd forget all about the off-handed comments he'd made to me.

"What's wrong?" Ryan asked as he kissed the back of my neck. He tucked his hand between my waist and the mattress, effectively trapping me against his body.

I wasn't complaining. If I had my way, we'd stay like this until it was time to check out. I knew he wanted me to tell him whatever was on my mind, but that was a level of vulnerability I wasn't ready for, so I settled for a smaller truth. "Today's going to suck."

"Just remember what I told you. If things get rough, you find me and I'll make sure to help you survive without killing anyone," he promised.

As much as I appreciated the gesture, that's not what I was talking about this time. I meant the entire damn day. We spent long enough curled up in bed, we were already cutting it close to being late for breakfast. Once we finished eating with the entire family, Ryan would go with Deegan and the rest of the groomsmen to do whatever it was guys did before getting married, while I followed Haley up to the bridal suite to help her and the bridesmaids get ready.

The next time I even laid eyes on Ryan would be when he walked into the ballroom that was already being transformed into a winter wonderland for Haley's dream wedding. And then, I'd be able to look but I wouldn't be able to touch. I'd seen him in a tux when he and Deegan had gone to senior prom, and that had sent me into my room, tearing off my shorts as fast as possible so I could tug one out. If he had that effect on me then, I didn't even want to think about how I'd feel now.

"We're not going to be able to spend any time together until early tomorrow morning," I explained. Why did Haley have to plan a wedding that would inevitably drag on for over fourteen hours between the pictures, wedding, and reception? "I know you'd help me if my family tries giving me a hard time, but that's not the *hard* I'm worried about."

"Oh, I see what this is about," Ryan chuckled. "You're going to miss your Daddy cuddles, aren't you?"

Yeah. I was. It was hard to believe that less than twenty-four hours ago the entire concept of calling someone Daddy outside of sex was completely foreign to me. Now, I was dreading today not only because I'd be forced to spend time with people who would always view me as less than, but also because it meant time away from Ryan. And time was one thing we didn't have nearly enough of.

Ryan pushed himself up, leaning over my body to press his lips against my temple. He kissed his way down the side of my face before sucking my earlobe between his teeth.

"Try not to think about it too much. It's not going to be any easier on me," he admitted. "And you'd better believe I'll be looking for every possible opportunity to either steal you away or send you a text message letting you know where to meet me."

He flipped me on my back. As if to prove a point, he combed his fingers through my messy hair before giving a sharp tug. He sealed his mouth over mine, pressing his tongue against the seam of my lips until I opened for him.

When he pulled away, he said, "I hate that I have to spend a single minute away from you today." He kissed me again, more quickly this time. "There's not a chance I'll be able to make it until midnight, without tasting these lips again. Are you going to wear any makeup today?"

Before Ryan stormed back into my life, I'd planned on sashaying into the ballroom in all my gay glory, with fierce eyes and a fuck-the-world attitude. But Daddy was right; this was Haley's big day, and it would be rude of me to do anything to upstage her. It would also be against the first rule Daddy had given me. He didn't want me doing anything that would draw negative attention.

"Let me rephrase that," Ryan said before I could respond. "You *are* going to wear your makeup today. It doesn't have to be over the top, but you're so damned pretty and you exude confidence. Your makeup is like armor for you, and you shouldn't pretend to be someone you aren't for anyone. And I want you to keep that cherry lip gloss in your pocket. Whenever I tell you to meet you somewhere, I expect you to freshen it up."

"You... You like my lip gloss?" The corner of my mouth tipped up in a smirk. I knew damn well he did. At the rate we were going, I was going to demand he buy me another tube before dropping me off at my apartment because I couldn't remember the last time I'd gone through so much gloss so fast. He said he liked the taste of it on me, but I was pretty sure he'd enjoy kissing me just as much without it.

"You know I do." He sat up, flashing me a pained grimace. "As much as I hate to say it, we need to get up. If we don't, we're going to have your mother to answer to."

Damn. He really knew how to dump ice water on my libido.

As Ryan got out of one side of the bed and I begrudgingly twisted to do the same, I realized that I'd been denying myself something amazing for far too long. One of my biggest rules was that I didn't spend the night and I didn't let anyone stay in my bed. When I hooked up with someone, it was exactly that. We got right down to business and then went our separate ways. Even those I hooked up with somewhat frequently understood my limitations.

But now, I was grateful that this was something I could share for the first time with someone who meant more to me than a quick fuck. And maybe it wasn't having *someone* in bed next to me, but having Ryan holding me as I slept that helped me feel ready for whatever the day threw at me.

"Ten!" The crowd started gathering around Haley and Deegan as the waiters wound their way through the mass of people, making sure everyone had a champagne flute.

"Nine!" I caught sight of Ryan standing next my parents. As much as I would have preferred staying with Haley's family, I didn't want to start the new year with anyone but him.

But this was how we'd agreed to handle things. Ryan was right; this was Haley's big day, and I wouldn't do anything to screw that up. Or I wouldn't have, but now, I couldn't imagine ringing in the new year with anyone but him. And the way he was looking at me, he felt the same. It was up to one of us to make the first move, and I knew that wouldn't be him. He was *far* too concerned with keeping up appearances.

"Eight," everyone screamed as I took my first step. Ryan did the same and the everything around us faded. Our gazes never broke as we closed the distance between us. Finally, Ryan was in front of me, and I felt steady for the first time since this morning.

He hadn't been kidding when he said he was going to find as many ways as possible to steal moments with me when no one was looking. I was pretty sure Haley figured out what was going on by the third time I had to excuse myself from hanging out with the girls, listening to them catch up on what everyone else had been doing since the last time they were together.

If there were cameras where we couldn't see them in the resort, someone in security had gotten one hell of a free peep show today.

But it wasn't enough. Nothing would ever be enough with Ryan. I wanted him to tell me it was time to go to bed. We could make use of that massive tub in the bathroom, relaxing after a day filled with tension. Then, he'd take me to the bed, where I hoped he'd trust that I wasn't going to break, and he'd be rough with me.

That was part of having a Daddy I definitely wanted to experience before he left.

"Is this okay?" Ryan asked as he snaked his arm around my waist, pulling me tight to his body. Tears welled along my lower eyelids and a lump formed in my throat.

"Seven!" This was one of those moments that felt like it was straight out of a movie. Without letting me go, Ryan brushed the hair away from my face. "I couldn't stay away from you any longer. I hated trying to keep my hands off you today when other people were around."

"Same," I admitted as the room erupted in a swell of cheering. I tipped my head back and closed my eyes as firm lips pressed to mine. My mouth fell open on a sigh, and Ryan held me so tight there was no space between our bodies as his tongue teased mine.

Soon, we'd have to deal with the fallout, but for a little while longer, I wanted to pretend the two of us kissing was as natural as anything.

Eventually, the need to breathe forced us to break the kiss. Ryan's fingers tangled possessively into the hair at the nape of my neck. He pressed his forehead to mine as he said, "I know it's too soon, but I want to figure out how we can do this again next year and every year after that."

"We'll find a way," I promised him. My need to be with this man overcame all of my reservations about being in a relationship. Sure, I might wind up getting my heart broken, and I was certain my family would blame me for somehow coercing him into being gay, but I didn't care about any of that. When he flew home, Ryan would be taking a piece of my heart with him. That wouldn't change if I insisted we were nothing but a fling.

"Tanner Patrick Fincham, what in the world do you think you're doing?" I tensed when I heard my mother shrieking behind us. "We're all aware of your proclivities, but you don't need to create a scene at your brother's wedding."

"Lillian, please," Ryan interrupted. She startled, as if it had only just now registered who had me safely in his arms.

"Tanner isn't the only gay man here, so it's upsetting that you're choosing to single him out."

"But this is Deegan and Haley's day," she protested. I buried my face in Ryan's chest, not wanting to see how much of an audience we had. "I expected behavior like this from him, but how could you, Ryan? He's your best friend's baby brother."

"He is," Ryan confirmed. "But he's also an adult, capable of making his own decisions. Once you're able to see past your own disdain, I hope you'll be happy for us. I hope you will be happy for Tanner, knowing he has someone who loves him and will do everything in their power to make him happy."

I let out a choked, high-pitched squeal. I had to be hallucinating. Ryan did not just tell my mother that he loved me. He couldn't. There was no way in hell he could possibly be in love with me after two days, no matter how hard we'd tried burning up the sheets. But maybe he could, because I sure as hell loved him. I just hadn't wanted to jinx anything by saying the words out loud. And it hadn't been two days; these feelings had been growing in both of us for years despite our best efforts.

My mom stormed off in a huff. Eventually, I might wish she could accept me, but I no longer needed her validation, not when I had this beautiful man willing to protect me.

Ryan cupped my face in his hands, tipping my head back so he could look into my eyes. "I know what you're thinking, but don't argue with me this time. I let you go once after convincing myself it was the right thing to do. But it wasn't. I was so fucking wrong, and now I need to prove to you that

I've learned my lesson. I love you, Tanner. No matter how hard I tried, I haven't been able to make myself stop loving you since the first time I truly noticed you."

"I love you, too," I sobbed. He pulled a handkerchief out of his pocket and gently dabbed along my eyelashes, careful so he didn't smear my makeup. "You know we're going to have to tell my brother about us."

"He already knows." My gaze shot up, then followed Ryan's to where Deegan and Haley were slowly rocking back and forth on the dance floor, both of them watching us. Haley beamed and flashed a quick thumbs up. Deegan glared at Ryan before his features softened and he gave a quick nod. That was the closest we were going to get to approval from him. "What do you say we go back to our room? We'll come down for brunch with them tomorrow and we can all talk then."

"That sounds perfect."

Ryan didn't let go of my hand as he led me through the ballroom. It felt like the crowd parted to let us through, and every single person had something to say. A few looked shocked as Ryan held his head high, silently showing them he wasn't about to hear anything those who were disgusted had to say.

I felt like I was living in a dream when Ryan stepped behind me, wrapping his arms around my waist as we waited for the elevator to arrive. It still floored me that I was his—and that he made it clear whatever we were doing was *not* going to end when he left for the airport.

"You're not going to regret that, are you?" My question echoed off the walls of the elevator. As badly as I wanted to look at him, I couldn't. I was afraid of what I'd see written on his face.

"Baby, the only thing I regret is not having the balls to claim you sooner." He hugged me tighter, pressing my face into his chest as he rested his chin on top of my head. "I don't know how I can make it up to you for letting you think I was upset that morning."

"Telling me again how you're in love with me while you do dirty things to my body would be a good start," I suggested. In a very un-Ryan-like move, he slid his hand into the back of my slacks, and shoved a finger into my crease. I arched back, leaving my neck exposed. Ryan clamped his teeth around my skin, biting hard enough I knew there would be a mark by morning. "Please, Daddy. Don't stop."

"Do you like being my dirty boy?" Daddy growled in my ear. I nodded. "Good, because, at some point, I'm going to do things to you that are going to make your entire body flush with embarrassment. Would you let me do that?"

"Like what?" I asked breathlessly. I was all down for some freaky fun, but I had my limits. If he was talking covertly getting me off while we were in a room full of people, I was totally game. If he meant parading me up on stage so he could fuck me in front of an audience, I was going to need one hell of an incentive.

"When the club opens, they're going to have a special area for Daddies to show off how well behaved their boys are," he explained. My eyes shot open, wishing like hell I'd asked for details about this club he'd invested in sooner. Ryan chuckled. "Oh, did I forget to mention that part?"

"Uh yeah, I'm pretty sure I would have remembered." The chime sounded, alerting us that the doors would be opening on our floor in mere seconds. I expected Ryan to pull away. It wasn't going to take long for me to realize expecting anything out of him was pointless. At every turn, he was shocking the hell out of me.

With his hand still stuffed in the back of my pants, he guided me into the hall. If anyone approached us from the front, it would just look like he had his arm around me. I glanced over my shoulder, hoping like hell no one we knew was about to sneak up on us.

When we reached the door, Ryan pinned me to the wall, grinding his erection against my ass as he growled in my ear. "Fuck, I can't wait to put you on display. You're so fucking hard already, knowing anyone could catch us. You like that, don't you?"

"Yes, Daddy," I whimpered. At that moment, I'd have agreed with anything he said. I could feel the wet spot at the front of my underwear already. If he kept this up, my first orgasm of the night was going to be right here in the hall.

"Fuck, you're gorgeous." He reached past me, sliding his keycard into the door. "Let's get you inside. It's time to see how far you'll go to make Daddy happy."

I wasn't ready to tell him I'd go to the ends of the earth to please him.

10

RYAN

"Do we really have to leave?" My heart broke at the way Tanner's voice cracked. I hugged him tighter, dreading the alarms that would be going off soon. The fiasco from Deegan's wedding reception hung over us like a dark cloud. While most of the family had pretended like nothing happened the following morning at breakfast, things were still tense with Lillian. His mom refused to see the damage she'd done or admit that *she* was the one who'd caused a scene.

Like Tanner, I wasn't ready to say goodbye. I needed him to believe me when I said this wasn't just a fling and the two of us would find a way to work things out once I went back home.

If I had my way, he'd be in the seat right next to me on the plane, but he'd refused. That was probably the mature decision, since it wasn't like I was asking him to move twenty minutes down the road, but that didn't mean I had to like it. Until I could convince him that nothing was going to come between us, I'd be racking up the frequent flyer miles, coming back to visit him as often as my schedule would allow.

"We've been over this, sweetheart," I reminded him. "If there was any way I could stay out here longer, I would."

"Have you even tried to see if the world can hold itself together without you? I just think it would be nice for the two of us to spend a couple more days here before letting reality crash the party," he complained. His hand drifted down my stomach, the tips of his fingers teasing the tip of my cock. "You said you can work remotely, right?"

"Yes, but there are some things I *have* to do in person," I pointed out. Later this week, Jack and I were meeting to go over the contracts for our partnership. Once that was settled and the financing was secured, he could start hiring contractors for the renovation. He was a decent enough man he'd likely be willing to do a video conference to settle the details, but I didn't want him thinking I was disinterested in the project before it even got started. I might not plan on being on-site every day, but that didn't mean I wanted to be nothing more than a checkbook. This was a sound investment, and if things went well it could lead to opening future similar clubs.

"Are any of those before Thursday?" The boy was relentless when he wanted to get his way. His hand curled around my shaft and he began lightly stroking me. "Just hear me out. If we stay here another day or two, we can get to know one another better without the threat of my family barging in on us. You said we'll be able to keep things going when you head home, but we haven't talked much about what's that's going to look like. Wouldn't it be easier to do that now?"

Tanner made valid points that were hard for me to dispute. I pulled up my phone, checking the calendar to see if there was anything I absolutely couldn't push back or do from the resort. I was trying to not tip my hand, but he wasn't the only one who didn't want to check out of the hotel and go back to the real world. I felt like I'd just gotten a second chance at happiness, and I didn't want to piss it away.

"Don't mind me, I'm being whiny," Tanner said when I didn't immediately blow off his suggestion. He buried his face in my armpit, peeking out his tongue to lick me. He did that a lot, and it was exactly the type of goofy, innocent gesture I'd miss when we were apart. "I feel like we've been living in a twisted dream and now it's time to wake up."

"I understand why you feel that way." I rolled to my side, kissing the top of his head. "But this isn't forever. And maybe you're right. We need to sit down and talk about the rules before I leave, and I don't want to rush through that."

"You know I hate rules," he grumbled.

"True, but I think it'll be different for you this time. You want to be able to tell me what a good boy you've been when I call to check up on you, don't you?" I teased. Tanner was a sucker for knowing he'd pleased me. Over the weekend, he'd pointed out times when he'd ignored his family rather than standing up for himself. I understood why he thought that was the right thing to do, but I didn't want him to go back to having his family's footprints all over his back once I wasn't here to keep an eye on him.

"Yes, Daddy." Just hearing him say those two words had my dick fully hard. I flipped over, pinning him to the bed. As I kissed my way down his neck, he squirmed, trying to grind our cocks together. "You're not really making a good case for needing to make your flight."

"Maybe I'm starting to realize you were right, and that we need a little more time together," I pointed out. I slid a hand between our bodies, wrapping my fingers around his shaft. "I haven't been able to tease you nearly as much as I'd like. If I stay, you'll have to do whatever I tell you. Is that going to be a problem?"

"No, Daddy," he promised. He wrapped his legs around mine, capturing me so I couldn't climb out of the bed. That was a mistake, because I wanted today to be about spending time together while both of us had our clothes on. Him trying to take control was only going to prolong his suffering.

It was too bad I hadn't imagined a scenario like this when I'd flown out. If I'd known Tanner and I would be such a perfect match in our sexual desires, I would have packed a bag with some of my favorite toys. Now, we'd have to settle for me sending him gifts to use on himself, knowing it was what I wanted.

I rutted against him until he was a panting, writhing mess beneath me. I sucked a mark at the base of his neck, a deep purple that would linger after we were separated. I tucked his hair back. "You're gorgeous like this. So desperate and needy for me."

"Need to come, Daddy," he pleaded. "I can't help myself when I feel your body against mine."

"But you'll wait, because it's what I want," I informed him. He scowled up at me as I pried his legs away from my body and hopped out of the bed before he could pull me back.

"Right now, we're going to get dressed and go down to breakfast. That way we can talk."

"I see no reason to put on clothes when the view is so much nicer from right here." He reached for his dick. I glared at him, and his hand immediately dropped to the mattress. "How do you expect me to go out in public looking like this? I know it's not a monster cock or anything, but people are going to know."

"You'll be fine," I assured him, tossing my hoodie onto the bed. I'd be shocked if that made it into my suitcase. Whenever we had time to lounge around the suite, he'd worn the sweatshirt that barely covered his bare ass. He did it to taunt me, not realizing how sweet and innocent it made him look. That mental image reminded me of something I'd wanted to try but hadn't been able to yet. "If you're a good boy, I was thinking we could go shopping today. I want to find a few things to remind you who you belong to even when I'm not here."

He perked right up at the mention of shopping. I sighed and shook my head. I used to think it was weird how he'd ask to go to the mall every weekend, but now that I saw him in a different light, I realized it was a way for him to find pieces that would allow him to express himself. Today, I was going to make up for all the times Deegan and I had teased him. And I fully intended on buying him some pretty underwear he could model for me during the nightly video chats I was going to insist on.

Tanner took his sweet time getting ready. He made a show of bending at the waist to pull clean clothes out of the suitcase he'd set on the floor last night when we'd planned on leaving first thing this morning. I pressed the heel of my hand against my erection, willing it to go down because I wasn't going to be able to resist him if he turned around and dropped to his knees.

There was something to be said for a boy who seemed most content when his mouth was full. It didn't even seem to matter to him if I was hard or not, sometimes he just wanted to suck on it as if it were a pacifier.

Fuck. I needed to stop thinking about that, otherwise we'd never get out of the room.

I spun around, determined to grab my own clothes and take a quick shower before he'd finished deliberating about how he wanted to dress for the day. Down the road, I hoped he wouldn't have a bad reaction to me taking that choice away from him. I loved the idea of picking out his outfits and helping him get dressed.

Nope. Not thinking about my possessive need to dress him up and take him out to show him off.

I didn't bother waiting for the water to heat up before stepping under the spray. The cold water would do me good, and the clock was ticking. I spent the minimum time possible scrubbing last night's sex from my skin, turning off the taps just as the bathroom door opened.

Tanner gawked at my naked form, rivulets of water cascading down my chest. "You're the worst," he grumbled. "How am I supposed to get ready to go when you're standing there looking at me like that?"

"Easy," I scoffed. To tease him further, I pressed my wet chest to his skin and bent down to rest my chin on his shoulder as he laid out his skincare products on the vanity.

His hand dropped to my flank, sliding around to cup my ass. I pulled it away before I could start grinding my way between the taut globes of his ass. "None of that. If you don't hurry, we're going to miss breakfast service. *Someone* made me miss dinner last night, so he might earn a punishment if I'm forced to skip another meal."

"You suck," Tanner complained. "You keep talking about spankings and punishments, but you're not very good on follow-through."

"Watch it, boy," I warned him. "Keep that up and you'll realize discipline isn't always sexy or fun."

I grabbed my towel off the bar and quickly wrapped it around my hips, ducking out of the room before he could tempt me more. By the time he got out of the shower, I was dressed in a pair of jeans and a sweater, sitting at the table poring over the contracts for the week.

I'd gotten enough accomplished while he showered and fixed his hair and makeup that I could relax the rest of the day and not worry about falling behind. I'd also paid an exorbitant fee to change my flight to a red eye Wednesday night so I could steal every possible second with him.

When we got to the dining room, I recognized a few of the guests from the wedding who had also decided to make an extended vacation out of the weekend. I waved to them, keeping my hand planted on the small of Tanner's back. No one was shocked to see us together, but some were better than others at hiding their judgment.

If I could go back to when we first arrived, I would have made it clear to everyone that he was mine. Trying to hide the first seeds of a relationship between us had been a horrible decision. The only thing that accomplished was allowing Lillian to think that Tanner had somehow managed to seduce me in the short time we'd spent together.

That ended now. When I went home, everyone was going to know that giving Tanner a hard time because he was gay or because we were together was unacceptable.

"Where would you like to sit?" I asked, leading him toward the back of the dining room. At least there, we'd have a little bit of privacy.

Tanner looked up at me, offering me a tense smile. He'd obviously noticed the whispers from some of their extended family who hadn't even had the decency to say good morning to him. "I suppose back in our room isn't a suitable answer?"

I tightened my grip around his waist, pulling him against my side. "Forget about them, sweetheart. If they don't want to accept you exactly as you are, that's for them to deal with. The only thing that you need to be thinking about is how happy I am to have you sitting next to me this morning. I want to show you off, make sure they all know this isn't a phase for me and you didn't try to seduce the guy they all thought was straight."

I found an empty table in the corner. My heart melted when he smiled as I pulled out a chair for him. He didn't hesitate before sitting, and when I tried to step away, he grabbed my arm.

"Thank you for helping me this weekend. I don't know if I could have done it without you."

"You're stronger than you give yourself credit for, baby." I bent down and pressed my lips lightly against his. "I think you just need someone to remind you of how confident you used to be. The Tanner I knew wouldn't let anyone make him feel bad for being himself."

"Yeah, well, that was when I had you to protect me," he admitted. I didn't think I done anything special before I left for college, so I was confused by his statement. "Now, I talk a good game and pretend like I don't care what they think of me, but I do. Why is it so hard for them to accept that I happen to like looking damn fine."

"And you're good at it," I mused. "I wish I knew why they have an issue with you expressing yourself. But I want you to remember that you *are* beautiful and there's nothing wrong with you, no matter what anyone says."

"Do you even realize you made that same speech time and again when I was a kid?"

It embarrassed me to admit that I was completely clueless.

Tanner scooted his chair closer and placed a hand on my thigh. "You were always sticking up for me. When Deegan or some of your other friends would start picking on me, you'd tell them to knock it off. Then, you'd pull me aside and tell me to ignore them because they were wrong. It was the only thing that got me through high school."

"Hell, sweetheart." I let out a deep breath, hating that I'd left him on his own for so long. I'd never realized how much of an impact it'd had on him to hear someone insisting there wasn't anything wrong with him. "I really don't remember that. In my defense, hearing them cut you down felt like they were saying the same things to me, even if they didn't know it. So maybe telling you that you were perfect was a way of reassuring myself at the same time."

"Why didn't you come out sooner?" He'd asked this question a few times, and I always dodged giving him a good answer. The truth was, I was a coward. I worried too much about what everyone would think of me, and I'd still be hiding if it wasn't for him.

I shrugged, not having a decent answer for him. "Not everyone is as brave as you, sweetheart. By the time I started to understand why I wasn't as girl crazy as the rest of the guys, everyone had made up their mind about me. It was easier to go with the flow, knowing I would be leaving for college eventually. If I'd known it would've helped you, I'd like to say I would have done things differently."

"Don't be ridiculous," Tanner scoffed. "I would've been mad as hell if you'd come out just to make my life easier. Coming out is something you can only do for yourself, and I'm sorry I forced your hand this weekend."

"First of all, *you* didn't force anything," I insisted. He tucked his chin against his chest, and I squeezed his hand to make him look at me. When he did, I leaned closer, brushing the backs of my fingers over his cheek. "The longer I kept my feelings for you locked away, the harder it was. It felt disrespectful to you."

"I would have been fine," he assured me. And he would have been. He'd have gladly suffered as long as his silence allowed me to stay safely locked away in the closet.

"Why do you always do that?" I asked, frustrated that he was willing to make his own life hell to appease me.

"Do what?"

"You're always trying to make everybody else's life easy, even if it means you're miserable."

Tanner shrugged. "I learned early on that it's best to not make waves that can pull other people under."

"You absolutely should make waves if it means people won't think they can push you around," I insisted. "I don't ever want you dulling your shine to make someone else happy. Not even me."

He stared at me, and I could tell he was about to say something I wouldn't like. I pressed my index finger to his lips and whispered, "There's only one right answer here. What do you say?"

The seconds dragged on, and I wondered if I'd pushed too far. He said the "Daddy stuff" needed to stay in our room, but I wanted to spend the next two days showing him that it didn't have to be hidden. I could be his Daddy, even when we were out in public, and no one but us needed to know.

"Yes, Daddy," he responded with a stuttering breath.

"That's my good boy," I praised him.

The server came by to take our order, and we spent the rest of breakfast catching up on idle chatter about what we'd both been doing over the past few years.

11

TANNER

There were worse things in the world than having a Daddy who wanted to spoil me before he had to go home. I'd made a couple of jokes about him being my Sugar Daddy and he hadn't appreciated those at all. To him, taking me shopping had nothing to do with wanting to spoil me, and everything to do with making sure I knew who I belonged to when we had to be apart.

And as it turned out, Daddy was even pickier about clothes than I was. At first, I worried he was trying to mold me into something I wasn't, but every time he pulled something off the rack, he looked to me to see how I reacted. He had a great eye for fashion and paid no attention to which section of the store we were in. The only thing I couldn't understand was how frustrated he was by early afternoon.

"You don't have to spend the entire day shopping," I assured him. "I know this isn't really your thing."

"It's not that I don't want to shop," he promised me. "I'm just not finding some of the things I'd been hoping get for you.

We may have to head back to the city tomorrow morning and go to some of the shops there. They have to have some specialty boutiques that have a better selection."

I couldn't believe it, but the idea of spending two days wandering from store to store trying to find whatever it was he was looking for irritated me. Normally, I was the one begging to look in just one more shop. But time was a finite resource between us, and I didn't want to waste all of it chasing down clothes he wouldn't even see once he went home.

"We've already got quite a few things for me to model for you when we get back to the room. Why don't we call it a day?" Ryan hadn't taken the bait when I invited him into the dressing room with me. I think we both knew what would happen if we were alone behind closed doors.

Even though the idea of sucking him off with strangers on the other side of the door pushed all my buttons, I didn't think either of us wanted to risk and indecent exposure ticket in a somewhat buttoned up town far from home. He was far too busy for having to fly cross-country for court dates.

"There's just one more thing I want to find," he insisted, squinting as he looked at the storefronts. "I'm not giving up until I find it."

"What if you tell me what it is you're looking for," I suggested. "Chances are I'll know if it exists and where we need to go."

"It's supposed to be a surprise." His shoulders slumped forward, and it was the closest to pouting that I had ever seen him. I reached up and flicked his bottom lip.

"I thought I was supposed to be the petulant one," I teased. "Come on, I promise it's not going to ruin things if you tell me what you're so obsessed with finding. Plus, it'll help us get back to the hotel sooner. I'm thinking we should spend the rest of the day naked, only getting out of bed to refuel before another round of sex."

"You're insatiable," he quipped.

"And you're the one who didn't let me get off before breakfast." I glared at him, still annoyed because he'd been amused by my pain. "Sue me if I want to live out as many of my teenage fantasies as possible before you abandon me."

I was only joking, but apparently that was the wrong thing to say. Ryan's brows pinched together, and his lips narrowed to a thin line.

"I'm kidding. I know you have a life you have to get back to," I added, trying to sound unaffected. After he dropped me off and I'd watched his car until he was out of sight, then I could bury my face in a pillow and cry myself to sleep.

"Still, I don't like the idea of being so far away from you," he admitted. "I just got you. What if I fly home and you decide it's too much work having a long-distance relationship?"

One of the things I loved about Ryan—had always loved about him—was that he never tried to hide his vulnerability. But he was worrying for nothing if he thought I was going to be the one to call it quits.

"It won't be long distance forever," I promised him. He let out a grunt. I tugged on his arm, spinning him around so he faced me. After trying to keep my hands to myself over the weekend, I didn't give a flying fuck who might see us. We were hours from home and no one else mattered. I pressed my chest to Ryan's, reaching up to cup his face.

I'd always thought of this type of relationship as being one sided with the Daddy always trying to look after and take care of his boy, but now I realized it was just as much my job to take care of him. I was the one who needed to reassure him when his mind was filled with doubts.

"Just because I said I'm not ready to pack my things and jump on a plane today doesn't mean I never will be. I just want to make sure we're solid before I do anything drastic. Despite what my family believes, I am capable of making mature decisions sometimes."

Ryan hugged me tighter. "I know that, and someday I'll get over myself and be proud of you for being the responsible one for a change. But you have to give me a little time. And can you really blame me for wanting to keep you next to me? I feel like the past five years have been one giant missed opportunity. Time that we lost when we could've been together."

"Weren't you the one telling me that things might not have worked out if we had gotten together back then?" I reminded him. "I was an immature brat back then. You would've gotten sick of me."

Ryan shook his head. "Not a chance in hell. And for the record, you're still a brat. The difference is you know how to work that to your advantage to get what you want from me now. The only thing that would've happened is your backside might have been permanently blistered from pushing the limits. I probably would have resorted to daily preemptive spankings just in case you were naughty while I was at work."

The jeans I was wearing were far too tight for dirty talk in public. I swatted his shoulder and groaned. "You can't say things like that to me when you can't do anything about it."

Ryan quirked an eyebrow. "I can't, huh? The last I checked, you're mine and I can do whatever the hell I want to you, unless you use your safe word."

"I still don't know why you insisted on a safe word. I won't use it," I insisted.

He let out a low growl. "I know you think that now. I've been taking it easy on you because I don't want to jump in too fast."

An undignified snort escaped me. I quickly covered my mouth to hide my amusement.

Fine, so we hadn't jumped headfirst into hard-core kinky stuff, but I wasn't sure you could qualify it as going slow when I'd lost track of how many orgasms I had, and housekeeping was probably going to have to burn the sheets after we checked out. Even industrial-strength cleaners weren't going to get the scent of sweat and cum out of the bedding.

Ryan swatted my backside, making me jump. "You know what I mean, brat. When you come out to visit me, I'll introduce you to some of the things I like doing to boys who push the limits."

"Is that a promise? Because I have to tell you, you're making it really damn hard for me to stand by my insistence that we not rush into anything. If I have to wait until I move in with you to get to the good stuff, that might sway my decision." I'd expected Ryan to laugh, not scowl at me.

"I'm not trying to manipulate you, Tanner." He led me to a bench in the courtyard of the open-air mall. I yelped when my ass met the frozen metal of the seat. What was it about him and wanting to have meaningful conversations while I froze my ass off?

"I'm really not upset with you for looking out for yourself. I understand that it's going to take time for you to trust that things between us will last. When you make that decision for yourself, I'll be the happiest man in the world. Until then, we'll have to settle for weekend visits when our schedules allow. If you can't take time off from work, then I'll be the one making more trips." He draped an arm over my shoulders and pulled me against his side. I was surprised that in all the shopping we'd done, he hadn't insisted on buying me a warmer coat.

Taking time off work wasn't going to be a problem. If my dead-end retail job wanted to fire me for requesting some weekends off, it wouldn't be a problem for me to find something else. It wasn't an exciting career that was holding me back from moving in with Ryan, it was the fear of the unknown and the fact that I'd never hear the end of it from my family.

Moving over two-thousand miles away to be with a man, even one I had known most of my life, would be the height of irresponsibility in their eyes. And despite the don't-give-a-shit attitude I tried to portray most of the time, I really did want them to see that I was capable of being a functioning adult. "How is it supposed to work for these weekend trips you're talking about? I thought you had all this important businessy stuff you had to take care of."

"One of the joys of being my own boss is the ability to set my own schedule," he explained. "And as you've seen, I can work from anywhere with a few exceptions. The meetings I have to get back for have been planned for months now and there are a lot of people waiting on the contracts to be signed. That's the only reason I didn't leave my return flight open-ended."

Something caught Ryan's eye and he jumped up. He pulled a twenty out of his wallet and handed it to me.

"Why don't you go over to that sports bar we saw earlier and get us a table," he suggested. "We'll get something to eat before we head back to the resort. That way, we don't have to waste the time we have with menial tasks like eating."

"Where are you going?" He was suddenly acting nervous and cagey.

"I think I found a place that might have what I'm looking for. But I want to surprise you, so you're going to do as you were told," he demanded. He glared down at me, and I didn't dare argue.

"I told you we don't have to keep shopping." I pointed at the bags stacked at my feet. "You already bought me more than enough."

"I think you're going to like this." The corner of his mouth tipped up in that cocky smirk he got when he had something up his sleeve. "I know I will. Now, go get us a table and order before I get there. You wouldn't want to waste any time, would you?"

"Of course not, Daddy," I responded, a bit sarcastically. "Are you going to tell me about this covert mission you're on?"

"Not yet. You'll see when I get back." He gave me a quick kiss and started to walk away. Just as I turned toward the sports bar, he called out to me.

I stopped, glancing over my shoulder.

"If you can, ask for a booth near the back." My cock twitched, hoping that meant we were going to get a head start on playing out some of those porn fantasies of mine.

The hostess didn't bat and eye when I asked for a booth that would give us some privacy and told her that I was still waiting on someone to join me. I barely looked at the menu, too distracted make sense of the words.

When the server came by, I asked for two glasses of water and ordered the lunch special for both of us. I wasn't even sure what that was, but it would be quick and probably not something gross.

While I waited for Ryan to get back, I sent Mav a quick text message, updating him on everything that happened. We talked a little bit over the weekend, and I knew he was dying for me to get home so I could spill all the juicy details.

Mav: He let you out of bed long enough to look at your phone? Mav responded after I sent a quick, "What's up?"

He's not that bad, I responded. Part of me wished it was like that. An image popped in my head of Ryan keeping me tied to the bed until it was time to check out. I could get totally down with that.

Mav: So things are still going well?

Better than I dreamed they could be, I admitted. Even though Mav and I didn't have many secrets, I didn't tell him about the Daddy kink stuff. It was fun, but the type of thing that a lot of people wouldn't understand.

Mav: When are you coming home? Or am I posting online to find new roommate?

Me: You'd better not give away my room, asshole. I'll be home late Wednesday night. He has to take a redeye for some important meeting.

Mav: I still think you're an idiot for not taking him up on the offer.

Me: You know why I can't.

As soon as I told Mav about Ryan and I discussing what happened *before*, he went from being cautious about me getting hurt to being Ryan's biggest cheerleader. He thought it was sweet how Ryan went out of his way to stand up for me to my family. Hearing that Haley had essentially set us up, even managed to thaw his opinion of her.

Mav: I know why you say you shouldn't, but I still think you're being an idiot. This is what you always wanted.

Me: Yeah, and if it's meant to be, then I'll move when the time is right. I'm not uprooting everything when we don't know if he's still going to want me after he goes back to his real life.

Mav: From what you told me, he's been pining after you just as long as you been crushing on him. This isn't a phase, Tanner.

Me: And once I know that for myself, then I'll tell you to start looking for someone to take over my share of the rent. You keep that up and I'm going to think you're trying to get rid of me.

Mav: *As if. How many people would put up with me? Besides, I'd have to trust on a hell of a lot to open up the apartment to them.*

Me: *See, that's another reason I don't want to rush things.*

Mav: *Don't you dare try to make this about me.*

I noticed Ryan following the hostess through the dining room. *Gotta go. I'll give you a call later tonight.*

No, you spend time with that sexy man of yours. We can talk when you get home. Unless you're going to finally listen to reason.

You're impossible, I sent back before tucking my phone away in my pocket.

"Who were you talking to?" Ryan asked as he slid in next to me on the bench. To her credit, the hostess quickly wiped the surprise off her face when she realized this wasn't just two friends hanging out for the day. She quickly turned Ryan's menu toward him.

He handed it back to her. "I think my boyfriend has already ordered for both of us but thank you."

I didn't hear what either of them said after that. My brain had short-circuited on the word *boyfriend*. It was silly how, even though we'd talked about the fact neither of us were willing to say goodbye when it was time for Ryan to head home, hearing him call me his boyfriend to a total stranger somehow confirmed that he wasn't trying to blow smoke up my ass.

Ryan clutched my hand. "I hope that was okay."

"More than," I reassured him. It felt nearly impossible to draw a full breath. The reality that he wasn't lying about this being more than a fling was starting to settle in.

He lifted our joined hands to his mouth. "Good, because I've been waiting years to call you that."

"You're right. You totally should have come clean a long time ago," I grumbled.

"Weren't you the one just telling me how immature you used to be?"

"First of all, that was you," I argued. "And second, if I was immature and a brat, that's all the more reason you should have done your Domly duty and just told me how it was going to be."

"My Domly duty?" Ryan chuckled, shaking his head. He twisted in his seat, holding my hand tightly. "We can wish all we want that things were different, but we both know it wouldn't have worked if we'd gotten together back then. And you wouldn't have been the reason for our demise. Yes, you were a brat, but I was just as immature. The pressure of what everyone expected of me would have been too much."

"And now?"

"Now, I'm old enough to realize it doesn't matter what anyone else thinks of me. I know what it's like to not have you next to me and I'd rather not spend the rest of my life miserable just to make other people comfortable."

While that was admirable, I still worried about his friendship with Deegan. I didn't trust that my brother's cautious acceptance of us the night of the reception would last forever. Once the honeymoon was over—literally, in his case—he'd remember all the reasons he was pissed off that his friend had not only lied to him but was also sleeping with me.

"Does that include my brother?" As much as I didn't want to know the answer, it had to be addressed. No way in hell was I going to be the reason for a permanent rift between the two of them. That would make family holidays hella awkward.

"I think he'll be okay once he gets over the shock. I'm sure he'll have questions for me, but those will likely be about how he never got the impression I was gay." He scrubbed a hand over his face and his shoulders slumped forward. "Looking back, I wish I hadn't tried to hide from everyone. It was selfish, and I'll understand if everyone's upset because I didn't trust them enough to come out."

"It's not like you didn't have a good reason," I scoffed. "You saw how they acted around me. I don't blame you for wanting to keep that part of yourself safe. Hell, I'm jealous you were able to."

He pinched the bridge of his nose and closed his eyes. "That makes me feel even worse. I shouldn't have let a kid bear that burden alone."

"I wasn't a fucking kid," I growled. Sooner or later, he was going to have to quit saying shit like that because it was really starting to piss me off.

"No, you weren't." He kissed my cheek and squeezed my thigh. "Forgive me?"

"As long as you let that shit go. It's annoying as fuck that you're still thinking of me as some sort of helpless kid." I sat up straighter and gripped his chin the way he did to me when he wanted to make sure I was listening. "I was plenty strong enough to deal with their bullshit then, and I'm not going to put up with it now. And you'd better fucking believe that means if they try saying anything about you when you're not around."

"My little fighter." The embrace was awkward as he hugged me tightly in the somewhat cramped booth. "But we're getting off track here. Even if it takes time for Deegan to come to his senses, he's not going to convince me to walk away from you."

"But he's been your best friend since the two of you were kids," I protested.

"Which is why he needs to get over his own shit and be happy for me. Wouldn't you agree?"

"I guess you're right." My stomach churned, and I wasn't sure I'd be able to eat my meal when it arrived. This was a hell of a lot to deal with when I'd spent most of my life trying to avoid getting into relationships. It felt like every possible complication was being thrown our way.

Ryan leaned over, pressing his lips to my ear. "One thing that will make life a whole lot easier on both of us is if you realize Daddy is always right."

He sucked and nipped my earlobe. When he started kissing his way down my neck, my jeans grew painfully tight. I squirmed in my seat.

When I reached down to adjust myself, Ryan chuckled. "Are we having a problem over there, sweetheart?"

"You know damn well what the problem is," I grumbled. "You kept me hard all day."

"Did you want me to do something about that?"

"I swear, if you're teasing me right now, I'm going to make sure you go home with the worst case of blue balls ever."

Ryan bit down on my neck. We both know that won't happen. "You're way too greedy to deny yourself the pleasure of having my dick stuffed inside of you." He dropped his hand to my lap, squeezing the front of my jeans. "What if I offered to help you out with this right here at the table? Would that cross a line?"

"Not at all," I responded breathlessly. He quirked an eyebrow, silently waiting for the response I knew he expected. The man got off on hearing me beg. "Please, Daddy. I need to come."

"Even if that means I make you wait longer when we get back to the hotel?"

"I think I proved I'm capable of waiting until you give me permission." It would've been so easy for me to rub one out in any of the dressing rooms I'd been in earlier today. I was so turned on it would've only taken a few strokes, and I could be quiet when I needed to. But Ryan had instructed me to keep my hands off my cock.

I wasn't a fan of delayed gratification. Except, apparently, when I knew it was going to make Ryan look at me like he was proud of me.

He picked up the deep purple bag and handed it to me. "Go into the bathroom and put these on. When you come back, you're going to show them off for me."

"How's that supposed to work?" I was down for a bit of semi-public fun, but the bag weighed practically nothing, giving me an idea of what was inside. A lingerie fashion show in the back of a restaurant might just be on the other side of my limits.

"Trust me," he insisted as he slid out of the booth. I followed, my dick feeling like a steel rod in my pants as he kissed me deeply. He shoved a hand inside the back of my jeans. "I've been dreaming of seeing you in something like this since the second I pulled up and found you in those fucking heels. When we get back to the hotel, I'm going to fuck you wearing nothing but this gift and those shoes."

Yes please, Daddy. Fuck, maybe I should hop on that plane with him. But I wouldn't, because for once in my life, I was going to do things in the right order.

12

RYAN

I was well and truly screwed. I'd expected Tanner to call my bluff when I sent him to the bathroom to change. I reached down, squeezing my shaft, trying to keep from firing off like a Roman candle inside my pants before he even got back.

I couldn't help but think about the club, and all the things he'd let me do to him there. What Sam and Jack had envisioned with some areas for public play, had intrigued me the first time I'd seen rough sketches of what they hoped to create. I'd always gotten off on pushing my play partners to their limits where anyone could catch us, but that had all been within the safety of private parties. There'd never been anyone I trusted enough to push their limits in public like I could with Tanner.

When Tanner came back to the table, he was practically strutting. Some men would be uncomfortable wearing lacy lingerie, but it seemed to bolster his confidence even more. He looked so damn sexy, I couldn't wait to get him back to the hotel and strip him out of the trunks I'd picked up.

When I got home, I was definitely going on another shopping spree because an ass as gorgeous as his deserved to be framed in nothing but the finest fabrics.

"How do they feel?" I asked as he approached the table. His cheeks flushed crimson red. He checked over his shoulder as if he expected someone to be walking up behind him.

"Why don't you ask a little louder?" he grumbled. "I'm not sure they heard you out on the street."

I gripped his cock tightly through his jeans. He was still hard as nails.

"You don't seem to be too upset about the idea of everyone knowing how far you'll go to please your Daddy," I observed. I nodded toward the booth. "Sit and open up. Let me see how they look."

"You seriously expect me to whip my junk out for you right here?" His breathing was fast and shallow, and I'm not sure he even realized when he started stroking himself over the denim.

"Have you ever known me to joke about something like that?"

Tanner smirked but didn't verbally call me on my lie. While we'd found plenty of places to sneak off to during the reception, I'd also teased him every chance I got. It was my way of making sure he knew I wasn't forgetting about him when he was out of sight.

Someday, I hoped the events before this weekend were nothing more than fading memories, but I obviously still had more work to do to fully gain his trust. I could deal with that, as long as he didn't give up on me.

"You're stalling," I scolded him. "Let me get a look at your dick wrapped in lace."

Tanner slid across the booth, slouching down as he unbuttoned his jeans. He spread the flap wide, giving me a peek at the lavender lace covering his cock.

I made a show of adjusting myself. "Damn, sweetheart. Going to get you a pair of those in every color."

I sat next to him and pressed my palm against his hard length. "Would you like that? Would you let Daddy play dress-up with you? You could model them for me when we video chat."

"Yes, please," he moaned. As I continued stroking him over the lace, he bit down on his bottom lip to keep from crying out.

I leaned closer, biting the side of his neck. If I wasn't careful, he was going to be covered in hickies and bite marks by the time I left. Then again, I wasn't too upset about that prospect since it would be a way for everyone to see that he was mine.

I glanced up, making sure we were still alone. The illusion of public sex was hot but that didn't mean I wanted us to get caught. I kept stroking, flicking my thumb over the damp spot seeping through the lace. "Do you think you can get off before the waitress comes back with our food?"

Tanner whimpered as he thrust his hips toward my hand. I pulled away, unwilling to give in until he said the magic words.

"You know what you need to do, sweetheart," I reminded him. I'd make him come harder than he had the entire weekend and then force him to clean my hands with his tongue, but not until he asked nicely.

I needed to know that he would always ask Daddy to fulfill his needs, especially if we were going to survive the next few months apart. Because I had every intention of proving we didn't even need to be in the same state for me to play his body like a perfectly tuned instrument.

"Fuck, Daddy," he whimpered when I started stroking him even harder. "I need to come so bad."

"So, what do you need to say?" I teased him.

"Please, Daddy," he cried out, bucking his hips hard, chasing his orgasm. Whether I gave him permission or now, he wasn't going to last much longer. The fake leather of the bench creaked with every thrust. Anyone who was within earshot would know what was going on back here, but my boy was too close the edge for me to care.

"You've been a very good boy today," I praised him. "You've earned this."

I pushed aside the lace and curled my fingers around his shaft. It was impossible for him to remain silent when I pressed a fingernail into his slit.

"So damn needy for me," I praised him. "You like hurting for Daddy, don't you?"

"Love doing anything for you, Daddy." His head lolled to the side, his cloudy, lust filled gaze meeting mine. "Please, Daddy can't wait any longer."

I pressed my lips against his ear, muttering encouragement as he fucked my fist. "That's it, sweetheart. Take what you need. Let Daddy make you feel good. Give me everything you've been holding in all day."

That was exactly what Tanner needed to shoot off like a fountain over the top of my fist. I cupped my other hand over the head of his dick, capturing his release. His body sagged against mine as he gasped for breath.

Without giving him a chance to regain his composure, I lifted my hand to his face. "Look at this mess you've made. You'd better clean me up before somebody comes back here," I warned him. "Otherwise, everyone's going to know what a dirty little slut you are.

Tanner's gaze never left mine as he offered me the flat of his tongue. He hummed as I fed him his own release.

"You like that?" He nodded. "I figured you might. You try hard to act prim for me, but underneath, you can't wait to see what I'm going to do to you next."

I lifted my other hand to my own mouth, letting out an exaggerated moan as I licked his cum from my fingers. "Damn, sweetheart I'm going to miss how good you taste when were apart. I might need to forbid you from coming just so you can save it up for me."

Out of the corner of my eye, I noticed the server approaching with our meals. "You'd better get yourself put back together. Unless you want to give that poor server a show."

Knowing Tanner, anything was possible.

I chuckled as he struggled to close his jeans over his already growing erection. He really was insatiable. Once I had him somewhere we wouldn't be interrupted for a good long while, I was going to see how many times I had to get him off before he was finally exhausted.

Neither of us wanted to talk about what would happen after I went back to Annandale, but we couldn't put the discussion off any longer. Tanner craved structure in his life. Having spent the past few days with him, it was easy for me to see that most of his acting out had been a cry for attention.

"Wake up, sleepyhead," I whispered. He burrowed his face even deeper into my armpit. For whatever reason, that seemed to be his favorite position. "Come on, sweetheart, we have to get ready to check out."

"Can't we stay here forever?" he whined.

"As much as I wish, no, baby. We talked about this." Last night had been rough on both of us. He'd grown increasingly irritable, to the point I wound up having to step out onto the balcony, ignoring the fact it was snowing and I was barefoot. He'd worked himself into a tizzy, certain that the moment we left the resort, the spell would be broken, and I'd realize it was too much work to be with him.

"Real life sucks," he grumbled as he kicked the blankets off his legs. "Don't want to go home. Want to stay with you."

I bit my tongue to keep from pointing out that there was a way he could do that. I didn't want to push him, but it was ridiculous that he was so insistent on staying here until our relationship was secure.

Realistically, I knew he had a point, but it was going to be even harder to prove to him how serious I was with all those miles between us. If Tanner would have agreed to it, I would have suggested a detour to Vegas on the way back home just so I could make him one-hundred percent mine.

I had no doubt that was where we would eventually wind up, but I also understood that saying as much to him too soon would scare him off.

"Do you really have to go home?" he asked as he pulled out a pair of skinny jeans and my sweatshirt that I'd already resigned myself would be going home with Tanner.

That was fine by me. He could keep whatever of mine he wanted so he'd always have a piece of me with him.

"If there was any way I could stay, I would," I told him for the thousandth time. "But I can't miss this meeting tomorrow. The sooner we have the contracts signed, the sooner renovations can begin."

"Will you tell me more about the club on the way home?" I'd tried explaining the structure of the club to him, but it was unique enough that he wasn't fully grasping what we were trying to achieve.

It was difficult for me to talk about Club DeSires when I was here. It wasn't that I was embarrassed about my latest business venture but, again, I didn't want everybody feeling the need to give me their unsolicited opinion about me being a partner in a kink club.

It wasn't something I'd consciously had on my list of possibilities, but when Jack mentioned how much more he could do if he had an investor, it felt like the right time to do something with the money I'd squirreled away in savings. This project wasn't for anything other than my own personal interests.

It wasn't a company I bought into with the intention of turning things around and then selling it for a profit. It had nothing to do with how the success or failure would impact my net worth. My investment in the club was solely because I believed the community needed more safe places for people to learn about and express their authentic selves.

"I'll tell you whatever you want to know," I promised Tanner. "But only if you get your lazy bones in gear. We have other things to talk about today, too."

Tanner grunted, knowing what was coming.

"Don't be like that, Tanner. We need to make damn sure both of us are on the same page before I have to leave tonight. You know this." Yes, things were more complicated with me living in another state, but there would have been rules regardless of geography.

"Doesn't mean I have to like it," he grumbled. "I don't want to think about anything that makes me admit you're leaving me."

"I'm not leaving you. I'm simply getting back to everything that has been waiting for me while I been taking care of my boy. And before I leave for the airport, we'll figure out when we'll be able to meet up. Do you want me to come to you or are you willing to visit and see where I live?"

"I don't have a lot of money for flying back and forth," Tanner admitted. He leaned against the small table, shoulders rounding as if he was embarrassed to tell me he wasn't in the same place financially as I was.

I grabbed his arm and dragged him over to the bed. "You think that's going to stop you from coming to stay with me? I have enough money that if you agreed to go all in with me, you wouldn't have to rush to find a job you actually wanted to do instead of busting your ass to get from one paycheck to the next.

"I don't want you feeling like you have to support me." He lifted his gaze, jutting out his chin and squaring his shoulders. "I might be okay with you taking care of me in the bedroom, but you have to treat me like your equal, too. Otherwise, you'll eventually resent me and grow tired of me mooching off of you."

"But what if that's exactly what I want to do? I love you, Tanner. And that means I'll do anything I can to make you happy." I understood what he was saying, but even if I never worked another day in my life, it was unlikely Tanner would catch up to me financially. That was the result of working hard enough to try to ignore everything that wasn't right in my life.

"But I won't be happy if I'm mooching off of you." He relaxed a bit and wrapped his arms around my waist, using my head as a pillow. "You know how I was raised. I need to earn my keep."

"That's a difference of mindset we'll have to figure out a way past." In an ideal world, he wouldn't have to do anything to contribute to the house, but he'd never agree to that. And I respected the hell out of him for his work ethic. "But that's not something that needs to be addressed today. There are other things that are far more important."

"Like the rules?" Tanner slumped harder against me. "I'm probably not going to be any good with whatever these rules you keep threatening me with are," he warned me.

"Well, that'll work out perfectly for me then because I have no problem putting disobedient boys in their place. It'd be a shame if the first thing I have to do when we're together again is paddle that pretty behind until you can't sit down."

"Doesn't sound like much of a threat to me."

"True. I might have to think of something more fitting for you. It's crazy how much you crave the pain. When you come out to see me, are you going to let me test your limits?"

"I'll be disappointed if you don't," he replied. Surprisingly, it was Tanner who wiggled out of my arms and stood. "We need to get a move on. I don't want to miss breakfast before we get on the road."

"Oh? Do you have big plans for today?" I'd expected him to be reluctant when I asked if it was okay for us to spend part of today at his place. I wasn't sure if he was ready for his roommate to know about us, and he seemed hung up on the fact that he was still living like a college kid. It was ridiculous to me that he expected to have his life in order when he wasn't much older than someone who'd recently graduated. The only thing that mattered to me when it came to his home, was that it was safe for him.

"If this is my last chance to have you fill me up, I want to get back to my place as quick as possible," he informed me.

Maybe I shouldn't let him tell me what was going to happen, but there were times I was more than willing to follow his lead. And in this case, it seemed both of us were on the same page, so it was safe to let him think he was in control.

I slipped the keycard into my pocket and my hand into Tanner's. I hugged him tightly while we waited for the elevator, wanting to stay connected to him for as much of today as possible. We somehow managed to keep our hands off one another while riding down to the first floor, not wanting to make the elderly couple already on the elevator uncomfortable.

The dining room was already clearing out, as most of the guests during the week were here for conferences and such. I sent Tanner to find a table and order for us while I checked out.

One of the benefits of knowing Tanner for as long as I had, was knowing all the ways he'd try to avoid doing what he was told. If things weren't written down, there was no doubt in my mind he'd try to claim he'd forgotten the rules. That was why everything would be clearly spelled out on the legal pad the front desk clerk had offered me when I asked if there was someplace close by to purchase a notebook.

Tanner jumped when I dropped the pad of paper onto the table. "What's that for?"

I quirked an eyebrow and chuckled. "You know damn well what that's for, sweetheart."

Instead of sitting next to him, I sat across the table. It pained me to put distance between us, but I couldn't let my boy distract me this morning.

"I figured this was as good a time as any to discuss the rules. That way we both know what to expect when I go home tonight," I explained, already jotting down some of the rules we'd agreed to when we'd first arrived.

"Fine," Tanner grumbled. "What are these rules you're so hellbent on giving me?"

"You might want to check the attitude," I scolded him. "You knew this was part of the deal, and you said you were willing to do whatever I wanted. Have you changed your mind on that?"

"No, Sir," he mumbled, keeping eyes lowered. He curled in on himself and wrung his hands. "I'm sorry. Today's just a shitty day and talking makes me realize you're really leaving."

"Which is why we're going to talk about expectations now. We'll get that out of the way so I can spend the rest of the day showing you how much you mean to me," I reminded him. Knowing him, that meant as much sex as possible, but that wasn't all I wanted to do. The routines we'd set up would help him stay focused, and knowing that he was following the list to please me, would center him. The time we spent curled up on the couch later today watching TV would imprint his home with memories of our time together, so he had more than just a vacation fling to think back on.

While we sipped on our coffee, I ran him through the basics. He gaped at me when I rambled about the importance of eating right and getting a decent amount of sleep. I didn't miss the smirk when I informed him he was allowed to go out with his friends, but only if he sent me a picture before they left and called when he got home to let me know he was safe.

"But with the time difference, that means it's going to be after four in the morning your time," he protested.

"Then I guess I'll start work early on those days and take a nap in the afternoon." Anything having to do with his safety was non-negotiable. And maybe that would keep him from going out as often as he had been. It wasn't that I didn't trust him, but I'd been concerned when we'd been talking about our lives and he'd confessed to going out most Fridays and Saturdays. That wasn't good for the body or the bank account.

"I'm only going to agree to that if you promise you'll tell me if it's too hard on you," he countered. "I don't want you getting rundown, either. As someone recently told me, it's important to make sure you're getting enough sleep so you're healthy."

"Cheeky brat," I scoffed, offering him a wink and a smile.

We weren't able to finish talking about the rules because the server came back with our meals. French toast and bacon for him, and a veggie omelet and turkey sausage for me. I glanced at both of our plates, debating swapping them to see how he'd react. The only thing that stopped me was knowing my body would revolt if I put that much sugar in my system so early in the morning.

As we ate, I continued scribbling notes on the paper. We could talk more about them once we were on the road, but I needed to get them out while I could give my thoughts my full attention.

"Man, these rules aren't anything like I thought they were going to be," he admitted when I was finished writing out everything we discussed and slid the paper toward him. This is just, like, the things any normal couple would agree to.

I chuckled. "I'm not sure what sort of couples you're used to but there are definitely some differences."

I pointed to one of my personal favorite rules.

"Tanner agrees to call Daddy anytime he wants to play with himself. Playing without permission will lead to consequences." Tanner squirmed in his seat as he read the rule. It wasn't until a few seconds after he'd stopped speaking that he realized we were in a public dining room. His head whipped to one side and then the other, checking to see if anyone had heard him.

"I figured you'd like that one."

"But what if I can't get a hold of you?"

"Then, I guess you're just going to have to wait."

"Can I text you instead? You could send back a simple yes or no to a text message, even if you were in a meeting," he suggested. Luckily, I was prepared for this. He'd always been a master at trying to find loopholes. If he'd shown any interest in it, he'd have made a damned good lawyer.

"Nope." I slid my finger to the next rule.

"Tanner will only play with himself if he's on the phone with Daddy to tell him what to do." His face scrunched up and he shook his head.

"Do you have a problem with that?" I asked, keeping my tone as level as I would during any contract negotiations for work. "You seem to like it when I tell you how I want you to touch yourself."

My eyes flicked toward his waist, wondering what he'd do if I suggested he touch himself now, just to prove a point. We were the only ones left in the dining room and the employees bustling around were too wrapped up in their own conversations to notice us. I resisted, only because we'd already checked out of the room and I wanted to be the one to make him come after he'd edged himself to the point of tears.

"That one isn't going to be easy," he admitted. "I usually rub one out in the shower in the morning."

"I'm well aware." His cheeks flushed, only then realizing that I'd heard him jerking off while he cleaned himself up. I'd let it slide because he got so into what he was doing, he hadn't noticed me opening the door to watch him. "But I suggest you get comfortable with your roommate being able to hear what's going on so you can have me on speakerphone, otherwise you'll have to do it before or after. You've already gotten away with breaking that rule more than once."

"But again, what if you're in a meeting? It'll be later where you're at, and you'll already be at work," he protested.

"Then you'll have to hold it for me." Maybe long distance wasn't going to suck as much as we both assumed it would. There was a heady thrill knowing that he'd be completely at my mercy, even from nearly two-thousand miles away. "If you text me to let me know you'd like to play with yourself, I'll call you as soon as I'm someplace I can help you."

"But what if I'm already at work?" He was really working hard to figure out a way out of this rule.

"Then you'll go to the bathroom and listen while Daddy tells you how to touch yourself," I informed him. My dick pulsed in my pants, aching with the need to be inside of him again. "Hurry up so we can get on the road. Read through the rest while you eat."

After a few more bites, Tanner pushed his plate aside. He'd eaten more than half of his breakfast, so I wasn't going to give him too much of a hard time. He tapped the end of the pen against his teeth as he read through the rest of the rules.

"Do I get to give you rules, too?" he asked as he handed the pad back to me.

"What sort of rules do you want to set?" I asked. I was secure enough in my position as his Daddy that I had no issue abiding by whatever stipulations he might set.

"I don't know. I'm just wondering if you'd be okay with that."

"I'll do whatever you need to feel safe with me, Tanner." I took his hand, staring at him from across the table. "This isn't about me having all of the power. I set the rules because it's what we both need to be happy while we're apart. You need to know someone cares enough to tell you what you can and can't do. I need to know I'm taking care of you in some way. It's a balance that I think will work well for us. If there's something you need me to agree to, that's fine by me."

"Fuck, every time I think you can't get any more perfect, you go and say shit like that," he groaned, pushing his chair away from the table. "Can we get out of here? My bed's not as comfy as the one here, but I want to make it smell like us before you go."

"Whatever you need, love." I shook my head as I rose, wondering when I'd turned into such a sap.

The answer: the first time I realized how easy it would be to fall in love with Tanner. But then I'd pissed away years I could have been taking care of him because I was too worried about what people might say.

That ended now.

13

TANNER

Every day that passed without Ryan next to me sucked a little bit more. No matter how much I loved and appreciated him for not pressuring me to say screw it and move across the country with him, part of me wished he had. At least then I wouldn't have to feel this soul crushing loneliness every day.

Wasn't that something Daddies were supposed to do? If he'd made a valid argument for why it was stupid for me to hang onto my dead-end job and my crappy apartment, he could have convinced me to follow him.

But he hadn't, because he respected that I needed to do things on my own time, and neither of us wanted to do anything that would lead to resentment down the road.

The multiple calls daily helped, but they weren't enough. Seeing him on the other side of a computer screen wasn't the same as feeling his strong arms around me. Using my own hand, even as he guided me, wasn't the same as him manipulating my body, making me cry in pleasure, pain, and frustration before I came for him.

In short, being without him was hell.

He seemed to be trying to make up for the absence by sending me almost daily care packages. I'd given up fighting with him about those. As he liked to point out, what good was having a thick bank account if he couldn't spoil me a little bit?

And, okay, maybe I didn't mind the special deliveries as much as I had when they first started arriving at my door. I set today's package on the bed, staring at it while I waited for my phone to ring. Ryan was busy with getting everything lined up for the club he'd invested in, which meant I spent all of my days off waiting around for the phone to ring. The only thing that made the silence bearable was knowing he'd promised to visit as soon as he could break away.

Mav barged into my room without knocking. "You going to stare at that thing all afternoon or do you plan on opening it?" He'd become almost as excited for the presents as I was. He said it was a way for him to live vicariously through me.

"I'm waiting for Ryan to call," I told him. He knew damned well I wasn't allowed to open his gifts until he was on the other end of the line. It was sweet how much seeing my reactions meant to him. And it was hot as fuck when it was a sexy present and he wanted me to show off for him.

"How would he even know if you opened it just long enough to peek?" Mav taunted. "You could open the bottom of the box, and then he'd still see you opening the top."

"He'd still know." I waved Mav off. "If you're just here to annoy me, could you come back later?"

"Damn, someone's touchy," he sniped.

"You would be, too, if you hadn't seen your boyfriend in almost a month," I shot back.

"If only there was a way you could have saved yourself this pain." Mav tapped on his chin and rolled his eyes before snapping his fingers. "Oh wait, that's right. You had a chance and decided you'd rather be an idiot."

I gave him a playful shove away from the side of the bed. He'd been cautious when I'd first introduced him to Ryan. All he'd known was the stories I'd told him about how I'd angsted over my brother's best friend and totally made an ass of myself when I was a teen led around by his hormones. Luckily, he kept an open mind, and by the time Ryan and I walked down to where he'd parked on the street for a tear-filled goodbye, Mav had given him his seal of approval.

"Since when is trying to be responsible the same as being an idiot?" It didn't matter that I'd been calling myself the same things recently; I didn't like having my mistakes thrown back at me. And I didn't want to think about this right now. If I did, Ryan would sense how miserable I was and he'd suggest, yet again, that I put in my notice and join him.

He'd even offered to give me a job during last week's conversation, but that was something I wouldn't take him up on, no matter how badly I wanted to be with him. Mixing business and pleasure was a surefire way for things to explode in spectacular fashion.

"I'm just saying that maybe you were a bit shortsighted when you told him you couldn't follow him out east. It's a really cool area. I think you'd like it."

"How would you know?" Mav wasn't exactly a traveler, and his judgment of a city's worth directly related to the party scene. That used to be fun, but I'd realized over the past month that I didn't miss it as much as I thought I would.

"Remember, I visited out there last summer," he said, as if that was all that needed to be said. Yes, he had flown out to meet a friend he knew from online, but there was a difference between visiting and living somewhere.

"You do understand the entire eastern side of the country isn't all exactly the same, right?"

"True, but it's a different vibe out there. And you wouldn't have to worry about the fam coming down on you all the time," he pointed out, knowing how they suffocated me. And it had been even worse since the wedding.

My mother had been giving me the silent treatment ever since we got home, insisting that I had hooked up with Ryan just to try and steal the spotlight from Deegan and Haley. It didn't matter how many times Haley told my mom she was happy for us; my mother was still holding the king of all grudges. She wouldn't rest easy until I admitted that I'd somehow seduced Ryan and convinced him to help me ruin their weekend. There was no convincing her that Ryan coming out to everyone by kissing me at the stroke of midnight was because of a mutual attraction we couldn't deny a second longer.

"Maybe after I visit him we'll talk about it some more," I told Mav. "You know me, I'm not a spontaneous guy most of the time."

"That's such total bullshit." Mav made himself comfortable at the end of my bed, alternating between staring at the box like it might be a bomb and checking his phone. "You're the one who used to be up for just about anything. You were the ringleader, once upon a time."

"You can't even try to compare moving to be closer to someone I spent one weekend with to running off into the woods and getting lost," I scoffed.

"You're right, but it's not totally different, either. It's an adventure, and that's something you used to always be up for."

My phone chimed before I could ask Mav what the hell he meant by that.

I pointed at the bedroom door. He lingered a moment too long and I glared at him. *Go*, I mouthed as I picked up the phone.

"Hey. Did I catch you at a bad time?" Ryan asked. It was possible I had a tendency to answer the phone before it even rang through on his end. I didn't give a single shit about possibly coming across desperate to him.

"Not at all," I assured him. "Mav and I were just talking about some things."

"Everything okay?"

"Yeah, everything's fine. I flipped the box over and lifted it to my ear, giving it a shake to see if I could figure out what he'd sent today. "Just roommate stuff."

That wasn't completely a lie. Even if we hadn't been arguing about what an idiot I was to not trip over myself as I packed to follow Ryan home, bickering was pretty typical for us.

If this shoe had been on the other foot, I probably would've been saying the same things to him.

"Do you have something to open for me?" Ryan asked, changing the subject. His voice echoed, and I wondered where he was calling from.

"I do," I confirmed. I could hear the clicking of his dress shoes across the floor. "If this is a bad time for you, I can wait until later."

"That's sweet, but now's fine," he reassured me. "I've been waiting for you to get this one and open it. You're not the only one who can get impatient."

"You know you don't have to buy something for me every single day, right?" It was a weak protest that had become part of our routine. I told myself that, as long as I made a halfhearted attempt to get him to stop, I didn't have to feel guilty about the collection of toys and clothes I had amassed since he left.

"Sooner or later, you'll realize you're not going to keep me from spoiling you," he teased. "Sue me if I'm enjoying the hell out of finally having a boy of my own who's more than just someone I meet up with at the club when I need something."

I grunted, hating hearing him talk about what he did before we got together. I trusted him completely and knew that wasn't something he was still doing, but I wanted him to be going to the clubs with me so he could forget about those other boys. I was way better than them.

"What you say when you get a present, sweetheart?" he coaxed, completely ignoring my petulant reaction. That was way better than the times he'd chuckled. For some reason, he thought it was cute that I was jealous of men who were nothing but memories for him.

"Thank you, Daddy." My eyes shot toward the door, hoping Mav wasn't still on the other side eavesdropping. For some reason, I hadn't been able to bring myself to tell him about this aspect of my relationship with Ryan yet. I didn't want him judging me if it was too weird for him.

I chuckled at that thought. Mav was one of the most sexually adventurous people I knew. What he hadn't already tried, he had on a mental kinky bucket list, and I knew he'd eventually try just about everything. No, he probably wouldn't have any problem with me calling Ryan Daddy. Still, it was something that felt special between the two of us.

"What's so funny, sweetheart?"

I shook my head, forgetting he couldn't see me. "Nothing, I was just thinking about something Mav said. Can I open my present now?"

"Someone's anxious. You didn't peek at what's in the box, did you?"

"No, Daddy. Mav told me I should, but I knew you'd be upset with me if I broke the rules," I rambled. Just thinking about what he'd promised to do to my backside the next time he saw me, had me squirming on the mattress.

The first time I'd earned a punishment, had been less than two weeks after Ryan went home. There was nothing worse than hearing his heavy, disappointed sigh across the line. I'd gone out with some friends from work and had forgotten to call him ahead of time.

When we stayed out longer than we planned on, I also missed my call to say good night. Those happened long before I was ready to go to bed, because I wasn't willing to have him staying up until three in the morning just to tuck me in, but they were something he insisted on.

It seemed so weird, at first, to have him say he wanted to help me get ready for bed, even though he was on, what felt like, the other side of the world. But eventually, I found that I couldn't settle down for the night until we'd talked, and he talked me through my nighttime routine and instructed me on how to take off my clothes while he watched. Most nights, that wound up with a mutual jerk-off session while he told me all the things he wanted to do to me.

"And are you in your bedroom already?"

"Yes, Daddy," I whispered just in case Mav was listening in. The text message from him earlier, telling me to make sure I cleaned up and closed the bedroom door before he called, hinted that this was going to be a sexy unboxing.

"What are you wearing?" I chuckled again. That was such a corny line, straight out of bad porn, but I knew he was truly interested in knowing what I had on so he could undress me.

"Just a pair of sweatpants," I informed him. "That's what you told me to wear tonight."

"You're such a good boy." Ryan groaned. "Switch to video for me, baby. I want to see you."

I already had the tripod Ryan picked up before he left town, set up on the edge of my nightstand. My hands shook as I tried to get my phone into the holder. Something about tonight felt different, but I couldn't put my finger on why I was such a ball of nerves.

I pouted when I settled back on the bed and noticed that Ryan hadn't turned on his camera. "Don't I get to see you too?"

"I'm sorry, sweetheart. I'm not someplace I can do anything just yet. You'll have to wait a little bit longer for that." He sounded genuinely upset about letting me down.

"It's fine," I quickly reassured him. Ryan was constantly looking out for me, and he truly went above and beyond what most men would to make me happy. It wasn't his fault he'd been burning the candle at both ends so he could finish up his current project and come out to see me. He had likely stolen away a few minutes to call me.

"Do you have your present with you?" His question snapped me out of my mini snit. I knew going into this, that it wasn't going to be easy, and these packages were a way for him to be close to me from a distance.

"Duh," I scoffed. "That's a silly question. I've been staring at it ever since I brought in the mail."

"Do you have any guesses what might be inside?" he teased.

Knowing Ryan, the possibilities were endless. So far, he'd sent me everything from a set of anal plugs in various sizes and a huge bottle of lube to a small prostate massager that included a remote control at that allowed him to torture me from across the country. That was a genius invention because it allowed me to feel like he was still close, even when we couldn't be together. Of course, I didn't think that on the days he told me to wear it to work, which led to me trying to pretend I wasn't having my ass played with while helping customers find the right size pants.

And then there were the nonsexual gifts as well. One time, he sent a sketchpad and expensive set of pencils with a note reminding me about all the days I used to spend sketching while pretending I wasn't watching him playing football in the backyard with Deegan. Drawing wasn't something I'd ever be good enough at to turn it into a career, but it *was* something that quieted my mind. He'd even sent some of my favorite cookies and snacks from when I'd been younger, along with reminders for me to eat.

"Why don't you go ahead and open the box to see what we're doing tonight," he suggested. My eyebrows scrunched together when I lifted the flaps on the box and noticed a blindfold at the very top.

"Um, okay," I muttered as I lifted the blindfold out of the box and held it up for him to see.

"Trust me, baby," he pleaded. "I haven't steered you wrong yet, have I?"

No, he absolutely hadn't. Somehow, my sex life over the past month was better than ever, even though I had to rely on bits of silicone as a substitute for having the man I loved next to me.

"Keep going," he urged me. A door closed somewhere near him. There were muffled voices alerting me to the fact Ryan wasn't alone. He said something, but I couldn't make out what or who he was talking to.

I stiffened, worried I was going to get him in trouble.

"If you need to go, we can pick this up again later," I offered again, even though my nuts were ready to explode.

"Who's in charge here, Tanner?" The clipped words and gravelly tone of his voice had my dick twitching.

"You are, Daddy," I responded.

"That's right. And if I say this is the right time for us to play together, do you get to question me?"

"No, Daddy." He groaned, and I imagined him reaching down to adjust himself. He loved hearing me call him that. It wasn't something I could do easily in casual conversation, but when we were like this, it was the most natural thing ever.

"Glad we settled that. Now, what else is in the box?"

I pulled out a small bundle of wrapped tissue paper. I grew even harder, like some sort of Pavlovian response to the dark teal paper. This wasn't my first gift from this particular store, and everything Ryan had bought me so far made me feel beautiful. I unwrapped the paper, revealing a royal blue satin jock.

"Do you like it?" I bit down on my bottom lip to hold back a snarky response. Daddy didn't mind snark, but there was only so much he'd take before adding another punishment to the tally for when he saw me next. He *had* to know how much I loved it, based on my beaming smile and the fact I couldn't stop rubbing the soft fabric over my cheek.

"I love it, Daddy. Can I put it on now?"

"In a minute," he told me. "First I want you to open the rest of your presents."

There was only one thing left in the box. This was bigger and heavier, so it had to be whatever toy Ryan planned on torturing me with tonight.

I pulled out a prostate massager like none I'd ever seen before. I flipped it over my hands, taking in the shape and ribbed texture at the center of it. My hole clenched, imagining the curved end of the toy nailing my prostate just right while the swollen area at the center worked my nerves from the outside. It didn't surprise me when the toy started vibrating in my hand.

"Where do you keep finding things like this?" I slipped my fingers into the holes at the front of the massager, knowing exactly what they were made for. He was going to make me work for my orgasm tonight.

"A good Daddy never tells his secrets," Ryan teased.

"I had no idea there were so many toys you could control from anywhere in the world." The buzzing stopped, then started up again with a different rhythm. I sucked in a sharp breath, wrapping my hand around the shaft of the massager, imagining how it would feel against my inner walls.

"Neither did I," he admitted. "But now I have to admit, I have a long list of things to eventually add to our collection."

I like the sound of that. *Our* collection. Even though everything was tucked away under the bed in my room, they were just as much his toys as they were mine. It was a way for us to share connection while we were forced to be apart.

"Can I get changed now?" There was a wet spot at the front of my sweats, and I was eager to get the first orgasm out of the way so he could tease me.

Yes, I was impatient today. Ryan hadn't been available when I'd tried calling him this morning, and he'd been busy for more than a quick goodnight call last night, too. When he said he promised he'd make it up to me tonight, I hadn't realized something like this would be in my mailbox this morning.

"Stand up and take off your sweatpants, sweetheart. I want you facing the door so I can see that gorgeous ass of yours," he demanded. He truly had an obsession with my backside.

I hooked my thumbs into the elastic and slowly pushed the pants over my hips, glancing over my shoulder. This was when I normally got that first glimpse of Ryan's glassy, unfocused gaze. It was like watching me strip for him got him so turned on he could barely help himself. But tonight, I stared at the blank screen.

"Where are you?" I asked before stripping myself any further. My heart raced, imagining Ryan sitting with his friends and me putting on a show for all of them. We'd talked about playing where others could see me a couple of times, but I couldn't imagine him doing something like that without giving me a bit of advance warning.

"I'm in a stairwell right now," he told me. "There's nobody else here."

"Then why can't I see you?"

"You will, soon, baby," he promised. "You just need to trust me a little bit longer. Can you do that for me?"

"Of course," I responded immediately, trying to hide my disappointment and frustration. I'd do anything Ryan told me to, even if it frustrated the hell out of me.

"Good boy. Now, I want you to put the ring of the massager over that sexy cock. You can face the camera so I can make sure you're going it right."

It wasn't easy since my dick was already hard enough that I was on the verge of orgasm. I tried thinking unsexy thoughts while stretching the silicone ring over my length. Thanks to the stretch of the rings, I was able to get one looped around my sac and the other around my shaft.

"That's not too tight, is it?" Daddy asked. I shook my head. "Let me see."

My face flamed with embarrassment as I stepped in front of the camera, turning to the side so he could get a good look at my restrained junk.

"Clean up that dripping bit. You wouldn't want to waste it, would you?"

"No, Daddy," I agreed, flicking my thumb over the head of my cock before sucking it clean. Daddy groaned, just like he always did when I tasted myself. A stabbing pain in my chest had my cock deflating. Most days, I could deal with the distance, but today I was struggling. I didn't want to be the one eating my cum. I wanted him sucking me dry, the way he kept saying he couldn't wait to do.

I wanted to fall into his arms as post-orgasmic exhaustion pulled me into sleep, instead of staring into a cold, hard phone screen until he disconnected the call.

I just wanted for everything to be different.

"Hey, what's going on, baby?" Ryan asked when he noticed my distress.

Damn video chat.

"Nothing, Daddy," I lied. Telling him how upset I was wouldn't do anything to change the situation, and it would upset him, too.

"That's five more. Do you want the tally to go up?" My ass clenched reflexively. I wasn't sure how many with the paddle I was up to so far, but it was enough I wouldn't be able to sit right by the time he was done. "I'm going to ask you one more time... Where did your head go just then?"

I flopped back on the bed and then jolted off of it when the massager stabbed against my taint in a very much not good way. I pressed my lips together to keep from crying out loud enough that Mav would come running in to see what was wrong.

I couldn't blame Ryan for the stifled laughter on the other end of the line. If the toy had been on the other cock, I would have been the one fighting inappropriate amusement. At least he pulled himself together enough to ask if I was okay.

"Fine. Just one more thing not going the way it's supposed to," I muttered, climbing back onto the bed, carefully this time, and rolling to my side. I still wanted to get off—I was still a very sexually driven man in my prime, after all—but I no longer felt the same sense of urgency.

For a change, it was Ryan hurrying things along. "Grab the lube, sweetheart. I'll make you forget about everything that's worrying you."

I followed his directions as Daddy guided me through prepping my hole and then slicking up the toy. My eyes rolled back in my head as I pushed it past the ring of muscle. Just the shape of it was hitting all the right spots; I couldn't wait until he turned on the vibration again.

"That feels good, doesn't it?" he asked once the toy was seated fully inside my body.

"So good," I panted.

"Put on the jock, sweetheart," he instructed next. "I want to see that gorgeous ass framed for me."

I hissed as I tried to arrange my junk in the cup. It wasn't easy with as hard as I was, and even with the pressure from the rings, I felt ready to lose control.

"Fuck, you're beautiful like that. So needy for me."

"Always," I admitted. Knowing what his next direction would be, I climbed onto the bed with my ass facing the camera. I spread my legs so he could get a good look at what he was doing to me. My back arched when my insides were jolted by the vibrator. "Fuck, Daddy. I'm too close."

"But you'll wait until I give you permission, won't you?" he demanded in his bossy, gravelly tone. "You wouldn't want to come before you're allowed and then have to go even longer before the next orgasm, right?"

"No, Daddy. I'll wait," I promised.

"Good boy." Another door closed. "Put on the blindfold and fold your arms in front of you. Stick that ass in the air for Daddy."

I closed my eyes behind the blindfold, imagining Daddy really was standing behind me. Any moment, he'd reach out and tease his fingers through my crease. My breathing grew slow and steady, and my mind drifted to that peaceful place only Ryan could achieve.

14

RYAN

It took every ounce of self-control I could muster to keep from breaking down the door. I'd paid an outrageous amount of money for a last-minute flight this morning when Jack declared everything was good to go at Club DeSires. It had been an agonizing month away from my boy, and it was killing me to be so close but so far away.

"Hey," Mav greeted me as he slipped out of the apartment, leaving the door cracked open. I pressed a finger to my lips, reminding him that Tanner was on the line. Of course, I had my boy so worked up, I wasn't sure he'd have noticed if Mav had been shouting that I was standing in their hallway. Mav lowered his voice to a whisper. "I'll be out all night."

Thank you, I mouthed before turning my attention to the remote in my hand.

"Do you have the blindfold on, sweetheart?" I asked as I stepped into the apartment. It was a longshot that this would work, but so far, everything was going according to plan. Before today, I'd planned to play with him over video chat, but this was a million times better.

"Yes, Daddy," he whimpered. Fuck, I loved it when he was this turned on. He sounded about a minute away from sobbing, begging me to let him come.

Soon, my sweet boy.

I quickly toed off my shoes as I continued telling him how pretty he was and switched the massager to a more intense setting. I had to turn down the volume on my phone to keep him from noticing the echo until my earbuds connected. "That's it, Tanner. Fuck yourself for me. Let me see how you want me to drill into that tight hole."

Tanner reached between his legs, pulling the toy out as much as his position would allow, before slowly gliding it back into his passage. His face was buried against the mattress between his arms. A flimsy door was all the separated us, and I hoped he'd forgive me for not rushing in there the moment I arrived. This was too much fun.

"What else do you want Daddy to do to you, Tanner? Would you let me slide a finger in next to my cock?" I pressed the heel of my hand against my dick to take the edge off. Round one wasn't going to take long tonight. But that was okay because I didn't plan on leaving his cramped bedroom any more than absolutely necessary for the next few days.

"Oh fuck," Tanner cried out, loud enough my ears rang. "Please, Daddy. Want to feel you stretching me wide, owning my ass."

"I *always* own that pretty ass," I reminded him. "Whether I have you stuffed so full you think you're going to split in two or so empty you think you'll die if I don't let you put something up there."

"Are—Daddy?" he stammered, and I realized I'd fucked up. I'd made sure he couldn't hear the echo of his own pleasure, but in my lust-addled mind, I'd forgotten to keep far enough away he couldn't hear me.

So much for surprises.

I slowly pushed the door open, bracing myself when Tanner bolted off the bed and practically flew into my arms. "Hey, sweetheart."

"What are you doing here? I thought you were supposed to be in big, important meetings all week. How long are you staying? Why did you make me play with myself when you were right outside the door?" The questions never seemed end, but they were sprinkled in between the sweetest, sloppiest kisses, and I couldn't help but laugh.

I toyed with his ass as I carried him across the room. He moaned and writhed against me, making it nearly impossible for me to set him down gently before stripping off my pants.

"I wanted you to play with yourself because I knew I wouldn't be able to wait long before burying my cock deep inside of you." We'd both agreed to get tested after our first week together. The relationship might be a new development for us, but the emotions were something we'd both held close to our chest for years. Whenever I talked to Tanner on the phone, it was hard to believe it had only been a month.

I kicked my shoes across the room and stepped out of my pants before falling into bed next to him. The remote for the massager was hidden in my hand. I sealed my mouth over his, savoring those first sips of him in far too long. While I would hold to my promise of not pressuring him into moving, feeling the strength of his lean body under mine and swallowing every whimper and moan he fed me, I knew it would be even harder to leave him this time.

He threw his head back and screamed when I pushed the button to turn the vibrator on full blast as I started fucking him with it. "Yeah, you like that, don't you? I might have to see if it's possible for me to fit inside of you without taking it out."

"Too much," Tanner pleaded. "Oh fuck, Daddy. You can't say things like that to me. Now, I can't stop thinking about it."

"Good." I bit the side of his neck before rolling to the side and flipping him onto his stomach. I pressed the length of my dick into his crease and started rutting against him. "I want you thinking about it. With every thrust, I want you holding your breath, waiting to see if this is when I stretch you even wider."

"Do it, Daddy. Please." He craned his neck, fisting the back of my head and pulling me in for a kiss. "Own me."

How could I deny him when he was all of my fantasies come to life? I stretched to reach the lube on his nightstand, squirting a liberal glob next to my shaft. As I started working a finger in next to the massager, I circled my thumb and index finger around myself, hoping like hell it worked to fight off my own climax.

He tensed as I slipped my middle finger into his ass, cupping the base of the toy with the rest of my hand. I leaned over, kissing the back of his neck. "Tell me if it gets to be too much."

"I...will...so full...hurts, but want more, too," he slurred, his voice raspy and distant.

"So damn needy all the time," I teased as I stretched his hole further. "Are you going to let Daddy double stuff you tonight?"

"Anything you want," he promised me. "Want you to fill me until I think I'm going to break in two."

As tempting as it was to trust that he knew how much he could take, a niggle of doubt crept into the back of my mind. That was going to be a lot for his body to handle. Maybe it would be for the best if we saved the toy and my dick for another night. It could be something we worked our way up to.

The primal need I felt for Tanner was dangerous. He made me forget my rules, had me ready to throw caution to the wind.

Tanner's body seized and he let out a pained cry when I added a second finger. When I tried pulling back, he threw his arm back, latching onto my wrist. "Don't stop. Please. I can do this, I just need..."

"There's no rush, sweetheart," I reassured him. His voice was panicked, as if he expected me to walk out of the room and his life if he didn't give this to me immediately. "I'm not going to push your body further than you can handle."

"I want it all," he insisted.

I smoothed my free hand over his back, bending down to kiss his neck. "I know you do. You're my good boy, and you want so badly to please Daddy, even if it hurts you. That's when I have to step in and do what's best for you."

"You're what's best," he insisted through a choked sob. "And you should get what you want, too."

"Baby, just being here with you is everything to me," I promised him. A peace had settled over me since Maverick opened the apartment door for me. Just knowing that I was breathing the same air as Tanner made life better. "Even if you said you weren't up for having sex, I couldn't possibly be upset with you."

"But you want to have sex, right?" The fact we were having this conversation while Tanner's hole was filled with my fingers and the newest toy I'd bought for him was absurd.

As if there was any question what I wanted. To prove the point, I pressed my length against his crease. "Unless you're too sore or tired by the time I finish playing with you, I fully intend to fill your ass tonight. You still want that, don't you?"

"Oh fuck!" He pushed back against my fingers. His hole clenched, trapping me where he wanted me. "Yes, Daddy, please. Want to feel you running down my legs by the time we're done."

"That's what I hoped you'd say," I praised him. "So how about we table this for the time being? I'm not sure I can wait long enough to properly stretch you to take more than a toy *or* my cock. I've been waiting too damn long to be back inside of you again."

"Me too," he moaned. "I hate being away from you."

"I know, baby. But it won't be forever." I planted a line of kisses along his spine as I pulled my fingers from his body. Next, I carefully eased the massager out of his passage. "But let's not think about that right now, okay?"

"You're the Daddy, and I'm supposed to listen to whatever you say." He settled on the bed with his head pillowed on his arms, ass wiggling around in the air.

"Cheeky little brat." I cracked his ass and the sound that came out of his mouth was somewhere between a moan and a yelp. "Don't think I've forgotten about the mother of all spankings you've got coming."

That only encouraged him. He wiggled his butt again, this time letting out an exaggerated moan. "Do it, Daddy. Spank me for being a naughty boy and then fuck me hard. Make it hurt."

I squeezed his cheeks, spreading them so I could see his gaping hole. "Who's in charge here?"

"You are, Daddy," he responded immediately.

"So do you get to tell me when you should get your spankings?"

"No, Daddy. I'm sorry. It's just...you talk about them all the time, and I want to know what it's like to feel my ass burning for you."

"Oh, you're going to." I chuckled, biting back a groan as I slicked up my shaft. "But it will be when I decide I'm ready, and not a moment before. Got it?"

"Yes, Daddy."

I pressed the tip of my cock against his hole, stretching him but not fully entering him. He rocked back, trying to take more and earning himself another smack on his hip. "Try to take control and this is going to be over quick, but not in the way we both need."

"I'm trying, Daddy. I promise I am, but it's hard. I've been thinking about this since you told me to get tested. Even before that, really." I loved seeing Tanner when he was this uninhibited. Whenever we talked on the phone, I got the impression he was trying to hold back from me. I couldn't get on his case too much about that because I did the same to him. It was as if neither of us wanted to admit to the other how much we were hurting. "Please, don't make me wait any longer."

"How can I resist when you're so sweet for me?" I covered his body and bent down to kiss him as I eased my way into his passage. It was an awkward position, and I could already feel my body protesting, but I couldn't *not* kiss him. His muscles clenched around me and he whimpered into my mouth. There were so many things I wanted to say to him. Being fully seated in him felt like coming home. *This* was where I belonged; deep inside of Tanner, over him, protecting him, loving him.

Tanner laid perfectly still, allowing me to make love to him slowly and passionately. He wasn't a passive lover, but a compliant one. His muscles rippled with the effort he was putting into not arching off the bed.

"So damn good for me," I praised him. "I expected you to be greedier."

"Oh, I'm definitely greedy," he quipped. "But I don't want to do the wrong thing and have you stop."

The admission broke my heart. Yes, I wanted him obedient, but not to the point of panic. I stilled, pulling out long enough to flip him onto his back. I needed to see him, needed him to look into my eyes as I made love to him, so he'd know how happy he made me. I cupped his face in my hands. "Nothing could stop me now that I'm here. I love you, Tanner, and that includes when you're an impatient little brat. Maybe especially then, because it gives me something to punish you for. You're strong-willed, and that's not something I ever want you to lose."

"I love you, too, Daddy. So much." His eyes turned glassy, and he sucked his bottom lip between his teeth.

"What is it?" I rocked my hips gently, not actively fucking him, but drawing out our connection. "Tell me, boy. You promised you'd let me know what was going on in that beautiful head of yours so I wouldn't have to worry."

"I keep waiting for you to wake up and realize this isn't working for you," he admitted. "You're always trying to take care of me."

"And that will never change," I promised him. "You're my boy, and it's my privilege to be the one to make sure you have everything you want and need."

"Even if I'm too scared to move in with you?" His head fell to the side, and I could practically feel him pulling away from me.

Ahhh, so that's what this was about.

"Maybe especially because of that." I withdrew before slamming into him again, harder this time. His back arched off the bead as I pounded into him, proving with my body what he wouldn't believe in my words. "You're *mine*, Tanner. And until you realize I don't mean you're mine *for now*, but *forever*, I have to work that much harder to prove myself to you. I have to make sure you know every day how much you mean to me."

"Even if it means flying cross-country to surprise me?"

"Yes, even then," I confirmed. I'd known he'd been struggling, so I'd pushed up my plans by a few days. When I told Jack what was going on, he agreed that there was nothing for me to do in Annandale and promised he'd call if he needed me. What Tanner didn't know yet was, I'd purchased a one-way ticket so there wasn't a deadline for us this time. "You think you're good at pretending you're okay when you're not, but I know you, Tanner. I know every single one of your tells and I know when you're lying to me."

"But you lied to me, too," he shot back, a bit of that fire returning to his eyes. "I don't like making you sad, and I know you are because I won't be with you."

"When the time is right, you will be." Keeping on as we had been forever wasn't sustainable, but I meant it when I told him I'd never pressure him before he was ready. When he moved into what I already thought of as *our home*, we'd both know he was there because he wanted to be. "Until then, I'm okay with working on airplanes as I go back and forth."

"But the money," he protested. I sealed my mouth over his again, unwilling to have this argument.

"Is well spent if it means being inside of you."

Understanding Desire

Somehow, nothing ever went according to plan when Tanner and I were together, but maybe that was how we were supposed to be. I gave him the security he craved, and he forced me to let go of itineraries and carefully choreographed scenes. The only thing that truly mattered was that we were finally together again.

We held each other tightly as I thrust in and out of his body, his cock trapped between our bodies, leaking a steady stream of precum. Time dragged on, in the best possible way, as I made love to my boy the way I'd dreamed about for so long. Later, there would be time for hard and kinky fucking, but first, we needed this. The connection, the reminder of who we were when pretenses and titles were stripped away.

"I love you, Tanner. Always," I promised him as I felt my orgasm threatening to send me hurdling over the edge. My pace became erratic as passion claimed me. I fisted my hands in his hair, holding him tightly so he couldn't look anywhere other than into my eyes. "You're mine, and I'm not fucking letting you go again."

"Please, Daddy," he cried out. I wasn't sure what he was asking me for, but I'd give it to him. His release, my heart, everything that was mine was his. I spilled into him, and my brain short-circuited at the feeling of my cum filling his body. I pulled out slowly, my eyes fixated on his spasming hole, my release leaking out of him.

If I was a younger man, I would have been ready for round two as I watched Tanner reach between his legs and scoop up my release onto his fingers. His gaze never left mine as he lifted his fingers to his mouth, sucking every bit of my cum clean.

"I should punish you for taking that without permission," I teased, bending down so I could nip his ear. "Lucky for you, it was too fucking hot for me to think of a suitable punishment."

"I'm sure you'll think of something." Tanner curled his legs around mine and wrapped his arms around my back, pulling me on top of him. "Now, I think we need to take a nap because there's not going to be much sleeping tonight."

"Smart boy." Tanner tightened his grip on me when I tried sliding to the mattress beside him. I couldn't help but chuckle as I kissed his forehead. "I take it my boy has me right where he wants me?"

"Always." Tanner sighed, and it wasn't long before his breathing steadied, and he was asleep in my arms. I should have listened to his advice to nap while I could, but that would have meant time spent not trying to refresh my memory on all of the sounds he made as he slept or missing out on the way he twitched as he dreamed.

Sleep could come later.

15

TANNER

"How long are you in town for?" I asked as Ryan pulled out the eggs and a loaf of bread. Last night had been better than any reunion I had fantasized about. I'd spent more time than I should've, thinking about what it would be like when I finally saw Ryan again, but never had I imagined the silly man would surprise me by flying out unannounced.

We hadn't done anything hardcore but that was okay. In a way, it made me feel like what we had was that much more real, as opposed to role playing our fantasies. Getting freaky in bed was great, but it was nothing compared to the tender way we had made love twice more before Ryan claimed he was too tired for a fourth round.

"That depends a lot on you," he responded. I took the loaf of bread from him and started making toast while he worked on the eggs. I was ashamed to admit that even the most mundane tasks in the kitchen were above my skill level. Luckily, it seemed Ryan was right at home in my kitchen.

"I mean, when do you have to be back for work?" If I had my way, he'd never leave, but that wasn't feasible. Every time we talked, he was eager to tell me about the latest progress with the club renovations. He swore he had no plans of being hands-on with the business, but it wouldn't surprise me if that changed down the line. It was probably killing him to not know what was going on.

"I talked to Jack and he agreed this is where I need to be for a little while." Ryan stepped up behind me and wrapped his arms around my waist. My body relaxed against his as he kissed his way along the back of my neck. "It's quite possible I've been a bit insufferable being away from you."

"Same," I admitted. "Mav has been threatening to kick me out if I keep snapping on him."

"You mean to tell me my boy has a bit of an attitude when he doesn't get his way?" He chuckled and I turned to glare at him. "Come on, baby. You've never been the patient type. When you feel like you're missing out, you're like a toddler who missed naptime."

"Well, this is your fault, too," I accused, even though it was a lie. Almost weekly, Ryan offered to buy me a plane ticket to come out and see him, and every week, I refused.

I was starting to realize my stubbornness was hurting more than it was helping. And that was something I needed to figure out how to talk to him about before he left. I wasn't ready to uproot my life just yet, but I'd feel better if we had a plan in place to make that happen.

Look at me, being all adult and shit.

"How do you figure it's my fault?" Ryan released me, going back to his pan of eggs.

"You're the one who moved all the way across the country. If you were still close by, I could see you all the time." In my head, it made perfect sense. When we were kids, I'd foolishly thought Ryan and Deegan would remain close, and I'd be stuck pining after him the way I had through my teen years. He'd never struck me as the type to spread his wings and fly.

"You still could," Ryan pointed out. He turned off the heat and moved the pan of eggs to the back burner.

I swallowed hard when he leaned against the counter next to me. Despite wanting to talk to him about the distance between us, I felt my hackles rise when he broached the subject first.

"What's really holding you back? What do I need to do to make you see this isn't a flash in the pan for me? Because I'll do it. I'll do anything for you." The inches between us felt like miles. He wasn't holding me in his arms, kissing every inch of my body that was exposed and in reach. He was giving me space, trying to have an important conversation without hormones taking control.

I'd never doubted the lengths Ryan would go to for my happiness. Hearing him say the words out loud only made me feel even worse.

"I know it sounds cliché, but it's not you, it's totally me," I muttered, paying far more attention than necessary to the toaster. If I looked at him, I'd see that I was hurting him, and then I'd fall to my knees, begging for him to take me home with him. I wanted to, but there were things that felt unresolved keeping me from giving in.

"Then talk to me," he pleaded, reaching up to brush a finger over my cheek. "Tell me what's holding you back so we can get past it and really be together."

I wasn't sure if Ryan would understand my hesitation. It had nothing to do with us as a couple anymore, and everything to do with the world around us.

"Have you talked to Deegan recently?" The fact it was difficult to say my brother's name was a huge red flag for me. It was like the subject of their friendship was off-limits now that we were together, which was exactly what I had feared would happen.

Ryan averted his eyes and that was all the answer I needed. I'd been serious when I said I wouldn't be the reason a friendship that had lasted decades fell apart, and I meant it. "Is that what this is about?"

I nodded.

"What happened to the tough as nails boy who didn't give a damn what anybody else thought?"

"This is different," I insisted. My determination to be happy, despite my family's judgment, was as strong as ever and I wasn't looking for my big brother's approval. "You and Deegan have been friends for a long time, and I need to know that you're going to be okay before I make things even worse."

Ryan didn't say anything for a long minute. He pushed away from the counter and poured himself a cup of coffee before opening the fridge to get the orange juice for me. I didn't even realize we *had* juice.

"I might have done some online shopping before I got here last night. Maverick told me the two of you live off fast food and frozen pizza," he explained, sensing my confusion over the sudden presence of actual food and drink in our kitchen. The crease in his brow grew deeper. "And we will be talking about that. I'm pretty sure I told you that you needed to start taking better care of yourself."

"I try," I insisted. "But you don't understand how expensive it is to eat healthy."

"Then you tell me so I can help you out." Fuuuuck, I wished we were back on the subject of my brother. I always felt like I was disappointing Ryan when I argued about him spending money on essentials for me, but I felt weak when I caved. I was *not* going to cave about this.

If Ryan wanted me to move in with him, he'd have to get used to my new steely backbone.

"That's not going to happen," I protested. "I love you, but I have to be able to stand on my own two feet. That's not going to change no matter what."

"You also need to learn what it means to have a partner who only wants the best for you." His expression softened as he opened his arms to me. "I don't want to fight with you, Tanner. I'm sorry if you feel like I overstepped. I wasn't checking up on you, but Mav thought I should have a warning if I was going to be spending time here instead of getting a hotel room."

"I suppose that makes sense." I buried my face against Ryan's neck, a bit embarrassed about my tantrum.

"Let's eat and you can tell me why you're so worried about how often I'm talking to Deegan," Ryan suggested.

I quirked an eyebrow, silently calling him out for skirting around the truth. The two of them used to talk weekly, and now it had been over a month since he'd mentioned a conversation between them. And my darling *Daddy* had apparently forgotten that I was besties with his best friend's wife, so I knew damn well the two of them were being stubborn asses and avoiding one another.

"From the very start, I told you I didn't want to come between the two of you," I explained as I pushed the eggs around on my plate. I felt oddly vulnerable this morning. Having Ryan sitting across from me at the wobbly dining table made me realize just how miserable I was being apart from him. Part of me was starting to feel like Deegan was nothing more than a convenient excuse for me to not make the big, scary move.

"You haven't," Ryan insisted.

"Please, let me get this out," I pleaded, holding up a hand to silence him. "You promised me what we're doing wouldn't affect your friendship but it's obvious that it has. I'm not saying that you lied to me or anything like that, because I truly believe you had good intentions."

"I get what you're saying, but what does that have to do with you and me?" He wrapped his fingers around my wrist, stopping the clattering of my fork against my plate. "I don't like seeing you upset, but it doesn't make sense to me that *this* is what you're dwelling on when we're supposed to be spending time together."

"Yeah, well, welcome to my brain," I scoffed. "You'll probably think I'm being stupid, but I was thinking about how nice it was waking up with you again. And then I came out here and you were making breakfast, and it was like all of my dreams come true. I want that to be real life. But it would be easier for me to jump in with both feet if I didn't have to worry about my entire family blaming me for coming between the two of you."

Breakfast wasn't happening. He could punish me for it later, but there was no way I could eat now. I pushed back from the table and set my plate on the counter. I should scrape the eggs into the garbage, but he'd gone to the trouble to make them for me and that seemed disrespectful. I curled my fingers around the edge of the counter and hung my head. I knew I was talking in circles, but I couldn't get my thoughts in order.

Ryan wrapped his arms around me from behind and rested his chin on my shoulder. "Baby, I don't think that's stupid at all. It's sweet, actually. But you need to remember that Deegan isn't the one I'm in a relationship with. You're the man I love, and they'll have to get used to that at some point."

"Again, that's something that's easier said than done. Let's say things fell apart between us..." Just thinking about an end to this had me feeling queasy. I shivered, and Ryan wrapped me tighter in his arms. "They'll never let me live it down if the two of you still aren't talking."

"This really bothers you, doesn't it?" I closed my eyes and relaxed into his embrace as Ryan started kissing the side of my neck. If I turned around and dropped to my knees, I could distract him from talking.

But no. It was time for me to show him I was capable of being a responsible adult. "Yeah, it does. Probably more than it should, but I can't help it. I want everything to work out for the best, which is somewhat weird for me. I know I talk a good game about not caring what other people think about me, but it would be a hell of a lot easier for me to follow you home if things were settled here."

"Is that what's holding you back?"

I shrugged, not wanting to admit that the nights spent alone gave me far too much time coming up with the thousand and one excuses why moving to be with Ryan would be a bad idea.

"If it's this important to you that we make sure Deegan isn't pissed off at me for taking advantage of his baby brother, then let's get together with them," he suggested, phone already in his hand. He quirked an eyebrow as if trying to call my bluff. I nodded for him to connect the call.

While he and Deegan chatted, I disappeared into the bedroom. This was a conversation that needed to be between just the two of them, and it wouldn't do my good mood any good if my brother started talking shit and trying to convince Ryan he could do better than me.

He totally could. Ryan was one hell of a catch who could have any man he set his sights on, but for some odd reason, he wanted me. Complications and all. Unless he woke up and realized he was settling, he was stuck with me.

Understanding Desire

The bedroom reeked of sex. Sleeping on the sheets he'd slept on sounded romantic, but they were crusty from the amount of cum he'd wrung from my body last night. I pulled off the sheets and tossed them toward the door before digging through the closest for a clean set. Once that was done, I figured I might as well make the bed. Ryan liked things organized and I liked making him proud. It seemed like a win-win for me to spend a bit of time tidying up.

When I worked up the courage to leave my room to see how things were going, it was completely, terrifyingly silent. There was always some sort of noise in the apartment, but now...nothing. I peered through the living room and found Ryan standing out on the balcony, leaning against the railing I was afraid would separate from the floor if we looked at it wrong. I debated going outside to warn him, but if he needed more privacy, I'd give it to him.

I was almost through with my shower when Ryan opened the door. "Damn, baby. Are you trying to melt off your skin in here?"

"As if," I scoffed. "It only steams up like that because there's no ventilation. The water heater in this place sucks."

I'd bet Ryan had one of those fancy tankless water heaters that never ran out of hot water. And water pressure. I'd suck him off ten times a day if he had a showerhead that felt like the high-pressure spray at the car wash.

"You're not going to ask how it went?" Through the fogged-up glass door, I could see Ryan leaning against the vanity. The man seriously needed to realize that you didn't lean on anything in our apartment. The management company was all about doing as little as possible without drawing fines for building code violations. I would *not* miss this place.

Funny, twenty-four hours ago, I was still insisting I wasn't ready to move, but here I was thinking about *when* I left, not *if*. I'd have to talk to Mav to let him know my plans were changing. Our lease wasn't up for a few more months, but I didn't want to renew.

"Nah, I figure you'll tell me if there's something I need to know," I responded, feigning a casualness I certainly didn't feel. Deegan could be a stubborn bastard when he wanted to be, and I didn't believe for a second, his acceptance the night of his wedding would last.

"Come on, brat." Ryan reached in and turned off the water before holding out a towel for me. When I tried snatching it from him, he held on tighter and narrowed his eyes. "Let me take care of you. I've been horribly deprived since I went home."

"Well, then maybe we'll have to find a way to keep you from suffering in the future," I teased. I wouldn't admit how nice it felt having him kneel before me, drying every droplet of water from my skin.

"Don't toy with me, boy," he warned me.

"Who says I'm playing around?" It was almost comical how Ryan lost his balance and crashed into me. I reached down, helping him off the ground. "Man, if I knew you'd react like that, I would have waited to say anything. If I'd lost my balance, I would have cracked my head on the faucet, then you'd have to nurse me back to health from a concussion and a gaping head wound."

"Such a little drama queen." As Ryan stood, he reached around and swatted my ass. "I ought to take you over my knee for making me put you in danger."

"How in the hell is this my fault?" I jumped out of the way when he tried swatting me again. "You know, I've heard balance is one of the things that goes to hell as you age."

It was fucked, but this was the first time Ryan and I had really played around without any stress between us. He was relaxed, like he hadn't been the week at the resort, and I finally trusted that we were both committed to making things work. I liked joking with him, almost as much as I liked fucking around with him.

"I've got your age right here," Ryan scoffed as he cupped his dick. "Then again, I'm so old I'm not sure I'll be able to get it up. Will you still love me if I can't fuck you until you forget your name?"

I scratched my chin, pretending to think for a moment. He narrowed his eyes and pursed his lips. He was cute when he was trying to mean mug me. I draped my arms over his shoulders and pressed my naked, still damp body against his. "You know there's nothing that could make me love you less, not even a wilted, wrinkly dick."

"That's either super sweet or disturbing as hell, but I'm not sure which." Ryan moved out of the way when I stepped up to the mirror. I'd gotten lax about shaving, too busy throwing myself a pity party, but now that Ryan was here, I wanted to look my best for him. "I'll find you something to wear while you get ready."

"I thought we were hanging around the apartment today," I grumbled. Mav had texted in the middle of the night to let me know he was crashing at a buddy's house for a few nights to give us some private time. I'd intended to make every minute of our privacy count, but apparently Ryan had other plans.

"Yep, but that was before you blackmailed me into calling Deegan," he informed me. My mouth watered when he leaned against the door frame. "Haley freaked when she heard I was in town, so apparently we're spending the day with them."

Leave it to Deegan to fuck up my plans. But that wasn't fair; I was the one who made Ryan call. Even though I didn't agree to him calling it blackmail, I could see how he might have felt like it was.

"I didn't realize you and Haley were close," I choked out, trying to find something to say that wouldn't make me sound like a petulant turd. This was my fault, plain and simple. Now, I had to pretend there was nothing I wanted to do more than hang out with my brother and my boyfriend, who were trying to repair their friendship that I'd helped fracture.

"We're not, but apparently the two of you have been royal pains in her ass."

Fair enough. I tried to not put her in the middle of things, but it was tough because she'd always been the person I talked to about my shit. I didn't bother taking relationship problems to Mav; he was allergic to anything more than a one-night stand.

"And when we get back here, we're going to talk about when you're at least coming out to visit me," Ryan warned me. I was surprised he hadn't insisted that we spend the night packing my shit so we could drive across the country. It was something small, but it proved to me that he was trying to respect my need to do things in my own time.

"I don't think I need to visit," I told him. His face went as white as the towel I scrubbed over my face, and I realized how that might have sounded. I tossed the towel onto the vanity and threw myself into his arms. "Hey, I didn't mean it like that. I'm just saying that wherever you are is where I want to be. It might take a bit to get everything in order, but you flying out here made me realize I need to be willing to meet you halfway."

"Are you sure, baby?" Ryan's tight embrace said he really hoped I wasn't about to tell him I was kidding. "Moving isn't exactly a halfway sort of move. This is a big step and, as much as I want you with me, I don't want you to feel pressured."

"And that's exactly why it's time for me to pull my head out of my ass. You keep going out of your way to make sure I'm happy and taken care of. It's time for me to do the same for you." I was so damn proud of myself; my voice didn't even crack as I said it. The raw vulnerability I felt diving into this with him was nothing compared to standing naked in front of him while he was fully clothed.

"Then that's what we'll talk about later." He laced his fingers with mine and pulled me across the hall to my room. My hopes that he wanted to celebrate with a quickie were quickly dashed when he guided me to the bed and then started rummaging through my dresser to find something for me to wear.

If letting him dress me wasn't a sign of how much I loved him, I wasn't sure anything was. That was a level of trust no one achieved.

16

RYAN

Tanner telling me he wouldn't consider moving to be with me until I fixed things with Deegan was an eye-opening moment. Yes, he was my boy, and I was Daddy, but that didn't mean he was a pushover who would hesitate to tell me what was on his mind. And it was exactly the threat I needed to pull my head out of my ass.

He was right; I'd been avoiding Deegan since shortly after the wedding. I was riding the high of a new relationship, he was still in the honeymoon phase of his marriage, and I didn't want both of us crashing to reality by talking about all the shit we hadn't addressed. There'd been a void across the line where we used to shoot the shit every weekend, and I'd made the decision to stop picking up the phone. When he hadn't bothered calling me, I figured he had the same thought. If we didn't talk, neither of us could say something we couldn't take back.

"You ready for this?" Tanner asked as I followed the GPS deep into the suburbs. I'd been to Deegan and Haley's place a dozen times in the past few years, but this felt like the first time all over again. And in some ways, I supposed it was. This was the first time I was bringing someone with me. The fact it was Tanner, only set me that much more on edge.

After today, Deegan wouldn't be able to pretend he didn't know I was into guys. I wouldn't have to act like my world didn't revolve around Tanner, which it had since long before I pulled up at the curb in front of his building. Tanner was the man all others were measured up against and found lacking.

I placed my hand over Tanner's and squeezed his fingers. "Yeah. This is going to be good. In case I haven't already said it, thank you."

"Thank *me*? What the hell did I do?" He gaped at me like I was insane.

"You were right to tell me I needed to be the one to reach out to Deegan. He might be the only person out there more stubborn than you are." They liked to pretend they were polar opposites, but the brothers were more alike than they'd ever see. Extending the olive branch wasn't something I was only doing for our friendship. They needed to heal and move on, too. "I missed him. It was weird to not talk to him."

"Why *did* the two of you quit talking? Haley used to tease him about your bromance, and I know you talked a couple of times after you went home, but then nothing."

"Honestly?" I didn't *want* to tell him about that final call, but he deserved to know. I doubted it would surprise him, but he had a much more tender heart than he let on.

"No, I want you to lie to me," he deadpanned as he rolled his eyes. "Yes, honestly."

"He worried that you had somehow convinced me to pretend we were together to piss off your parents," I admitted. The notion that I would have gone along with a fake boyfriend scheme to shock his family was laughable. It *was* the sort of thing I could see Tanner doing, but not for the wedding, and not with me.

"Is that why he was so chill about us at the reception? Figures, the one time I have someone I actually care about with me, and he thinks it's all some big fucking joke." Tanner ground out.

Okay, so apparently we were going with anger to mask the hurt today. Strangely, I could deal with that. "It caught him off-guard, Tanner. He didn't know I was gay; I hadn't exactly found a good way to come out and confess to him that I jerked off to images of his little brother, and he'd had one hell of a long day."

Tanner slumped back in his seat and crossed his arms tightly over his chest. "And now?"

"Now, he knows that shit won't fly." I pried his arm free and lifted his fingers to my lips. "It might take him a bit to get used to seeing the two of us together, but I made it clear I won't put up with him talking shit about the man I love."

"Did you actually say that?" His mouth fell open, but he sat up straighter. "Man, I wish you'd waited to tell him that until we were standing in front of him. That would have been epic."

I rolled my eyes and shook my head. "And then you wonder why everyone accuses you of trying to stir up shit. If you want people to accept us, you need to act like the mature adult I know you are."

"Mature sounds boring," he scoffed, jutting out his bottom lip.

I quirked an eyebrow. Tanner was cute, but this was a game to him. He pretended to be immature and vapid, so no one got to know the real him. But I saw what others didn't bother digging deep enough to find. He was a kind man with a tender heart. His life was spent on the offensive, trying to cut others before they could hurt him.

"Fine. I'll be on my best behavior today, *Daddy*." He smirked when I had to adjust myself. The boy knew how to turn me on with a single word in that sweet, innocent tone. I was beginning to regret not letting him suck me off when I laid out clothes for him.

And believe me, he'd tried. When we got to the bedroom, I'd pulled out one of the scraps of lace he'd modeled for me the night it arrived in a care package. He reasoned it was only fair for me to get the *full experience* of him wearing the bikini briefs that barely restrained the hard-on that seemed to be a permanent condition for him.

But no, I was the one who insisted we needed to get going. When he asked why I made him dress in sexy underwear if we weren't going to fool around, I told him it was so he wouldn't forget who he belonged to if he got uncomfortable.

Just like I had the day of Deegan and Haley's wedding. Fuck, it was hard to believe that was just over a month ago. It felt like Tanner and I had been together forever in some ways, but maybe that was just because every day dragged on for an eternity when I was waiting for our nightly video chats.

"You'd better behave, otherwise you'll be going to sleep in the cage tonight and you won't get to come until I believe you're truly sorry for teasing me," I warned. The threat would have held more weight if I wasn't just as desperate for him as he was for me.

"Yes, Daddy." He tilted his seat back and rolled his head to the side, watching me as I drove. Tanner usually grew restless when it was quiet, but this morning he seemed content. He still held my hand, and every once in a while I gave his fingers a squeeze to let him know I was thinking of him.

When we pulled up in front of the little bungalow Deegan and Haley had bought cheap and remodeled, my boy tensed. His fingers were curled around the door handle, and I wondered if I would have to pry them free and drag him into the house. This had been his idea—sort of. He might not have known Deegan would insist on the four of us getting together to clear the air, but part of him must've had an idea it *could* happen.

"Come on, sweetheart. It's not going to be as bad as you're trying to make it seem," I reassured him. "Deegan's not the enemy here. If you play your cards right, he'll defend us to your mother when she tries to accuse you of turning me gay."

"I mean, her assumption might not be totally wrong," he quipped. My brow furrowed, wondering what tangent his mind was going to latch onto. "After all, you *did* say you realized you were gay shortly after I came out. And then there was that morning you woke up next to me and freaked. I believe the word you used was unforgettable. So maybe she's right."

I curled my hand around the back of Tanner's neck and pressed our foreheads together. "Don't do that, Tanner. You don't need to put on a brave face with me. I know how badly it hurt to hear her saying that shit and I won't let it happen again."

This time, it was Tanner adjusting his dick. There was no hiding his arousal in the skinny jeans I'd paired with a flowy top and heels. The only thing better than Tanner's ass in jeans when he was wearing his pretty shoes was Tanner wearing *nothing but* the shoes.

And maybe the lace. We'd have to test that theory tonight. Maybe I'd have to get him a lace jock that left his ass exposed so I could fuck him in lingerie and high heels.

Great. Now both of us were hard. Tanner's gaze dropped to my lap and he licked his shiny lips. "You'd better put that thing away, Daddy. I'm pretty sure my brother's acceptance has limitations, and you dragging me to the guest room would be rude."

"It's your fault," I shot back.

Great, now you sound just like Tanner.

"Uh, no. I'm not the one who got all growly and possessive. And I sure as hell didn't make you think about whatever has you ready to shove my face in your lap right here in the car where anyone could see."

"You like it when I get pissed off about people mistreating you?" I knew he did, but I wanted to hear him say it.

"Fuck yes, I do." He squeezed the bulge at the front of his jeans. "You look like the boy next door, but then you do that caveman shit, and I almost bust a nut."

He glanced toward the house, and I thought I saw a curtain moving in one of the front windows.

"Come on. We can call them and tell them we'll be back for dinner instead," Tanner suggested. "They know what it's like to be in love. Hell, they'll probably do things I *really* don't want to imagine my brother doing to my best friend as soon as they know they won't get caught."

"Oh, but we should put those thoughts in his head about what *his* best friend is going to do to his baby brother?"

"After all the times I've had to listen to him brag about the girls he's banged, I think it's time for a little turnabout," he quipped.

I shook my head and kissed the tip of his nose. "Baby, we are not going to torment Deegan. Now, let's get in there so you can apologize to Haley for being a miserable brat."

I gave it about fifteen more seconds before she threw open the door and ran across the yard to find out what was taking us so long. Tanner gave me shit for not talking to Deegan, but I'd learned earlier that I wasn't the only one trying to avoid their best friend. The difference was Haley wasn't content to wait for him to get his head out of his ass and she called to check up on him.

I slid my hand to the small of Tanner's back as we walked up the front steps. It was a small gesture, but one that would remind Deegan that we were really together and there was no room for him saying anything stupid. I finally relaxed when it was Deegan who opened the front door and immediately pulled me into a one-armed hug.

"It's good to see you, man." He ushered us into the house, greeting Tanner the same way. My heart rate slowed seeing him acting like nothing was horribly different. "I hear I have you to thank for reminding him how the phone works?"

"Well, if we'd had to wait on you, technology would have advanced so far, phones were non-existent," Tanner teased. Deegan put him in a playful headlock and his squeal had Haley rushing into the foyer.

"What in the— God, would the two of you knock it off before you break something?" She turned to me, hugging me tightly. "Thanks for calling. He's missed you."

"It's only been a little over a month," I protested. A lot of people would never understand how it had been natural for the two of us to keep in touch every week, even when our lives led in very different directions. And those who did thought I was an idiot for hiding my sexuality from my best friend for as long as I had. I was beginning to agree with them, but Tanner and I had both promised we were through living with regrets.

"If you think about it, it's been closer to a year since the two of you really got to hang out," Haley pointed out as she dragged me through the house to the kitchen. "The wedding doesn't count. We were all so busy, trying to keep their mom from making a scene, that no one got to relax."

I chuckled, taking the beer she offered me. "I suppose that's a fair point. I still think you're crazy for marrying into that family."

"And *you* still have time to save yourself," she teased. "Things are going good for the two of you?"

"They are," I confirmed, not even trying to hide the dopey smile on my face. "We're both trying to live in the present instead of beating ourselves up over lost time. And it's not easy being so far apart, but he's worth it."

"I'm happy to hear you say that." She hopped onto the counter, so we were eye-level. I tried to keep from busting up when she pursed her lips in what, I was pretty sure, was supposed to be a scowl. "Remember, if you hurt him, you'll have to deal with me."

"And by that, you mean you're going to make Deegan beat me up?" Haley was about as intimidating as a church mouse. I knew she had spunk, but she was teeny and sweet enough to give a person cavities.

"Whose ass am I kicking?" Deegan asked as he and Tanner joined us. I smiled when Tanner approached, lifting up my arm so he could cuddle up against me. "Shit, do the two of you have to be all mushy in front of me?"

"Basically, yeah. We'll call it payback for all the times you drunk dialed me, pissing and moaning about how much you liked Haley, but she wouldn't give you the time of day."

Deegan threw a towel at me. "Traitor! What happened to the bro code? You're not supposed to spill my secrets like that."

"Well, then you shouldn't give me shit for hugging my boyfriend." Just like that, any awkwardness evaporated. Deegan and Tanner joked around like I hadn't seen them since they were young, and Haley and I stood back and gave them time to reconnect.

"How are you going to convince him to move?" Haley asked as I helped her put together a late lunch. My brow furrowed, wondering if Tanner had said something to her about our ongoing disagreements about if and when he'd move closer to me. "Oh stop. He hasn't been whining, if that's what you're thinking. But face it, one of you have their shit sorted out and the other works at the mall. It wouldn't make sense for you to come home, even if we'd all love it if you did."

As I listened to Deegan and Tanner bantering back and forth as they played a video game, guilt washed over me. This had been the only place he'd ever called home, and with him starting to get along with his brother, it didn't feel right to pull him away from that.

I knew Tanner would follow me anywhere, but I felt my priorities shifting. It wouldn't be easy for me to uproot my life, but both of us could be close to the people who mattered to us.

"Dammit, Ryan, what are you thinking? I know that look." Haley leaned against the counter, holding a spatula in her hand.

"Maybe he's not the one who needs to move," I admitted. Saying it to Haley felt safer than either of the brothers. "What if I moved back, and we could build something of our own together?"

Haley pursed her lips and shook her head. "Hell no. That's the last thing either of you need. If you're here, you won't be able to let down your guard, and you'll both be living a half-life. He needs a bit of upheaval in his life, too, because until now he's been content with the path of least resistance. He needs to be challenged to reach his potential."

Damn, someone had big time thoughts and feelings on the situation. I'd been so focused on feeling like I was forcing Tanner to change his life to suit me, but maybe Haley was right. Maybe it was up to me to make Tanner see that moving was best for him, too.

I hugged Haley and kissed the side of her head. "Thanks, Hales. I hadn't thought of it that way."

"Yeah, well, that's because all you boys are the same. You waffle between thinking with your dicks and focusing on all the wrong things. Now, get the meat in the marinade, otherwise we're never going to eat."

"Yes, ma'am." I saluted her on my way to the fridge. If there was any sort of power exchange in their relationship, I had no doubt Haley would be the one putting Deegan on his knees. The thought of my best friend submitting was funny as hell, but not impossible to imagine.

The rest of the day went better than any of us had probably expected. Haley and Tanner took off after lunch for an afternoon of shopping, while Deegan and I kicked back with beers and basketball the way we had throughout college.

Tanner was right. The chasm between Deegan and me was holding us back. We'd needed today, and I was finally looking forward to getting on with the future.

17

TANNER

"So, what's it going to take to get you to agree to come home with me?" Ryan asked one morning, almost a week after he'd shocked the hell out of me. This was the subject neither of us wanted to address, but I knew it was inevitable.

Ryan spent every morning making calls and attending online meetings while I slept, and every evening he came to the mall with dinner in hand. He didn't bitch about eating fast(ish) food and he didn't tell me I could do so much better if I just applied myself a bit. He was one of the few people in my life who understood that—for the most part—I liked what I did. I didn't need a fancy degree hanging on the wall or some pretentious title. I *liked* helping people look and feel their best.

Still, it was a job I could get in any city in the country, so the job wasn't a viable reason for me to stay on the west coast. If anything, I would be better off with a fresh start because my area manager had a bad habit of hiring and promoting his buddies, and I would never be an ass-kisser.

"Making me breakfast in bed every morning is one hell of a way to start," I quipped. It wasn't that I expected him to wait on me hand and foot, but once I got past my reservations that he'd see me as needy or codependent, I realized he actually meant it when he said taking care of me was what did it for him. He was happy when I was happy and, to him, nothing beat knowing that he was the one to fulfill my needs.

And, damn, did he ever fulfill *all my needs*. It probably sounded shallow as hell, but I was pretty sure I was turning into a sex fiend, and the sad reality that my dick on demand would be going away when I dropped him off at the airport was also a pretty convincing reason to get over my bullshit fears.

I sat up straighter and humored him, letting him fluff the pillows behind me. I looked up as he bent down to kiss my head.

"Damn, you smell fuckable." He kissed his way down my neck before latching his teeth into my collarbone. That was going to leave a mark. "I'm serious, Tanner. Name your price. What do I need to do to make you see we're both happier when we're together? I don't know about you, but I get awfully damn sick of my right hand."

I pressed my lips together to keep from blurting something out before thinking. I'd imagined telling him I'd made my decision over a romantic dinner or while we walked along the perimeter of the lake with only the moonlight to illuminate the path. I don't know why, but this felt like the type of thing I didn't want to say when my hair was sticking up at every angle and I still had a raging case of morning breath.

"I know you worry about what you'll do for work, but you don't need to," he reminded me. "If you want to take a bit of time to figure out where you see yourself, you can do that."

"So you've said. And, like I keep telling you, I don't know if I'm cut out to be your kept boy." Certain parts of me were on-board with that fantasy. Sexy images filled my head of him texting me, demanding that I be waiting when he got home, naked and on my knees. But I knew myself; thanks to the work ethic drilled into us by our parents, there was no way I'd be able to overcome the feeling I was taking advantage of him.

Ryan nuzzled his nose into the crook of my neck. I pushed him away, making exaggerated gagging sounds because—eww, I reeked like stale sweat and sex.

"Come on, baby. It doesn't have to be right this minute, but I want to know we have a plan in place before I leave, something for both of us to work toward."

I could imagine it now; Ryan would have a checklist of everything I told him needed to happen before I moved, and he'd get more excited with every box he could fill with a check mark. He was nothing if not obsessively organized.

Maybe it'd be fun to email him a list after he was gone, just to see how he'd react.

"What if we put a time limit on how long you can be out of work? Would that help?" Ryan settled onto the bed next to me and pulled me onto his lap. He held out the bagel he'd toasted, and I took a bite. "I don't want you to feel like you're there to be my live-in sex toy..."

"But I can be, right?" I flipped around to straddle his legs, grinding against his dick. "Even once I have a job, you'll still go good and hard on me? I don't want this to be one of those situations where I move in with you and suddenly our sex life dies. I'm way too young and hot to be celibate."

Ryan kneaded my ass cheeks, guiding my body back and forth against his groin. "Baby, that's something I can promise you will never happen. When I'm old and can't get it up, I promise I'll go to the doctor to get a pill to help me out. I can't think of anything worse than not being able to feel your ass clenching around my dick like a vise."

"Damn, and you accuse me of being dramatic," I teased. He popped my hip and I yelped, even though it didn't really hurt. "I'm just sayin', that was one of the sweetest things anyone's ever said to me, but it was cheesy as hell, too."

"I think you're rubbing off on me."

"Well, I'm trying, but for some stupid reason we're still sitting here talking." Ryan shoved his hands down the back of the tiny underwear he'd dressed me in last night. I would have preferred sleeping naked so I could wake up with his erection nestled against my ass, but Ryan had a thing for seeing my cock and balls encased in pretty, luxurious fabric.

"Tell me what I want to hear, and then we'll see what we can do about this," Ryan offered as he slid a hand around the front to drag his thumb over the head of my dick that was peeking over the waistband.

"I'm pretty sure they call that blackmail, and that's no way to start a healthy relationship," I pointed out. Before Ryan, I'd never joked around during sex before, mostly because it took a certain level of familiarity to do so.

"I wouldn't have to blackmail if you'd just spit it out already," Ryan complained. He hooked his feet around my calves, and in some sort of trick maneuver out of a porn or something, he jerked his legs up and managed to pull me flat on my back. He pinned me to the mattress, his mouth right next to my ear. "The bossy part of me wants to force you to spell everything out for me, but *that* feels much more manipulative."

True. But again, hot. And maybe that was what I needed. Sometimes, I got so caught up in my head that I needed Daddy around to pull me out. "Would you?"

"Would I what?" My cock chafed against the front of his sweatpants, but I didn't care as long as I got to feel his length against mine.

"Tell me it's time," I clarified. "Maybe what I need is for Daddy to make the rules. Everything's easier when I just have to do what you tell me," I admitted.

"You have to be sure about this, baby," he insisted. "I don't want you coming back six months from now when you're pissed off at me, accusing me of trying to control your life and forcing you to move away from your family."

"You and I both know damn well I *need* to get away from them." Well, most of them, anyway. Nana was pretty cool for an old lady, but she wouldn't be around forever. It was a morbid thought but the simple truth. And once she was gone, there wouldn't be anything for me here.

Deegan and I were getting along better since we'd gone to their place for dinner, but we'd never been the best buds sort of brothers. Our lives were too different, and the only things we had in common were a genetic bond and the fact we were in love with the other's best friend. Seeing him a few times a year would be plenty.

"You know what I mean. Do you want me to tell you what to do more often instead of asking you?" I nodded, feeling tears welling along my lashes. I'd been trying since the beginning of January to figure out a way to tell him this. It was completely at odds with everything I'd been raised to want out of life, but when he was Daddy, I felt free.

"Thank you for telling me, sweetheart. I know that wasn't easy for you." He blanketed my body with his, so we were connected from the tips of our toes to our foreheads. "After you shower and get dressed, we're going to sit down and make a list of what needs to happen so you can come home to me."

"Mmm, I like the sound of that." Somehow, a place I'd never even seen felt more like home than this apartment or even the house I'd grown up in. "I so knew you were going to want to make a list."

"You say that like it's a bad thing." Ryan groaned as he rolled off of me and sat up. I almost made a crack about his old age, but I was in too good of a mood to be snarky.

Don't get me wrong, I was still scared shitless, but it felt amazing having him take the decision out of my hands. I wished I'd been able to tell him that's what I needed when we'd first reconnected. But that wasn't important now; Ryan wanted me with him, and he wasn't going to take no for an answer.

That was fine by me.

After a solid week of marathon sex and more orgasms than I could count, the shower was little more than a way to get clean. The urge to rub one out quick was non-existent. And even if I'd been tempted, I'd been given clear instructions that I wasn't allowed to touch myself unless *Daddy* told me to.

I was practically flying by the time I dressed in the jeans and tee Ryan had pulled out for me and made my way to the kitchen. The apartment was filled with the scent of bacon and fresh coffee.

My steps faltered when I heard Ryan talking to someone. "Shit, tell me what you need from me, man... Yeah, I get it... You did the right thing... Don't worry, I'll tell him. Thanks." My heart raced as I tried figuring out what had him sounded so somber after his jovial mood earlier. I mentally bitch-slapped myself, trying to push away the worst-case scenarios.

That lasted until I stepped into the kitchen and was met with Ryan's furrowed brow and glassy eyes.

He held out a hand to me. I shook my head, not wanting to hear whatever it was he had to say. "Baby, come here."

He turned off the stove and grabbed my wrist when I backed away. "Whatever it is, just tell me. Are you heading home? It's okay if you are. It'll suck sleeping alone, but we both knew you couldn't stay here forever. We'll video chat to plan Operation Relocate Tanner."

The air was knocked out of my lungs when Ryan yanked my arm so that my body crashed into his. He wrapped me so tightly in his arms, I worried he might crack a rib.

"Okay, now you're really starting to freak me out." I hated the way my voice shook, but I was about a second away from completely losing my shit.

"Come sit with me," Ryan suggested, backing out of the kitchen while still holding me captive.

"We don't need to sit down," I argued. "I can take whatever it is you have to say."

Oh, if only that had been true.

Luckily, Ryan didn't listen to me and he remained silent until I was curled up on his lap. He swallowed hard when I cupped his cheeks. "Whatever it is, we'll get through it, right? I waited so long to have you; I'm not going to give up without a fight now that I'm yours."

"Baby, I need you to let me talk for a minute," Ryan pleaded.

I felt my throat closing and I couldn't form words. Deep lines were etched in his face, and a deep sense of foreboding washed ever me.

"Okay," I whispered. I rested my chin on his head and closed my eyes.

"First, you need to believe me when I say everything's going to be okay," he reassured me, but not really at all. Telling me everything *was going to be okay* meant something *wasn't* okay now.

"I swear, Ryan, if you don't get on with it already and give me a fucking heart attack, I'm going to kick the shit out of you." It was an empty threat and we both knew it. Beyond the fear, I loved him even more for being so careful with me.

"I'm sorry. This... Baby, I hate knowing I'm about to upset you. But, again, everything's going to be okay," he repeated. He lifted my hand to his mouth and kissed each of my fingers before looking up at me. The position was weird, and I really didn't like looking down at him. "They had to take Nana to the hospital this morning."

"Is she okay? What happened? I can't lose her, Daddy! I can't," I sobbed. Tears streamed down my cheeks and I hated myself for thinking about how she wouldn't be around forever. I tried jumping off Ryan's lap, but he held me tight. "Why are we sitting here? Let me get my shoes on so we can go down there and see what's going on."

"Baby, listen to me." The growly tone of his voice made it clear that was a demand, not a request. "Deegan is waiting to hear more, and then we're going to meet up outside the hospital. We thought it was best if he and Haley walk in at the same time as us to avoid any potential drama."

"Fuck her, man." Ryan's gaze narrowed, and I remembered he didn't want me cussing so much. But seriously, fuck that noise. If my mother wanted to say dick about Ryan and me, she could step off. Still, I needed Ryan to be Daddy today, and that meant no cussing unless it was me begging him to fuck me hard, which wasn't going to happen now. "Sorry, but only a little bit. I mean it though. If my mom says anything about us..."

"You'll let Deegan and me handle it," Ryan finished. That hadn't been at all what I was going to say, but whatever. "You're right that she's not going to say anything, but your brother suggested presenting a united front. If *he* doesn't have an issue with us being together, then she really can't say anything."

"She should be happy that both of her sons found kickass partners and have great taste in friends," I grumbled.

"You're right, she should. But you know your mother." Ryan wiped the tears from my cheeks and hugged me one more time before patting my hip. "Now, we're going to finish breakfast and coffee. When Deegan calls, we'll head straight to the hospital. When we get back here, we'll make that list, because there's no way in hell I'm ever going to let you get bad news without me there to hold you."

18

RYAN

It was after noon by the time Deegan called to let us know Nana was awake and it was okay to visit. The wait had been hard on both of us, but I was happy to spend the morning on the couch with Tanner curled up on my lap, alternating between sniffling and dreaming up every worst-case scenario and napping. I shuddered when I thought about how he'd be coping if I wasn't here. Luckily, that was never going to be an issue because, now that I had his clearance to push him, he'd be coming home with me if we could make the necessary arrangements for his apartment.

"Baby, it's time to get ready to go," I whispered, shaking him awake. I hated to do it, but he wouldn't forgive me if he knew I'd gotten the call and decided to let him sleep.

Tanner startled awake, his entire body stiffening. He looked up at me, sucking his bottom lip between his teeth. "This morning wasn't a bad dream, was it?"

"I'm sorry, sweetheart, but no," I confirmed. His eyes turned glassy again, and I worried how he'd take it if Nana wasn't going to be okay. She was a tough old bird, but she was getting up there in years and had been dealing with a number of health issues for as long as I could remember. The relationship Nana and Tanner shared was special, and when he lost her, it was going to kill him.

No. Don't even think like that right now, I scolded myself. We had to stay positive, no matter what the doctors had to say when we got up there.

"The good news is she was on the phone with your dad, and he was concerned for her. He called the ambulance and then raced over there," I explained. Deegan and I had been texting all morning, and I didn't want to hold anything back from Tanner now that he was awake. "They got her to a hospital that specializes in stroke care, which is likely why her prognosis is what it is."

"And that's a full recovery, right?" Tanner asked hopefully.

I didn't want to lie to him, but I also didn't want him spiraling back into scenarios of doom and gloom. "Things are hopeful right now. That's as much as we can ask for so soon. You know your Nana, if there's a way for her to come back from this even better than she was before, she will. She's almost as stubborn as you."

"She's *way* more stubborn than me." He batted his eyelashes and tried giving me puppy dog eyes. "I'm perfectly sweet and innocent."

"Yeah, and I'm the fucking Pope," I quipped, easing him off my lap. "Now get your shoes on so we can head out. Deegan said we'll stop in to see Nana, and then the four of us will grab some lunch. Haley's worried about you and wants to see for herself that you're not melting down, but she knows you wouldn't agree to lunch before the hospital."

"Is everyone worried about me losing my shit?" Tanner grumbled. He stomped to the front door and shoved his feet into his shoes without untying them. That said a lot about his state of mind. He was obsessive about keeping his shoes looking pristine, whether they were his Chucks or the glossy black stilettos he kept wrapped and in their original box on a shelf in his closet. He shrugged into a hoodie, and I couldn't help but smile. He looked adorable, even if he resembled a moody college student. "I *am* a full-blown adult, capable of taking care of myself. I'm okay with you worrying about me because you're Daddy, but the rest of them need to realize I'm not going to fall apart."

"Baby, people worry about you," I explained as I swiped my keys off the kitchen counter. "I know you're not used to that, but Haley and Deegan love you. And all of us know how close you are to Nana. Are you ready?"

"No, but I'm not sure this is one of those things you can ever be ready for." Tanner grabbed my hand and leaned against my side as I locked the apartment. "I'm glad you're here with me. I don't know if I could do it otherwise."

"You could," I reassured him, kissing the side of his head. "You're stronger than you give yourself credit for, and if I was back home and you were still here, I'd spend the entire day on the phone with you so you knew I was there as much as I could be. You don't have to go through anything alone ever again."

"Promise?"

"Cross my heart, hope to die." As soon as the words were out of my mouth, I realized what a colossal mistake it had been to use the childish phrase. I quickly added, "But for the record, I have zero plans on going anywhere for about a hundred years. We're going to be old and gray, and you'll be wishing I'd kick off already."

"That'll never happen," Tanner insisted. "Even when you're so old your dick is wrinkly and you can't get it up, I'll still want you."

"Same, baby." I shook my head, amazed that this was real life. He was a goofball who could make a dick joke about just about anything, and I loved him just the way he was.

As promised, Deegan and Haley were waiting for us outside the main entrance of the hospital. Haley pulled Tanner away from me, wrapping him in a tight hug as she whispered something in his ear. He nodded and held her tightly while Deegan and I watched on.

Deegan gave me a much more manly bro hug and a thump on the back. "He's holding up better than I expected. I still don't get what you see in my annoying as fuck little brother, but there's no denying the two of you are happy together."

Even a week ago, that comment would have pissed me off, but now I knew he was playing around. We'd spent a lot of time trying to reconcile after everything I'd kept from him until the wedding. He wasn't pissed that I was gay, only that I hadn't trusted him enough to tell him sooner. He wasn't *happy* about me being with Tanner, but that had nothing to do with thinking his brother wasn't good enough for me. Deegan worried that I'd hurt Tanner somehow, and he'd be forced to choose between his brother and his best friend.

That wasn't going to happen. I'd seen Tanner as his bratty, immature worst, and now I was looking forward to seeing him flourish once we got back to Annandale. I'd been serious when I told him being so close to his family, constantly worrying about what they thought of him even if he wouldn't admit it, was suffocating him.

"Who all's here?" I asked as we entered the hospital. Deegan had gotten Nana's room number from their mother earlier. It pissed me off that she hadn't bothered to call Tanner, but it was par for the course. Lillian wasn't a bad mother most of the time, but I'd never forgive her for acting like Tanner was an afterthought.

"Mom and Dad, obviously, and I our uncle should be here by now, too." Deegan kept glancing over his shoulder to where Haley and Tanner were following us. "Have you convinced him to go back with you when you have to leave?"

I let out a sardonic huff of laughter. "Yeah. And it's the damndest thing...right before we were going to sit down and figure out what needs to be done so he can leave, some asshole called and detonated our plans for the day."

"Shit, man. I'm sorry." The elevator doors opened, and we all filed in. Deegan lowered his voice. "Don't let him use this as an excuse to stay. I know him, and this is going to fuck with his head, even if he won't admit it."

"Yeah, I'm already trying to anticipate his arguments. He acted like he's still excited, but you forget, I've known him most of his life, too."

Deegan shook his head. "I still think you're crazy. But I've never seen him so happy. Take care of him and we're going to be just fine."

"You have my word."

I took Tanner's hand when we stepped off the elevator. He held on tight enough my fingers throbbed, but I didn't mention my discomfort. If this was what he needed to make sure I wasn't going to turn and run, he could cut off the blood supply. Our shoes squeaked on the linoleum floors, catching the attention of a nurse at the station. "Can I help you?"

"Yes, we're here to see Estelle Fincham," Deegan announced. "We're her grandsons."

"Mrs. Fincham already has three visitors," she informed us. "You're going to have to wait out here until they leave. And it's supposed to be two visitors at a time."

"Thank you, ma'am," I responded as Deegan pulled out his phone. Tanner grunted, obviously unhappy about having to wait longer. I turned my attention to him. He leaned into my touch when I pressed my hand to the side of his face. "It's okay, baby. We're going to hang out with Deegan and Haley and wait our turn."

"You two should go in first," Deegan said, his nose still buried in his phone.

"We go in together," Tanner insisted as he flopped onto one of the couches, pulling me down next to him. "If they can make an exception so Mom could be there with Dad and Jerry, they can make one for us."

"Tanner." He quieted at the single word warning. I kissed his hair when he rested his head on my shoulder. "I know you're upset right now, but we have to follow the rules. Would you rather go in with Deegan while Haley and I wait out here? That way you don't have to worry about anyone being upset if you see her before your brother does?"

"No, I want both of you there with me." He glanced up at Deegan and smiled. "He's a jerk, but he's still my big brother. I'm going to need both of you. And Haley. She's my person, so she should be there, too."

"We'll see," I told him, not wanting to keep the argument going when we were never going to reach a compromise. Maybe he was right, and they'd make an exception for us.

Tanner dozed off again. I wasn't sure if it was the stress of the morning or the late night we'd had with me worshiping every inch of his body, but I was glad he felt comfortable enough in my arms to rest. Deegan and Haley talked amongst themselves, but every once in a while, I noticed Deegan glancing over at us, offering me a smile and a nod of approval when our gazes met.

Despite the circumstances, it was almost peaceful. This was the life I wanted, my best friend and the love of my life together in the same room without the sniping and bickering.

And then, Lillian appeared. She did a double take when she noticed me in the waiting room, then scrunched her nose when she saw Tanner sleeping against my shoulder. Before Deegan could say a word, she schooled her features. "Ryan. It's a surprise to see you here."

"It's good to see you," I responded, even though it really wasn't. After the shit she'd pulled at the wedding, I would have been okay with not laying eyes on her during this visit. "I've been here for the past week, visiting Tanner."

"And you don't have a problem missing work?" She crossed her arms tightly over her chest, manicured fingernails digging into her skin. "I would have thought you had responsibilities to attend to."

I couldn't help myself. I held Tanner tighter and kissed his forehead, hoping I didn't wake him up. He didn't need to be subjected to his mother's snit. "My primary responsibility is right here. Luckily, I am my own boss, and I can work remotely."

"Oh. Well, that's...good, I suppose." She held herself so tightly, I wondered if she'd snap. "Estelle is resting now. We're going to take Jerry back to the house so he can get settled in, but we'll be back this afternoon."

Tanner stirred in my arms. He opened his eyes and looked directly to me, not noticing his mother hovering in front of us. "Is it time to see her?"

"Soon, baby." I smoothed a hand over his hair. "Your mom said she's resting right now."

"I want to go sit with her," he insisted. "I won't wake her, but I need to see her."

"She's. Sleeping," Lillian bit out. "Just because you *want* to be near her, doesn't mean you get to. She needs to rest so her body can heal, Tanner."

"And she can do that just as well with him in there with her as she could if he's sitting out here," Deegan insisted. "Honestly, Mom, why do you have to be such a bitch to him all the time?"

"Deegan Michael," she scolded. "You watch your language. I'd expect that from *him* but you're better than that."

"No, I'm really not," Deegan argued. It was refreshing to see him standing up for Tanner the way he used to. "You put me up on this pedestal like I'm something special, but I'm not. You've always acted like Tanner is a disappointment because he's strong enough to not bow to what you wanted him to be. He's living his own life, and you can't deal with that. And, honestly, I think you're jealous of how close he is to Nana but you refuse admit the role you played in their relationship. Now, we're going to take him down to the room. If you can't act like a civilized human being, maybe you should stay home when Dad and Jerry come back to visit. Nana doesn't need this shit right now."

I choked back my amusement, hiding my laughter with a coughing fit. Lillian glared at me and I rolled my eyes, holding Tanner tightly. His body practically vibrated from pent up tension and heartbreak. I kissed his cheek. "Don't listen to her, baby. Pay attention to Deegan and remember that he's got your back. We all do."

"I know," he responded so softly I could barely hear him. "Can we go see Nana now?"

"Yeah, we can." I didn't pay any attention to Lillian as we passed her. Her vitriol didn't matter to me in this moment, and it wasn't going to do Tanner any good to see all of us fighting about him.

The nurse from earlier popped up from her chair when she noticed us walking past the desk. "I told you two visitors at a time. Two of you are going to have to wait."

"We're taking our partners to see their grandmother, and then we'll head back to the waiting room," I told her. I'd almost said our spouses and had to catch myself. Someday…

She huffed and puffed and crossed her arms over her chest but didn't tell us that wasn't allowed. I paused outside of Nana's door, wanting a moment with Tanner. I turned him to face me, bracing his shoulders. "Remember, she's had one hell of a day but she's getting the best care possible. Everything's going to be okay."

"I hope you're right." He practically fell against my chest, throwing his arms around my torso. I gently rubbed his back as he fought his emotions. "I can't lose her, Daddy."

Fuck, hearing him call me that out in the open crushed my heart. It was a testament to how upset he was that he didn't even trip over the honorific. And on the flip side, it filled me with pride knowing that's how he was thinking of me. He trusted me to be the one to take care of him.

"You won't, baby." God, I hoped I was right.

19

TANNER

Ryan was the best boyfriend and Daddy in the world. It was only because of him that I did things like eat, sleep, and shower in the week after Nana's stroke. Every morning, he drove me up to see her, and every afternoon he came back after getting some work done at the apartment.

I had one more week before we were supposed to head back to Annandale, and I hadn't gotten anything accomplished with packing up my shit so I could go with him. I felt like the worst boyfriend and boy in the world because Nana's slow recovery made it hard for me to be excited about moving away.

"Tell me...what's...on your...mind." Nana took my hand in both of hers. I closed my eyes and tried to memorize the feel of her paper-thin skin. It was a stupid thing to fixate on, but there was something about the silkiness of it that had always soothed me, ever since I was a little boy. I couldn't lay my problems on her when she was still sitting in a hospital bed waiting to find out where she'd be going when they let her out of here, but this I could absorb.

"Just thinking about life, Nana," I offered, hoping that would be enough. She was the one I'd always gone to for the heavy conversations. She'd been the first person in the family I came out to, and I didn't let out a breath until she said that she hoped one day I found a man who would love me the way I deserved to be loved. In light of everything that happened recently, I was grateful she was still here to see how well Ryan treated me.

"He makes...you...happy," she said, as if she knew the memory I had in my mind. I nodded, sucking my bottom lip between my teeth. "Love...isn't...easy."

"No, it sure isn't." I chuckled, because what else was I supposed to do? I didn't like complicated shit, and the one time I decided to truly say fuck it and do what was going to make me happy, she wound up in the hospital the same day. I didn't want to have to choose between being here to spend what time I could with her or being with Ryan. I wanted the two of them close to me, but that wasn't possible.

She pressed a hand to my chest. "Listen to...your heart. It knows...what...the brain...doesn't." It sucked watching the woman who always had something to say, struggling to find her words. But the one time I'd shown her how upsetting that was, she scolded me for pitying her. She was determined she'd make a full recovery given enough time, and like Ryan said, she was stubborn enough to will herself back to health.

But what if my heart is conflicted, too? I didn't give voice to the question because I was trying really hard to not exhaust her with my issues.

I heard my mother's voice before she even entered the room, my dad and Uncle Jerry in tow. "Oh good, you're here."

That was the most cordial greeting I'd had from her, but something about it set me on edge. She'd spent the past five mornings accusing me of avoiding my responsibilities to sit with Nana like a simpering child, and suddenly she was happy to see me sitting in the chair that would likely have my butt imprints in it after Nana was discharged? Yeah, she was up to something.

She pulled a chair to the other side of Nana's bed, forcing Dad and Jerry to stand. Dad rested a hand on my shoulder when I tried to get up, smiling down at me and giving me a curt nod. He'd gotten more chill recently while my mom was even more of a bitch.

"Estelle, how are you feeling this morning?" I pressed my lips together to keep from laughing when Nana rolled her eyes. Mom was talking slow and loud as hell, as if the stroke had rendered Nana hard of hearing and incapable of processing what people were saying to her. It just showed how performative her presence here was. She hadn't actually listened to a damn thing the doctors had said. Nana tensed when Mom took her other hand. "The doctors say you're ready to get out of the hospital today. Isn't that wonderful?"

"I...know. They talked...to...us...this morning." Nana sat up straighter and sucked in a deep breath. She'd never liked my mom, so it had to be killing Nana to see her sons allowing her to steamroll them and act like she was the one in control. Then again, we were all used to it at this point. Sometimes, I wondered what Dad would be like if he'd married someone normal. "I want...my...house."

Mom plastered on the fakest of smiles and nodded. "We thought that would likely be the case. But you know they won't let you go home unless you have someone to take care of you, right? They're worried you'll push too hard, and you're going to need help for a while."

"I'll...be fine," Nana argued. "Don't need...babysitter."

"Estelle, it's not a babysitter. You're not going to be able to do everything you're used to, and we all want to make sure you don't suffer a setback," Mom explained. Someone behind me cleared their throat. Mom glared past me, to whichever of them wasn't buying her sweet concern anymore than Nana and I were. "What if Tanner comes to stay with you for a while? It's not ideal, but perhaps you'd be comfortable having him there with you instead of one of us."

"He has...a...life. I...won't keep...him...here." My eyes nearly bugged out of my head. I hadn't told her about the plans Ryan and I had been making for me to go to Annandale with him.

My mother made a most unladylike sound and her entire face scrunched up. She leveled her gaze on me, silently daring me to dispute the words about to come out of her mouth. "Don't be ridiculous, Estelle. You're the most important person in Tanner's world. He'd be happy to stay with you until the doctors say you're ready to be fully independent again."

"No," Nana argued. "Let him...go."

She definitely knew. I wasn't sure how, but I also shouldn't have been surprised. Nana didn't miss a damn thing.

"This is the best solution, Estelle," Mom explained. It was so nice of her to talk to me about the decision she'd apparently already made. "If you won't allow Tanner to stay with you, we'll have to look at an inpatient rehab facility. You don't want that, do you?"

"Mom, you're upsetting her," I interrupted, not giving a damn if she decided to lash out at me for speaking out of turn. I wasn't a child, and I wasn't going to sit here and watch her treat Nana like one, either.

"Then tell her you'd be happy to stay with her." Mom pressed her lips together and cocked her head to the side. She was playing dirty. To her, this was a way to have her two least favorite family members out of sight and out of mind. "I'm sure you can tell your boss you'll need to take some time off to care for an ailing family member."

"And how, exactly, do you expect me to take care of my responsibilities if I'm not working?" She liked to throw that word in my face often enough, it felt good to turn the tables on her.

"I'm sure we can help you." She looked up at my dad. I followed her gaze and he offered me a silent apology with his eyes. "After all, we understand you wouldn't be missing work because you're irresponsible this time."

I closed my eyes and took a few deep breaths to keep from going the fuck off on her. Yes, I liked a good party as much as the next single guy, but I had *never* allowed that to affect my job performance. Of course, she'd never believe that because I was a total fuck up in her mind. And it was clear I wasn't *an* option for allowing Nana to go home, I was *the* option. If I refused, she'd have to go to the rehab facility and then she'd be miserable.

It sounded like my decision was made.

"I'll do it." I squeezed Nana's hand, hoping like hell she wouldn't keep arguing. This was a fight we weren't going to win.

"Oh good. I knew you'd eventually do the right thing." God, this woman was testing my patience. Dad's fingers dug into my shoulder, and Jerry mimicked his position to my left. "I'll go out and tell the nurses that we've sorted this out so they can start working on your discharge paperwork. Of course, Tanner will need a car so he can drive you to therapy. We can't have him carting you around town on the bus."

"He can...use...mine," Nana pointed out. "Not...like...I can...drive."

"Wonderful! See, I knew everything would work out," Mom declared as she stood and smoothed the front of her skirt.

There was a collective sigh of relief as soon as she was out of the room, my dad following dutifully behind.

"I'm sorry about that," Jerry apologized once it was down to just the three of us in the room. "I offered to take a leave of absence to help out, but you know how Lillian can be."

"Yeah, sadly I do." Nana looked more broken now than she had since the first day in the hospital. She hated needing others to take care of her. And from the sounds of it, she felt like she was holding me back from what I wanted to do. She was, but I'd never tell her that. Besides, until my mother had forced my hand, I was conflicted about whether I should tell Ryan I needed more time. I rose and bent down to kiss

Nana's cheek. "It's fine, Nana. You'll have more fun with me there, than you would if you had to deal with her."

"I'd kick...her...out. Pushy...bitch." The corner of Nana's mouth curled up slightly. "I'm...sorry...Tanner."

"Don't you dare apologize to me. Really, it's fine. Ryan will understand," I promised her. And he would, because he was the best boyfriend and Daddy in the world.

MOM WAS none too pleased when Ryan showed up at the hospital early that afternoon. She thought she would still get to control everything, but now that she'd offered me up to move in with Nana until she could be on her own, Ryan was taking the lead. "Lillian, I'm sure you have other things you need to do today. We can make sure Nana gets home and is resting comfortably."

Nana reached out, beckoning Ryan closer. She took his hand and smiled. "You're...a good...man. I'm...sorry...I...ruined your...trip."

"Don't be silly, Nana," Ryan scoffed, bending down to kiss her cheek. "I'm glad I was here. You need a sweet ride to spring you out of this joint. And this will give me a chance to make sure Tanner has meals he can heat up for the two of you after I have to go home."

"The doctor will be in shortly to discuss her discharge orders." Mom stiffened, obviously annoyed that she was being dismissed. "We need to find out what the therapy schedule will be and when her follow-up appointments are."

"And I'm sure Tanner will relay those to you," Ryan pointed out.

Dad and Jerry were already down at the nurses' station, finding out what the plan was. They were both exhausted, both from their mom's health issues and from dealing with my mother. I'd overheard them talking to Ryan in the hall, and nearly cried when I heard my dad tell Ryan he was happy for us. It would have been nicer if he'd said it to me, but I wasn't going to be picky at this point. It meant the world to me that Dad accepted us now that he knew Deegan was supportive.

"Once the doctor releases Nana, I'll make sure she and Tanner get to the house, and then I'm going to see if they need groceries or anything else," Ryan explained. "You have nothing to worry about."

"Well, I suppose it makes me feel better knowing you'll be here to help them for a couple of days at least. I'm sure you'll have to get home soon, too."

Sadly, she wasn't wrong. He had more meetings coming up for the club and other deals he was working on that he needed to be home to oversee. While I wouldn't be with him, at least this time I'd have Nana to keep me from missing him too much.

It surprised me when Dad and Jerry came back into the room after Mom had left. I'd assumed all of them would leave together which I'd felt bad about. They were her sons, and they deserved to be in the know more than Ryan and me.

"We sent Lillian home," Dad informed us as he and Jerry sat on opposite sides at the end of the bed. "Tanner, I'm sorry we weren't able to talk her out of offering your help. I know you don't mind, but you should have had a choice in the matter."

"It's okay, Dad. Really," I promised. "I know Nana wants to go home. We're going to have fun."

Nana looked to Ryan, who was now sitting across from me. "I'm...sorry...Ryan."

"No more apologies," Ryan insisted. "We're all going to make sure you get back on your feet in no time. Tanner and I can wait."

Wait a minute... why did it sound like Ryan knew what she was apologizing for?

Ryan's cheeks went bright red, and he curled in on himself slightly. He was usually so confident; it was odd to see him nervous. "She and I might have had a chat when you went for a walk to stretch your legs the other night."

"So, she *did* know..." I arched my back and threw my head back. I wanted to ask what in the hell he'd been thinking, but I wasn't going to have one of our first fights be in front of my family.

"I...know," she confirmed, freeing her hand for Ryan's and clasping mine again. "I'm...happy...for you. This...is...what you...need."

"What's going on?" Dad asked. He didn't sound upset, so much as confused.

"Tanner is going to move to Annandale with me," Ryan explained. "As I'm sure you can imagine, having a long-distance relationship isn't easy, and he can take some time to explore what he truly wants to be doing if he's with me."

"Were you going to tell us?" Again, the lack of disdain in Dad's question was confusing to me. "I'm not upset, son, but that's a big move to make without talking to your family about it."

I gaped at him. "You're kidding me right now, right? I mean, yes, I was going to let you know I was moving to the opposite side of the country, but I hadn't yet because of Mom. I didn't need her telling me how I was going to screw up not only my own life but Ryan's, too. And you know damn well she wouldn't have been able to hold back from warning me that Ryan would eventually get sick of me and I'd be on the streets without anyone to help me."

"As if that'll happen," Ryan scoffed. He turned to my dad. "Patrick, I love Tanner, and I will do everything in my power to make sure he's happy and well taken care of. He needs to be where he'll be supported rather than stifled."

"I agree." Dad cocked his head to the side, looking back and forth between us. "You know, I always wondered if there was something between the two of you when you were younger. I'm sorry if we've made it seem like we wouldn't accept you, Ryan. I know it's not an easy life, but if there's anyone I'd pick for Tanner to be with, it would be you."

I felt like I'd fallen into an alternate reality. Maybe I'd tumbled down the stairs and I was currently having drug-induced hallucinations. This was the most Dad had ever said about *his* feelings on my sexuality. Of course, it wasn't like we often had opportunities to talk without Mom hovering nearby.

"I'm sorry if we've put a kink in your plans."

I cackled and broke out in a fit of laughter before I could stop myself. Everyone looked at me like I'd lost my damned mind. Well, everyone but Ryan, who glared at me. *Behave*, he mouthed when our eyes met. I pressed my lips together, praying no one would ask what I'd found so funny.

"It's a delay, that's all," Ryan assured him, but he was looking at me as if reminding me that staying here a bit longer didn't mean I'd never be home with him. "And if he'd already moved, I'm sure he would have flown out as soon as he found out what happened, and he'd still want to stay with her."

"But he...didn't...choose," Nana argued.

"You're right, but that doesn't mean he doesn't want to help you."

"I hate to break up the party, but the doctor's going to be by in just a minute to talk to you, and then we'll let you get out of here." We all looked up at the sweet nurse who'd made sure to spend time with Nana every day. She also snuck food in for me, taking care of both of us. I was pretty sure she'd been upset when she realized Ryan wasn't one of the grandsons and that he had eyes only for me, but she hadn't stopped hanging out every chance she got.

"About...time," Nana quipped, and we all laughed.

Dad and Jerry wound up driving Nana home with Ryan and me following. That gave us time to talk about the abrupt change of plans. "You're really not upset about this?"

Ryan laced our fingers together and moved our hands to his thigh. "Baby, I never want to take you away from your family.

I know it sounds horrible, but in a way, we're lucky Nana had a stroke when she did. You would have been beside yourself if it had happened after we got you settled. And you can't tell me I'm wrong, that you'd want to be here with her no matter where you were living at the time."

"No, but you didn't answer my question." I turned in my seat to face him. "Are you upset that I didn't talk to you first?"

"You act like I don't know Lillian." He'd always called her Mom when we were kids, but since the wedding, he'd taken to using her first name. "I know she didn't ask if *you* were cool with moving in with Nana, either."

"No, but I just told you I wanted you to be the one to make decisions, and then I made a huge one without talking to you first." That was my real issue here. No, I didn't have a choice, but I still felt like I should have found a way to at least get his opinion before agreeing. I was damn lucky that buying plane tickets was on his to-do list for later in the week. He'd been delaying until we knew Nana was going to pull through, otherwise I'd get to carry around the guilt of that wasted money, too.

"Being your Daddy doesn't mean you lose the ability to make decisions for yourself," Ryan explained, squeezing my hand. "You're an adult, fully capable of making your own decisions. There will always be times when you have to do something on your own and that's when my job is to support your decision, unless I think it's going to be harmful to you. This isn't one of those times. You're doing what you need."

"But are you upset that I'm not going home with you right now?" He'd been so excited about introducing me to his friends and their partners, who he was sure would become my friends, too. Every night, he'd told me about some of his favorite places in Annandale to pull me out of my head. I'd been looking forward to him taking me to each of the businesses he talked about, but now that was going to have to wait.

"I'm disappointed, but only because I really like falling asleep with you in my arms and waking up to you draped over my body like my personal blanket." I laughed because it was a pretty accurate description. "But that doesn't mean I'm angry. I'm proud of you for doing what needed to be done, even if it wasn't what you wanted to do. As soon as Nana gets the all-clear, I'll be on a plane to come out here and take you home with me."

"That sounds like the best plan ever." I relaxed, confident that Ryan meant every word. Damn, I loved him.

20

TANNER

It was a toss-up as to who was annoying the other more at this point. Nana was mostly recovered but if you asked her, she was better than ever and didn't need me hovering over her anymore. She was pushy as hell about me getting on with my own life and letting her live hers.

Never mind the fact it had only been a month since she'd been rushed to the hospital for a fucking stroke. Yes, she was making progress faster than any of us could have imagined, but she still struggled with certain tasks. Until she was *fully* recovered, I wasn't going to ditch her.

Still, it wasn't easy being cooped up in the house I used to love visiting. Everything was the same as it had been when I was little, from the pale blue walls with a huge flowery wallpaper border at the ceiling to the pictures neatly arranged on every surface and wall. It felt like living in a museum dedicated to our family history. It was both comforting and a constant reminder that my life was on pause. Nothing was changing, just like the decor of her house.

My phone buzzed, and my dick perked up before I even pressed a button. Since I'd moved to this side of town, most of my friends had forgotten about me and Ryan was the only person who texted me. He'd decided keeping me in a constant state of arousal was the most effective way of reminding me who I belonged to. It didn't matter if he was telling me all the dirty things he wanted to do to my body, demanding that I sneak to my room to send him a picture of that day's sexy underwear, or simply reminding me to eat lunch, any interaction with him had me hard.

Being away from him sucked, but he was going out of his way to make sure I always knew he was thinking about me. He hadn't mentioned me moving in with him since I'd dropped him off at the airport, and sometimes I wondered if that was because it was one of those things that was a good idea when we were together but not so much once he was back in his own space.

I tried to not be upset when it wasn't Ryan. It was Mav. *Hey, you have time to chat?*

For you? Always. I hadn't done a great job living those words lately, but he understood it wasn't because I was ghosting him. Still, I felt like shit for leaving Mav on his own at the apartment. He didn't like being alone, even if he didn't admit that to most people.

"Hey, what's up?" I answered the moment my phone lit up with his incoming call.

"Hey." There was a ton of angst in that single word. As I'd feared, he wasn't dealing well with being completely on his own without warning. "I haven't heard from you in a while. How's Nana doing?"

"Stubborn as always." I chuckled and let out an exasperated sigh. "She swears I'm wasting my time babysitting her, but when I was at work yesterday, she decided to try and go for a walk. I found her sitting on her front porch without a sweater or anything. Her fingers were like wrinkled little popsicles."

"If you need, I could come and sit with her," he offered. It was sweet, but he'd be bored shitless here, and he wouldn't be comfortable. No matter how many times I told him Nana loved everyone just as they were, he felt the need to bury his femme side around her. Like, unnaturally so. It was painful to watch, and he was always drained by the time we went home.

Still, he'd be a face that wasn't mine. My dad visited every day, and Jerry called every evening but, other than that, it was just the two of us with the exception of her weekly card game. And let me tell you, there was nothing like a group of old ladies sitting around playing cards and sharing the town gossip to make me hide out in my room.

"I think she'd like that," I told him. "She keeps asking about you. She's worried you're going to leave me because I'm spending so much time with her."

We talked a bit longer before he told me he had to get some shit done before he came over for dinner later. The call left me with a pit in my stomach. Nothing about our conversation warranted a *can you talk* text, which meant there was something else going on with him.

"You know damn well, I'm...capable...of cooking...for myself." I jumped when Nana's shrill protest rang out from directly behind me. She still struggled with speech a bit, but she was getting much better, much to my chagrin. That meant it wasn't a struggle for her to chastise me for treating her like a child. "But I won't say no to some sweets. Damn this...diet...the doctor..."

"Nana, we've talked about this," I interrupted. At least she was in a good enough mood to call him a doctor today instead of a punk quack. As far as she was concerned, the doctors were trying to ruin her life by making her change her diet. She figured she'd lived this long eating the way she had, and no one was going to tell her any different.

"I'm not a child," she protested as she lowered herself into the recliner.

"No one's saying you are. But what if the doctors are right and this is the way for you to live a long, healthy life?"

"As opposed to the past seventy years?" she scoffed. "Tell me, Tanner, what good is living if you can't enjoy it? I understand what everyone is trying to do, but even if I hadn't survived the stroke, I would have died content that I had done all I'd been meant to do on this planet."

"Don't talk like that. You're probably going to outlive us all." I swallowed hard, regretting the words that she'd thrown out for as long as I could remember. She *wasn't* immortal. At some point, her health would decline to the point we'd lose her, and I didn't even want to think about that day.

"So, you agree there shouldn't be an issue with me eating what and how I damn well please?" She smirked, crossing her arms over her chest because she knew she'd won. "I know you're trying to make sure I follow the doctor's orders, Tanner, but at some point, you have to let me live my life."

Shit. The way she said that, made me feel like I was doing to her what I accused most of my family of doing to me. Granted, their motivations were wanting me to be the model son rather than taking care of my health, but the end result was the same.

Satisfied that she'd made her point, Nana lifted the footrest on the recliner and closed her eyes, leaving me with nothing to do but think about how to find a balance between what she wanted and what was best for her. I wished Ryan were here with me, because he'd know what to do.

When Nana woke from her nap, she hurried into the kitchen, insisting on making dinner for her boys. And I let her, because I was determined to prove I *wasn't* trying to smother her like she thought I was. I sat in the front room, watching out the windows for Mav to arrive. I'd been on edge since our call earlier. Something was up with him, and it wasn't just that he missed me.

I stayed out of view when he pulled up to the curb, watching him twist his hands around the steering wheel. A check of the time said it was just after five-thirty, meaning he was early. Mav was *never* early. He wasn't habitually late, but he was a master of arriving at exactly the time he'd been told to be somewhere. When fifteen minutes passed without him stepping out of the car, I realized I was going to have to drag him inside.

He jumped when I tapped on the window. "Dude, are you okay?"

"Yeah, I'm good." He opened the door, grabbing the pink bakery box off the passenger seat. There was only one place in town that used boxes so bright they practically glowed, and I was pretty sure Mav was going to be Nana's favorite as soon as she saw that he'd delivered the treats the rest of us had denied her. "I hope this is okay. It was slim pickings this late in the day."

I set the box on top of the car and pulled Mav into a tight hug. He stiffened, unaccustomed to me being so tactile. He was skinnier than when I'd temporarily moved in with Nana, and he didn't have an ounce to lose then. Now, he was almost gaunt, but I knew better than to say anything to him about it. This was partly my fault because I knew he struggled when he was alone.

"Are you *sure* you're okay?" I asked when I finally released him. He was quiet and had dark rings under his eyes. Again, I didn't say anything about his appearance because the Mav I knew would be mortified if people noticed him looking anything less than his best.

"Yeah, I'm fine." He worried on his bottom lip as I grabbed the box and motioned for him to follow me inside. He didn't move, so I stood there, giving him time to process what he wanted to say. "Actually, that's only mostly true. Before I say anything else, I want you to know that I'm excited about what I have to tell you, but I'm scared shitless at the same time."

"Mav, you're starting to scare me." I leaned against the hood of his car and he mirrored my position. "This isn't typical Moody Maverick, is it?"

He hated that nickname. I'd used it to get a reaction out of him, but he just kept chewing his lip as he twisted the hem of his shirt around his finger.

"No, it's not," he confirmed after a long silence. "I have something to tell you, and I don't want you trying to talk me out of it. Even without you there to hound me about it, I sat down and made my pros and cons lists, and it's a good thing."

"Maybe you should spit it out already so I can tell you if I agree." He glared at me and I held my hands up in surrender, backing away slightly. "Not that my opinion matters, but you know I'll tell you if I think you're being foolish."

"Yeah, I do know that." Finally, the corner of his mouth turned up slightly. When I resumed my position next to him, he rested his head on my shoulder. "So, you remember how I went out to surprise Sam last summer?"

"How could I forget?" I scoffed. That was one of those times when I'd told him he wasn't thinking things through. Who in their right mind flew across the country to surprise someone they'd never met? If it annoyed the shit out of me that this Sam dude knew more about Mav than I did, I kept that bitterness to myself. For as close as we were, there were some things he still didn't share with me and I respected him enough to not push. "I was surprised you didn't come back and tell me you were madly in love with him and running away to get married."

You know, sort of like you would with Ryan if he proposed. That little voice in the back of my head was a complete asshole sometimes.

I listened as Mav explained how free he felt when he was on the east coast. I knew it was hard for him, living in the shadow of his grandparents' reputation in town while trying to outrun the not-so-great memories of his parents. I think I knew what he was going to say, even before he quit rambling.

"I want that again, Tanner." He sounded like a little kid pleading for the hot toy at Christmas. There was a bone-deep longing that made me feel like an even bigger dick for not realizing he was wearing a mask, even around me. I thought he was happy enough most of the time, but the longing in his voice made me wonder how much of his suffering I had missed. "Not just for a weekend, but all the time. I want to wake up in the morning and not have to weigh what I want against what people will think. I want to be happy, and I don't think that's something I can find here."

Our situations might be different but hearing him talk about the life he wanted for himself, made me realize how I'd put my similar dreams on hold. Yes, I had reasons for it, but sometimes I wondered if they were excuses to avoid going after what I wanted.

"Where are you going to go?" I worried he *was* making a bad decision, even if for the right reasons, but realized I wasn't in a place to question other people's life choices. I was going to be the good friend and hear him out.

"Sam and his partner have offered me a spare room at their house, and he's going to help me line up a job once I'm out there," Mav explained. A pit formed in my stomach. One more person I needed in my life was running away to the other side of the country.

Fucking ducky.

Neither of them are running away. You're the one digging in your heels to stay somewhere you're not happy, that little voice chimed in. *You could follow them and let yourself be happy.*

We argued about whether this was a smart choice, and then Mav twisted that knife in my gut. "Besides, if you and Ryan stay together, chances are you'll be out that way eventually, too. So, I'm just ahead of the game."

There was no *if* to it—other than *if* Nana hadn't had a stroke, I would have already been gone. But Mav didn't know that because he'd been trying to give Ryan and me space to be together without worrying about him overhearing us, and by the time he came home, shit had turned sideways.

"And by jumping out of the nest now, maybe I won't be so codependent by the time you quit hiding at Nana's house," he continued.

"I'm not hiding," I argued. Except, I sort of was. As long as I was here taking care of her, I didn't have to make any decisions. Ryan wouldn't pressure me to leave her before she was ready, so I was able to enjoy his calls to make sure I was taking care of myself while letting my life stagnate like water in a pond.

"You are, but I think I understand it." Mav hugged me and I closed my eyes, realizing how much I missed the touch of anyone other than Nana. Her hugs were awesome, but they weren't the same. "At some point, you have to take a leap of faith, too. He's got roots out there now."

"And I have obligations here," I argued. "But we're not talking about me right now. I'm not sure about this, but I'm not going to be able to stop you. Where did you say they live again?"

"The name of the city is Annandale. You'd love it there." I stumbled, feeling like the world had just tipped upside down. I'd say there was no way this was a coincidence, but I knew it was. Mav kept rambling, but I didn't hear anything he said.

"You have *got* to be shitting me," I blurted out when my brain finally came back online.

"Uh, no. Why?" His brow furrowed, and I realized I probably sounded insane as I worked to stifle my amusement.

"It's definitely a small world." Nana poked her head out the door and asked if we planned on sitting in the cold all night. I pushed off the hood of the car and grabbed the box. "We're not done talking about this, but I feel better now."

Better was, of course, a relative term. I wasn't sure how I'd be able to stay here until Nana was cleared by the doctors, knowing that not only were Ryan and Mav on the same side of the country, but they were in the same fucking town.

21

RYAN

This is getting a bit excessive. I know you're loaded, but you're going to have to file for bankruptcy if you keep sending me things.

It wasn't exactly a thank you, but I'd gotten used to Tanner's worsening attitude over the past month and a half. He swore everything was fine, and every time he repeated that lie I added another mark on his discipline tally for when I finally caught a breath so I could fly out and drag his ass back here with me.

I'd tried being patient. When his mother volunteered him to take care of Nana, so she didn't have to go to an inpatient rehab facility, I kept my mouth shut. Even though it wasn't his choice, there was no way he would have been okay with Nana being miserable.

When he said he couldn't leave until the doctors fully cleared her, I agreed. He'd committed to being there for her, and I was proud of him for putting his own needs on the backburner temporarily, especially for someone who wouldn't be around forever. The two of them were close, and I knew it was going to be hard on him once he moved out here and couldn't see her every week.

But now, Nana was healthy and had kicked Tanner out of her house. It wasn't done maliciously, but Nana had always been fiercely independent. Other than the fact she had to rely on rides because she couldn't drive yet, she'd made a more complete recovery than anyone had expected.

And Tanner was still dragging his heels, swearing that she needed him to run her to the store and her appointments.

I knew that was a lie because Deegan confided in me that he'd tried offering to help out and Tanner had refused.

You're welcome, brat.

I waited for his response, watching the three little dots appear and disappear at the bottom of the screen.

Sorry, Daddy. It's been a day.

I started typing out a reminder that he knew how to fix whatever was wrong. Lately, he'd grown bored and restless. His job had stopped scheduling him when he was taking care of Nana, but that was no great hardship. The way I saw it, that was one less thing tying him to that town. And with Mav out of the apartment, Tanner had lost his party buddy. Again, not a huge issue since he hadn't been going out much, even before Nana's stroke.

I deleted my snarky response because that wasn't what my boy needed. He'd called me Daddy, and he only did that during scenes or when he was feeling especially vulnerable. I picked up the phone and pressed the call button.

Tanner picked up on the first ring. "You didn't have to call. I'm okay, promise."

The fuck if he was. I could almost picture him curled up on the couch, his favorite blanket tucked under his chin. "What's going on, baby? Talk to me."

"I hate it here," he admitted. Yep, definitely far from okay if he couldn't even pretend he wasn't miserable.

"Do you want me to come and get you?" I offered, already pulling up the travel site on my computer. Now that the club was open, I was between projects. I purposely hadn't started working on any other acquisitions because I wanted to have time to spend with my boy whenever he decided he was ready to commit to being with me one hundred percent. "I can send you a list of things to get ready and have a shipping pod delivered so we can pack everything up when I get there."

"Not yet." My heart fell at the same time I felt anger welling up in the pit of my stomach. It was ridiculous that he was pushing back on this. He'd said he wanted me to make the decisions, but if he wasn't ready, I couldn't force him to do anything he'd resent me for in the future. "I just want to make sure she's really okay, and then I'll be ready."

"Sweetheart, what's this really about?" I closed the lid of my laptop to keep from booking a ticket despite his objections. "The doctors released her and said she's as good as new."

"But what if she has another stroke and I'm not here?" He sniffled, and I wished I was there to pull him onto my lap and reassure him that wasn't going to happen. But I couldn't because there were no guarantees. "Or what if next time it's a heart attack or something else? Or what if she falls?"

"What if she's stubborn enough that she refuses to let anything bring her down and you're putting your life on hold for the worst-case scenario?" I pursed my lips, knowing what I was about to say could easily cause an epic meltdown. "Tanner, if your Nana heard you talking like this, she'd whip your hide. Do you think she'd be happy knowing you're refusing to live *your* life because you're waiting for something to happen to hers?"

"No," he mumbled, and I knew I was starting to get through to him.

"If something's going to happen, it's not going to make a bit of difference if you're here or there," I pointed out. My stomach flipped, hating the idea of anything happening to her almost as much as Tanner did. Nana was a grandmother to all of us, whether we were related to her or not. "*If* she has more health problems, I promise you we'll be on the first flight out to see her. I don't care how much it costs; I'll get you there as fast as I can. But I'll be there with you to make sure you're okay."

"I like the sound of that," he admitted.

Holy shit. That almost sounded like progress.

Neither of us spoke for over a minute. I closed my eyes, imagining that I could feel Tanner's soft exhales against my cheek. "Would you really send me a list if I said okay?"

"I will do whatever you need, if it means getting to wake up with you in my arms every day," I promised.

He grunted. "Anything?"

"You name it, and I'll do it," I confirmed.

"Can you find Mav? I haven't heard from him in a while and I'm worried about him." Okay, so that wasn't what I was expecting, but it *did* fall under the heading of anything. "I know he was seeing someone, but he was being cagey the last time I talked to him. I'm worried he might be in trouble."

"If I do, would you be willing to promise you'll come out here so you can keep an eye on him for yourself?" It was dirty as hell, but it just might work. He and Mav were attached at the hip from what Deegan said, and it made sense that Tanner's worsening mood directly correlated to how long it had been since he'd seen Mav.

"That's probably a good idea," he agreed. I wouldn't admit that it hurt to hear him change his mind when it was looking after a friend instead of being with me. He had a big heart, and as much as he needed me to take care of him, he was still motivated by looking after others. "So, you'll do it?"

"I'll try, but no promises." I didn't like keeping things from him, but I couldn't tell him I was pretty sure I already knew where to find Mav. It wasn't the most common name out there, and Jack had been raving lately about a new employee at the club. I justified not telling him by remembering that there was a chance it was a coincidence, and they weren't the same person. I didn't want to give him false hope any more than I wanted to lie to him.

Later that night, I headed to Club DeSires to look around a bit. On my way, I called Jack.

"Ryan, good to hear from you, man." He sounded so damn happy that I couldn't help but be jealous. He had his hands full, between the club and his boy, but he'd never sounded so full of life. *That* was what *I* wanted. And if I could get Tanner out here, I was certain we'd be seeing more of Jack and Slade. He and Slade weren't exactly the same, but enough they'd be fast friends. "To what do I owe the pleasure?"

"So, this is going to sound strange, but I'm hoping you can help me." I explained the situation with Mav ghosting Tanner. When I asked Jack to confirm if they were the same person, he was understandably reluctant. In this world, discretion was everything, and he didn't want to make a bad situation worse. Little did he realize, I was prepared to grovel. "Listen, I warned you it was strange, but I promise there's no bad blood between the two of them. They're both a bit lost on their own, and if this is the same Mav, I'm pretty sure he's not calling Tanner because he's worried that Tanner will tell him he's being impulsive and irrational."

"That's not the kid I know," Jack scoffed. "And if it is, I promise he's in good hands. I never pegged John as being into guys, but when you see the two of them together, there's no denying they fit. He'd kick the shit out of anyone who tries hurting Mav."

"Yeah, well you'd have to understand these two." I sighed heavily. Their relationship was a complicated one. It had been since they were kids, and I doubted Tanner would ever stop worrying about Mav. "They have a lot of history, and from everything you've told me, the Mav you're getting to know is a far cry from how he was back home. I just... If I can make sure he's okay and reassure Tanner, it'll go a long way toward making my home life a bit more peaceful."

"Speaking of, any update on getting him to move out here?" Leave it to Jack to ask the tough questions. The unforeseen benefit of investing in the club was he and I spent more time together than we used to. Even though I wasn't on-site every day, I was still involved behind the scenes.

Jack had become something of a sounding board for all of my frustration. I didn't want Tanner to know how much I struggled with the distance between us because that would influence if and when he moved closer to me. At the same time, it sucked knowing we'd been so close to him packing everything he owned to follow me out here, only to have life kick us down.

I grunted, still annoyed about the fact he sounded closer than I'd heard him since we'd originally talked about our living arrangements before Nana's stroke. And I knew it wasn't fair to assume it was Mav influencing his decision, but it sure as hell felt that way.

"Uh oh, trouble in paradise?"

"No, nothing like what you're assuming," I responded. "Just, earlier today, he promised he'd come out here if I make sure Mav is okay."

"And you're butthurt because it's not *you* he's rushing out here to be with," Jack guessed when I didn't fill in any other details. "Have you considered the fact, knowing both of you are out here is what made him change his mind? It's been a while since his grandma got sick, so the timing might be right and it's a happy coincidence."

"You could be right," I conceded. "But what if he gets out here and realizes he made a mistake?"

"What if he gets here and *you* realize things seemed more solid than they were? What if you're the one who feels like moving in so quickly was a bad move for your relationship?" Even though he couldn't see me, I flipped him off. Neither of those were going to happen. Yes, we hadn't spent much time together, and a lot of that was under less-than-ideal circumstances, but we'd loved one another longer than either of us realized. Failure wasn't an option. "You're going to hurt yourself if you bite down on that tongue any harder. My point here is, neither of you know for certain how things are going to work out once he's settled in and you're not just visiting. Living together is totally different. You're going to learn shit about him you'd rather not know. Are you ready for that?"

"I'd happily put up with his annoying habits if it meant having him here with me," I insisted. And I meant it. He couldn't be any more annoying now than he was as a teen, and that time hadn't changed how I felt about him.

"Then I suggest you pull your head out of your ass and book a flight to help your boy move out here."

Hell yes. That sounded like the best idea I'd heard all day. But first, I needed to lay eyes on Mav so I could reassure Tanner he was okay.

22

TANNER

I was self-aware enough to know I'd go insane sitting around my empty apartment while I waited for Ryan to call and let me know if he'd found Mav, so I picked up the phone to call in reinforcements. My promise to Ryan this morning meant I had a lot of work ahead of me.

When Mav moved, he only worried about his own shit because he figured I still needed furniture and everything else to survive on my own. I was even more annoyed that he'd moved out now, because it meant I had to clear the apartment so I could move. And the rusty Honda Mav had left so I'd have wheels, wasn't going to cut it.

Haley went above and beyond. She and Deegan arrived at the apartment a little over an hour later, arms heaped with boxes, old newspapers, tape, and markers.

"It's about time you quit stringing him along," Deegan grumbled as he dropped a stack of boxes in the middle of the living room.

"It's good to see you, too." Before, I would have assumed this was his passive-aggressive way of letting me know he still wasn't thrilled about me being with his best friend, but we'd spent enough time together that I knew he was just worried about both of us. "And I haven't been stringing him along. I would have happily flown home with him if it wasn't for Nana's stroke."

"You could have told Mom to shove it," he suggested, as if that was an option.

Sure, I could have, but she would have made everyone's life a living hell. "She wasn't wrong. I'm the one person in the family who could take the time off, and her paying the balance of the rent through the end of the lease made it worthwhile."

That was the reason I was able to leave with a moment's notice. I wouldn't have to worry about the management company giving me shit about moving out two months before the lease came up. She was going to lose her mind when she realized pressuring me into taking care of Nana made it easier to run off with Ryan.

"Either way, that doesn't make it okay for her to assume you didn't have a life of your own," Deegan argued. "You have to really stand up to her or she's never going to quit walking all over you. Trying to piss her off isn't the same as doing what's best for you."

"And you think that's moving in with Ryan?" It felt important to hear the words. I might not need my brother's seal of approval to change my life, but I *wanted* him to tell me I wasn't fucking up my life.

"God help me, but I do," he confirmed. Haley handed each of us a box, along with instructions to go through the apartment packing what I wanted to move and placing everything else in boxes to run to the thrift store later. Then, she disappeared into the bedroom, leaving us alone. "Listen, I'm not perfect. Once the rush of the wedding wore off, I *was* worried about the two of you getting together, but not for the reasons you might think. I was selfish, worrying about what would happen to me if the two of you had a shitty breakup."

"Good to know you were already preparing for the end when we were still trying to sort out the beginning." I pushed myself off the floor and grabbed a roll of garbage bags. There was some stuff that wasn't even in good enough shape to donate, and that was all getting shoved down the garbage chute. "And, for the record, I wouldn't have been pissed if you stayed friends with him. I might be a bitch sometimes, but I'm not that level of petty."

"I never said you were," he pointed out, cuffing the back of my head as he moved a box next to the front door. "You assume a whole lot of shit about me, and I probably deserve a lot of that. It sucks that you're going to be so far away because Ryan helped me see that I needed to make sure you knew that I don't look at you like the immature shit you used to be."

"I'm sorry. You're probably right." He was definitely right. I put up walls around my heart when my family disapproved of my choices when I first started exploring my identity, and I'd been unwilling to accept that they might change, too. Not Mom, of course. She was so set in her ways, she'd never accept me as I was, but Deegan and Dad were both way more chill than I gave them credit for. "But you can always come out to visit us. I might need my big brother to make sure I'm well taken care of."

"As if," Haley scoffed. "How is this all the further you two have gotten? Less talking and more working. The sooner we get done here, the sooner we can head back to our place for dinner. The bed's stripped and the dresser is emptied, so the two of you can load those into the truck. Tanner, I love you, but not nearly enough to touch your nightstand. There are some things I really don't want to know about my husband's baby brother's sex life."

"Oh please, there was a time when you wanted all the gory details." She threw a towel at me. "You know I'm right."

"Yeah, but that was before I was part of the family. Now that's like hearing about my brother's sex life, and that's just gross," she argued.

"If you're getting rid of my furniture today, where in the hell am I supposed to sleep?" I wasn't stupid. I knew this was Haley's way of making sure there was no way for me to back out. And maybe that was part of why she was the first person I called to help me empty out the apartment. By the time we were done today, the apartment would be ready for someone else to move into.

"You can stay in our guest room until we sort out flying you out to Ryan," Deegan offered. "It was Haley's idea, but I'm a smart enough man to go along with a good idea when my wife speaks."

"You're so whipped," I teased.

Deegan nodded. His eyes when all fuzzy and soft when he smiled at his wife. "Yeah, I am. But when you're in love, you realize that's not a bad thing."

No, it definitely wasn't. I was secretly jealous of him.

IT WAS NEARLY midnight before we had everything packed up and the apartment cleaned. I let Deegan and Haley hold me upright as I looked at the barren apartment one last time. While Deegan and I had taken the donation stuff to the thrift store, Haley went to town cleaning. There was no reason for me to come back here.

"This is a good thing," Deegan reminded me as I wiped a tear from my cheek. It was stupid to cry about leaving this dump, but it had been home. It was a symbol of my independence from the family I thought hated me.

But Deegan was right; it was time for me to move on. The future held so much more for me than this place ever could.

"Yeah, it is," I agreed. "Just not good with change, I guess."

"Yeah, you never have been." Haley kissed me cheek. "That's why you need Ryan so much. I have no doubt he's going to shove you out of your comfort zone."

If they only knew how much he already had. No one but him could get me to explore my interest in having someone to call Daddy. It was hot in porn, but the reality was beyond my wildest dreams. It wasn't even about the sex, although there was no comparing Ryan to anyone from my past. I couldn't wait to get to Annandale to find out what erotic scenarios he could dream up when we didn't have to wait on shipping and our schedules to line up perfectly.

It was nearly two in the morning when my phone rang. Deegan rolled his eyes as I excused myself and ducked into the guest room.

"Hey, Daddy," I greeted him when I answered the phone.

"Wow, you sound wide awake." I swallowed hard, wondering if I was going to be in trouble for staying up past the bedtime he'd set. He had to know it would be impossible for me to sleep when I was worried, and when I told him what I'd gotten done today, he'd forget all about how late it was. "Were you waiting up just for me?"

"Is it bad if I say no?" It sounded much sweeter if I *was* up all night waiting for the phone to ring but, honestly, Deegan had gotten my mind off what had me stressed before.

Ryan chuckled. "No, sweetheart, that's fine. You're in a much better mood than you were this morning. Want to tell me what that's all about?"

"I spent the day with Deegan," I admitted. It wasn't the whole truth, but it was enough for now. "Did you find Mav for me?"

"I did," Ryan confirmed. "And he promised he'll call you, but it's probably not going to be tonight."

There was a slight hesitation that had my spidey senses tingling. "Is he okay? Why can't he call me tonight?"

"Listen to me, Tanner." Oooh, he used his Daddy voice. My dick perked up, knowing that if he was here I'd be close to getting a spanking. "Mav isn't in any trouble, but that's all I'm going to say. He'll tell you as much or as little as he wants when he calls, but that's up to him."

"Can't you give me a hint?" I whined. Now I really wasn't going to sleep tonight.

"No, and you're not going to pressure him," Ryan insisted. "Just think about how you'd feel if people started trying to get you to talk about being my dirty boy when you weren't ready to open up about it. That wouldn't make you feel good, would it?"

"I guess not," I grumbled. And I supposed it didn't much matter as long as Mav was okay. For now. But once I was out there, it wasn't going to be so easy for him to hide from me. Which reminded me... "So, when you wanted me to promise I'd move out there if you found Mav for me, did you mean it?"

"Of course, why wouldn't I?"

So yeah, stupid question, but now that I didn't have the safety net of my apartment under me, I was second-guessing myself. Again. And that's why I needed Daddy to take care of the hard decisions for me. "I don't know, but I wanted to make sure."

"If you're not ready yet, you don't have to move. I didn't put a timeframe on things when I asked you," he reassured me. "It's enough to know you'll eventually be here next to me and I can quit having a relationship with my phone."

I laughed, imagining Ryan cuddling with his phone at night. I would definitely make a better snuggle buddy for him. "And what about if I'm ready right now? Would you help me get a flight to Virginia so I can prove how much I appreciate everything you've done for me? I know that sounds greedy as fuck, but if I have to get my own ticket, it's going to take me a bit—"

"Stop right there, sweetheart," Ryan interrupted. "Are you serious? Because I'm pulling up the airline as we speak to buy myself a ticket to help you pack the apartment. I don't want to make you feel bad, but you're not going to need most of it when you get here."

"Yeah, we sort of figured." This time, it was my turn to cut him off. "That's why Deegan and Haley came over today, armed with boxes and tape. The only reason I'll be going back to my apartment is to stop by the leasing office to drop off my keys and do the walk-through."

"Seriously?" I could almost picture him with his mouth gaping open. "Where are you staying now?"

"With them. Haley figured this way Deegan and I can hang out and make up for the years I was being a total shithead to him." She'd never say it that way, but I was pretty sure it was what she meant. "And when you get here, the four of us can spend a bit of time together unless you have to get home right away."

"When did you think you'd be ready to fly out?" I could hear him tapping at the keyboard. "I can fly out first thing tomorrow and we can be back by Friday."

My heart started racing and it was hard to swallow around the lump in my throat. Friday sounded so soon. Even if my mom was a total ass and would never believe I had Ryan's best interests at heart as much as he did mine, I didn't want to sneak away without saying goodbye. That would give her ammunition to claim I knew I was making a bad decision.

And Nana would be crushed if she didn't get the chance see us off.

Like it or not, I wasn't getting out of Oregon without a going away party of sorts. Haley was going to kick my ass, but I needed it to be on my turf to keep Mom in her place. And at least for a few days, their house was the only place I had to call mine.

"Flying out tomorrow sounds good, but do you think it would be okay to stay a few extra days? I'll see if Haley is up for having the family over for a cookout this weekend, and we can break the news to them then," I explained.

"That sounds like a very responsible decision," Ryan praised me. "I love you, and I'm so fucking proud of how you're taking charge of your life."

"I couldn't do it without you," I told him. It was the truth; if not for him pushing me to quit living a life of boring familiarity, I wouldn't be doing any of this. When I wasn't thinking of all the ways I could implode my relationship, I was excited to see what lay in store.

Mav painted a picture of a town that was so accepting, their mascot might as well be a unicorn with a rainbow mane and tail. It probably wasn't as much of a gay utopia as he acted like it was but being able to walk down the street in Ryan's arms without anyone saying a fucking thing would be an improvement.

"You could, but I'm glad you'll never have to." My heart melted at his sentiment. "Now, before you talk to Mav, there's something I feel like I need to explain to you."

I flopped onto the bed when the room started to spin around me. No way would Ryan be breaking my heart when we were so close to being together again, but explanations weren't required for good news. My chest felt tight, and I couldn't catch my breath.

"Tanner, I need you to listen to me," Ryan said, his voice low and words measured. "Breathe for me, baby. Imagine me there with you. You're sitting in my lap with my arms holding you tight."

"Will you rub my back?" It was a ridiculous request, but it actually was helping me feel better.

"Anything you need," he promised me. "I'm sorry if I said something wrong. This isn't bad, I don't think. And you already know some of it. It's about the club."

"Okay, I trust you, Daddy." I rolled to my side and hugged the pillow against my chest. I closed my eyes and listened as Daddy talked me through my anxiety. Slowly, I felt my muscles beginning to relax. "I'm better now. You can tell me."

"You remember when I told you how the club has an area for Daddies and their boys?" I nodded, then remembered we weren't on video. He continued as if he knew I'd answered him. "Well, there's more to it than that. The new part of the club is for all types of kinks. There are different themed rooms where couples can explore desires they might not be able to at home. Some of them are more intense than others."

"And that's where you found Mav tonight?" I guessed. I knew better than to ask him for any details, but this seemed safe enough.

"Yeah, it is," Daddy confirmed. "But there's more to it. His friend, Sam, is the manager of the other side of the club. That's actually where most of the Daddies hang out."

"Is that where you want to be with me?" My mind was overflowing with questions, but it felt safest to keep him talking instead of jumping to any conclusions. "Would you be okay if I wanted to see the other side, too? Is that even allowed?"

"We can do whatever you'd like," he promised. "Honestly, I think you're going to push my limits once you get used to everyone. There's even an area where we can play with the illusion of being in public."

"Dadddddy," I whined as I slipped a hand under the waistband of my shorts. I curled my hand around my shaft but didn't start jerking off. I couldn't do that without permission. "You can't talk to me like that. My brother is right down the hall."

"Then I guess you'll need to be quiet. Do you want me to tell you what I'm going to do to you if you agree?"

"Can we switch to video so I can see you?" Phone sex was fun, but not nearly as entertaining as when I could see Daddy's face as he came.

"Not tonight, sweet boy. We shouldn't be doing this at all," he argued. "I wanted us to have a very serious talk so there aren't any surprises when I take you to the club for the first time."

"No surprises," I repeated. "Got it. I already knew you were a kinky bastard, so it's not weird that you invested in a kink club. Does that mean we have a free membership there?"

I sure as hell hoped so. We'd barely scratched the surface of the kinky shit I got sucked into on the porn sites. There were things I already knew were better left in the realm of fantasy, but there was a whole fucking lot I wanted to try out.

Ryan laughed. "Yes, baby. We can go any time there's a members-only night. What do you want to do first?"

"I don't know. Maybe you'd better choose since I've never even seen the place," I suggested. Having Daddy play with me where others could watch was something I wanted, but also something I needed to work my way up to.

By the time my battery beeped, alerting me that it was about to die, Daddy had helped me come twice before warning me I wasn't allowed to touch myself again until I picked him up from the airport tomorrow.

Tomorrow. That meant tonight was the last night I'd have to fall asleep alone.

23

TANNER

I felt like I'd just fallen asleep when the ringing of my damn phone woke me up. Figuring it was Ryan calling to tell me what time his flight would land, I answered without checking the caller ID. "'Lo?"

The other end of the line was silent, other than the ragged breathing of the asshole who thought it was cool to call at an unreasonably shitty hour. And, of course, it wasn't anyone in my contacts list because they would have remembered you don't call me before ten in the morning unless your name is Ryan or someone's bleeding out.

"Dude, I don't know who in the fuck you are, but you've got three seconds to say something before I turn off the damn phone," I warned them. That was new; usually I would have hung up and turned the phone to silent.

"Hey Tanner, it's me." My eyes shot open at the sound of Mav's voice. "Sorry, I forgot about the time difference. John told me I needed to call you before doing anything else today."

"Who in the hell is John?" That was the sort of detail a so-called best friend should know. But at least this time it was because he'd been keeping shit from me and not because I was so caught up in my own relationship that I'd ignored him.

"He's... Okay, so I'm just going to say it. And you can ask questions if you want but if you'd rather call back after you're more awake, that's cool too," he rambled. I sat up, leaning against the headboard and turned on the nightstand light. He was fucking hilarious if he thought I was getting back to sleep at this point.

"Spit it out, Mav." I thumped my head against the headboard a couple of times. "Would it make it easier if I promise I'm not mad at you? Whatever it is you have to tell me, I'm just glad you're safe. And I'm sorry for asking Ryan to track you down."

"Yeah, well the timing on that could have been better," he mumbled. Both of them were being cryptic as fuck about what happened at the club last night.

Which room did Ryan find Mav in? What secrets was he keeping from me?

"I'm sure you'll laugh about it someday." At least, I hoped we all would, if Mav felt like he could tell me what he was into.

"Yeah. Maybe." He didn't sound convinced. "But anyway, I'm not upset you asked Ryan to make sure I was okay. I think I needed the reminder that there's a life outside of being Daddy's princess."

He gasped when he realized what he'd blurted out. My mouth fell open, but I was more surprised that he'd said it so easily than I was hearing that we had one more thing in common. It reassured me to hear that John called Mav his princess. That meant Mav had accomplished what he wanted out of moving: he was able to embrace his femininity without being judged or lectured about it.

"I'm happy for you, Mav," I reassured him. "I can't wait to meet your Daddy. He'd better be good to you."

"He's the best. You should have heard him last night, Mav. He was this big grizzly bear until he believed Ryan wasn't a threat to me or to our relationship," he explained. He was more animated now, and part of me wished we'd waited to have this talk until I was out there so I could see the excitement on his face. "And when we got home, he got into it with his brother. I love him, Tanner."

I cackled, then pressed a hand over my mouth when I remembered my brother and Haley were probably still asleep. If Deegan woke up, he'd get it. I'm not sure any of us thought Mav would ever settle down. "Sorry. That was rude. I'm so happy for you, Mav."

"Yeah, I know. Not something you expected me to say, but it's the truth. I think I just needed to find someone who really understands me and isn't trying to put me into the box they think I fit in," he explained. I didn't know this John dude yet, but I already liked him. "He goes out of his way to make sure he respects however I'm feeling, and the man has a serious shopping addiction."

"I think that might be a Daddy thing," I mused. "Ryan does the same."

"Believe me, I'm well aware." It felt like he'd been gone a hell of a lot longer than a couple of months. Maybe it was the lack of caffeine that made me forget that he used to be there, teasing me every time another package arrived from Ryan. "So, not to change the subject, but when are you going to get your ass out here? If you didn't already have enough proof that Ryan loves you, last night should seal the deal. I can't think of many boyfriends who'd hunt down their guy's friend in the back of a kink club and act like nothing weird was going on."

I debated turning the attention away from me because now I *really* wanted to know what was going on when Ryan found him. But I wasn't the only one who deserved answers. "Actually, Ryan's flying out this morning, and we'll be back there by next week. I'm heading down to turn in the keys and do a walk-through later today."

"You're shitting me! That's awesome." I listened as Mav rambled about all the people he wanted me to meet. If he had his way, I wasn't going to be moving to a place where I only knew him and Ryan. I had a ready-made group of friends waiting for me. And because they were all in the lifestyle, I didn't have to worry about what they'd think of Ryan being Daddy sometimes.

"I'll talk to Ryan to see if we can have you and John over for dinner once I get there," I offered. No way was I going to wait until I was settled to meet the man who'd turned the commitmentphobe into a hopeless romantic who couldn't help but gush about the love of his life.

"That would be cool. I'd like John to spend some time with Ryan outside of the club. Last night was…intense, and the testosterone and posturing was stifling," he admitted.

"Want to tell me about that?" He left the door wide open, and the curiosity was killing me.

Mav made a strange little squeaking noise. "Would it be okay if we waited on that until you're here? I promise, I'll tell you whatever you want to know, but this feels like a conversation that would be better face to face."

Gee, that wasn't unsettling or anything. I swear, if I got to Annandale and found out Mav was putting himself in dangerous positions for the sake of getting off, I was going to kick his ass. I didn't care how much he loved and trusted John.

And *that* was probably why Ryan made me promise I wouldn't pressure Mav into talking before he was ready. Damn him for knowing me so well. But I wanted him to be proud of me, so I wasn't going to complain about waiting. "Yeah, but while they get to know one another, the two of us are going to have a long ass talk. You fucking scared me, Mav."

"I really am sorry about that," he apologized again. "I got caught up in everything here. Being with someone like me isn't easy, and it's even more complicated for John. Again, that's a story for once you're here, so you can get to know him and not judge him, but I think it was easy for me to try and make his life easier. But that's no excuse for not checking in with you like I promised I would."

"No, it's not," I agreed. There were footsteps and low voices in the hall, signaling that Deegan and Haley were awake. That meant it was time for me to break it to them that we were hosting a family cook out here this weekend. "I hate to cut this short, but I need to talk to Haley. I might have offered up their place for family dinner this weekend so I can tell the family I'm moving and there's nothing they can do about it."

"Damn, I'd almost love to be a fly on the wall when that happens. Do you think Ryan would record the moment so I can watch your mom's head explode when she realizes it's going to be even harder for her to control you?" I laughed because that was such a typical Mav request. "Ugh, you're not going to, are you?"

"I would, but I think we'd better at least try to keep the peace." With any luck, Dad would keep her under control. Since Nana's stroke, he'd been busting his ass to make up for all the shit he'd let her put me through. He seemed truly remorseful, and I was seeing him in a new light. It made me wonder what he was like before he got together with her. "I'll call you once I know our plans for flying back."

"You'd fucking better. Man, I didn't realize how much I missed you until this morning."

"Way to make a guy feel special," I quipped, even though I understood what he was saying. If I'd been the one to move out there, we might have had the same lapse in communication. I needed to remember that and go easy on him. "See you next week, Mav. And, at the very least, I expect you to send me a picture of you with this new Daddy of yours."

"Done." Seconds later, my phone chimed with an incoming text. "Don't open it until we hang up, otherwise you're going to have even more questions and it sounds like you've got shit to do."

"Fine." That didn't mean I wouldn't text him my reaction as soon as I opened the picture. "Talk soon."

After we hung up, I grabbed the first outfit out of the suitcase Haley had packed for me. If I had to be up this early, there needed to be copious amounts of coffee. And I had to let Deegan and Haley know everything that had transpired since last night when I'd bailed on them.

24

RYAN

It was hard to believe this was the last time I'd fly home from Oregon without my boy next to me. Everything had changed so much since the end of last year, I sometimes had to pinch myself to remember it wasn't all a dream. The distance between us made it that much harder to accept that Tanner was really mine.

Sitting on Deegan's back deck with a beer in hand and Tanner sleeping on my lap was more than I'd ever dreamed I could have. I'd convinced myself from the first time I looked at Tanner as something other than my buddy's little brother, that Deegan would kick my ass if he so much as caught me looking at him the wrong way. But that wasn't the case. From time to time, I noticed Deegan watching us and smiling, and that silent acceptance meant the world to me.

"He feels safe with you," Deegan observed. "I don't think I've ever seen him that still before. Even when he's asleep, he's usually all over the place."

Funny, other than a couple of nights when Tanner was stressed out, I'd never had that experience. Yes, he was like an octopus wrapping his limbs around my body and holding on for dear life, but once he was comfortable, he stayed like that. It settled me to hear Deegan speak highly of the effect I had on Tanner. "He's been carrying a load of worry that wasn't his to bear for a long time. Maybe he finally trusts that he's not alone."

"I fucking hate that I didn't stick up for him sooner. I'm lucky he's giving me another shot." If it wouldn't have jostled Tanner, I would have smacked Deegan upside the head.

Yes, he'd been an ass for a lot of years, but he was trying to do better now. And really, it wasn't completely his fault. He'd basically been groomed from a young age to be their mom's golden boy, and if there was one thing I knew about the Fincham boys, it was that they were both people pleasers. He went along with what Lillian expected because it was the easiest way to gain her approval.

"He's got a heart of gold, man. After the way you stood up for him at the hospital, he understands that you're not the jerk he thought you were," I assured him. "It sucks that the two of you are just starting to get along and now I'm taking him away."

"I don't see it like that at all," Deegan argued. "You're giving him freedom. He'd never have that here. No matter how much he tries saying he doesn't give a shit what any of us think of him, there's something deep down that keeps trying to gain Mom's approval. With you, he won't be under her thumb. And it's not like you're getting away from us. I fully expect there to be a guest room ready when we come out to visit."

"You're welcome anytime." The alarm went off on my phone and I gently shook Tanner awake. The family would start arriving soon, and it wouldn't start the night on a good note if he was still napping. "Hey sleepyhead, it's time to get up."

Tanner tightened his arms around my torso and buried his face in the crook of my neck. He shook his head and grumbled. "Don't wanna. Comfy here."

Deegan laughed and excused himself, saying he needed to fire up the grill and check on Haley. She was the real hero of the weekend. She hadn't complained when Tanner asked if it was okay to invite the family over for dinner, and she'd insisted on doing all the food prep so he and I could make up for lost time. The eyebrow lift that followed that offer, suggested she thought there was going to be far more sex than there had been.

Yes, my boy had an exhibitionist streak in him, but he was oddly shy when it came to anyone he knew overhearing him begging me to let him come. Lucky for both of us, I knew this now, and I'd come armed with a gag. There was no way in hell I was going to be able to wait until we were home to sink deep into his body.

Home. Fuck, that felt good to think about. My house had always seemed big and lonely, like it was just waiting for someone to come along and share it with me. No, not someone: Tanner. It had always been Tanner.

I gave my boy five more minutes of dozing as I closed my eyes and savored the weight of his body on top of mine. This felt like another new beginning for us. I'd promised he was mine and that I wasn't letting him go, and tonight, he'd know how serious I was about that intention.

"Hey guys, I hate to bug you, but Pat is on his way over with Nana," Haley called out from the kitchen. It was still weird hearing everyone talk about Pat and Lillian as anything other than a unit. Since Nana had kicked Tanner out of the house, telling him it was time for him to get on with his own life, his dad had stepped in to help out with Nana more frequently. Lillian had to love the hell out of that.

"Is Lillian coming tonight?" Again, strange thing to ask, but it wasn't my business to pry into their lives. I was proud of Pat for finally standing up to his wife and forging a relationship with their son, despite her criticism.

"Of course," Haley grumbled, flopping into the chair next to me and stealing what was left of my beer. "But I swear, if she tries saying one fucking thing about Tanner, I have no problem kicking her ass out. This isn't her house, and I'm not going to put up with her cutting him down anymore. I should have said more before..."

"But you were trying to make a good impression on your future mother-in-law," I finished the sentence so she didn't have to come up with what she would think was a shitty excuse. Was it fair to someone she claimed was one of her closest friends? Nope. But I understood. Again, this was a group of people pleasers, and they'd always do what made others happy, even if they were miserable. I squeezed Haley's hand. "Having your support now is all that matters. He'd have been pissed if you tried standing up for him before because he thought it was his battle to fight."

"Logically, I know you're right, but that doesn't make me feel any better." She tipped back the beer and drained the bottle. I was surprised she wasn't switching to the hard stuff to help her get through the night with the monster-in-law. While we'd been hanging out this week, she'd complained about how Lillian was already hounding her about having kids because *someone* needed to carry on the family name, and it obviously wasn't going to be Tanner. The thing was, Haley and Deegan were united in not wanting kids right away, if ever. But no one had shared that bombshell so far. "You do realize there's still time for you to make a clean break, right? It's too late for me, but you don't have to be stuck with this bunch."

"That's a lie," Tanner mumbled, sitting up and rubbing his eyes. "He's stuck. I'm not letting him go."

"It's not stuck if I'm exactly where I want to be," I pointed out as I combed my fingers through his outgrown hair.

Haley responded by making gagging noises. Tanner flipped her off and she threw a hand towel at him. "God, I was never that lovesick over Deegan. Maybe we're doing things wrong."

"Nah, you just didn't have the right parts to fall in love with the better Fincham brother," Tanner quipped. "I still don't know what you see in him, but I'm happy you were silly enough to marry him."

The front door opened, and Nana's voice echoed through the house. I couldn't help but smile because it was good to see how she'd recovered since the hospital. Tanner jumped off my lap and rushed into the house to meet her. Haley pulled another chair over, this one a solid folding chair rather than part of the outdoor furniture set. It was cute to see how they all jumped into action when the real matriarch of the family appeared.

"Nana, it's good to see you." Okay, so *they* included me. I held out a hand, steadying her as she cautiously took the two steps down to the deck. I bent down and kissed her cheek, then recoiled when she scowled at me.

"What's this I hear you're taking my boy to the other side of the world?" Her lips remained pressed in a tight line as I escorted her to her seat.

"I am, Nana. I would apologize about that, but I can't move back here," I explained.

Something shifted in her expression, and there was a glint in her eyes before she threw her head back and laughed. She patted my cheek. "You're too easy, Ryan. You always were. I'm happy for you. It's about damn time you make an honest man out of him."

My eyes widened, wondering whether Deegan or Haley had spilled the beans to her. It was supposed to be a surprise. "I'll always do my best by him."

"I know you will." She was winded by the time she sat down, but that likely had to do more with trying to walk and talk at the same time rather than failing health. She nodded at the chair next to her and I sat. "Everyone knows he's always been special to me. If I didn't think you were capable of treating him like the treasure he is, I wouldn't have kicked him out of the house. Deep down, he wants to take care of people. Don't let him get so wrapped up in making you happy that he forgets his own needs."

"Never." She wasn't telling me anything I didn't already know, and I was looking forward to helping him find a way to balance what he thought he was supposed to do and what he truly *wanted*.

"Good boy." While Tanner changed and freshened up after his shower, Nana and I talked a bit about her recovery, including the fact she was considering giving up the house. There was no way she'd shared that with Tanner. If she had, he'd have lost his mind. To him, that was home more than the house where he was raised. His grandparents' place had always been his sanctuary.

Nana smiled when Tanner joined us and settled on my lap. I hugged him tight, grateful that he was comfortable enough to stick close to my side.

He stiffened when his mother arrived. When she noticed us, her nose turned up and she visibly shivered. God, she was a frigid bitch sometimes, and time only seemed to make her caustic personality worse. I patted Tanner's thigh. It was time for her to realize she wasn't going to treat him like shit on the bottom of her shoe anymore.

I stood and whistled to get everyone's attention. Tanner's eyes were practically bulging out of his head. *What are you doing?* he mouthed. I held out my hand, drawing him closer to me. "Thank you, everyone, for being here tonight, and thank you to Haley and Deegan for hosting this family dinner for us."

"Anything for you," Deegan called out from the grill. Our eyes met, and he gave me a quick nod.

"Thanks, brother," I responded. We'd called each other brothers for a long time, and now, we would be as long as

Tanner gave me the answer I wanted. I turned to face the man who'd captured my heart when he was still a boy. "Tanner, the past few months have been a wild ride. I'm pretty sure Deegan never expected this when he asked me to drive you to the resort for their wedding, but I owe him for that request. If things had happened differently, we might not have had the chance to clear the air. And I might not have realized how much I've always loved you."

Tanner swallowed hard. He swayed slightly, warning me that he was holding his breath. I slipped an arm around his back to steady him, leaning in to whisper, "Breathe, sweetheart. You have a bad habit of forgetting to do that sometimes."

That got the response I was hoping for and Tanner chuckled. "What in the hell are you doing?"

Instead of answering him, I kissed his cheek. I turned, trying to find Pat. He was keeping his distance from Lillian, who was perched on one of the rattan chairs as if it was her damn throne. And her face was still puckered like she'd sucked on a bag of lemons. Part of me wished she hadn't come, just so I didn't have to worry about her shitting on what I hoped would be a memorable day. Seeing that everyone was accounted for, I turned my attention back to Tanner.

"I know we haven't been together long, but it feels like our entire lives have been leading to this moment. When I look around my house—*our* house—I realize that you're the piece that's kept it from feeling like home to me." My hand shook as I reached into my pocket. "I know I promised I wasn't going to rush you into anything you're not ready for, and I still mean that. There's no deadline, but I want you to know that you're it for me. Until now, you've been the man

I've measured all others up to and they've fallen short. For the rest of my life, I want you to be the only man. Tanner Patrick Fincham, taking you home with me is only the first step in the rest of our lives. Will you take the next step and marry me?"

"Holy shit! Are you kidding me?" Tanner exclaimed as he leapt into my arms. I stumbled backward but caught myself before we tripped over Nana's walker. "Yes, I'll marry you."

Not giving a damn who was watching us, I cradled the back of his neck and pressed my lips to his. Tanner's lips parted, inviting me to deepen the kiss. I spun him around, the platinum band I'd purchased as soon as I flew home from my last visit fisted in the hand supporting his ass.

"You seriously want to get married?" Tanner asked, leaning back when we broke the kiss. I nodded. "This has to be a dream. No way are you really mine *and* want to spend the rest of your life with me."

"Don't try to talk him out of it, you idiot," Deegan hollered from the other side of the deck. He yelped when Pat smacked him. "I'm just saying, if he gives Ryan too much time to think about it, he might change his mind."

"Not a chance in hell," I promised, staring into Tanner's eyes. "There's nothing that could push me away from you, Tanner. I'm so fucking proud to call you my boy."

"And I'll spend the rest of my life knowing that you're my Daddy," Tanner whispered. "Do you think we can move up our flight? I want to get home so you can show me what the next step is going to be."

"Patience, baby," I urged him. "Let's enjoy the rest of the evening with your family. I have the rest of my life with you, but I'm also taking you away from them."

"That's where you're wrong," Tanner argued. "You gave them back to me. You didn't let me make a fool of myself at the wedding, and you taught me the difference between living my own life and trying to shock and offend those I thought didn't accept me. It's because of you that everyone is here tonight."

I looked around, noticing that Lillian was mysteriously absent. That hurt but, at the same time, I was grateful she'd excused herself rather than causing a scene. If she couldn't accept that her youngest was just as deserving of love as her golden boy, that was a failing on her part.

I set Tanner on the ground and crouched in front of Nana. "Did I do a good job?"

She patted my cheek. "It took the two of you long enough to get your heads out of your asses."

Haley choked on her water, and Pat stifled his amusement behind a cough. Now that Lillian wasn't here, it seemed everyone was able to let their guard down.

"I'm not sure I would have put it quite like that, but she's right, son." Pat draped an arm over my shoulders and the other over Tanner's. "We're not as blind as you might think. There were times I've wondered about the two of you, but you always swore you were straight, so I convinced myself it was wishful thinking. Tanner's always thought the world of you, and you were exactly the sort of man I hoped he'd someday find. You've been a part of the family for a long time, but congrats on making it official."

"Thank you, sir." I swallowed hard, trying to keep my emotions in check.

Pat noticed Tanner's quickly deteriorating mood at the same time I did. As I pulled my boy into a tight hug, Pat said, "Don't let her ruin your day. It's hard for her to let go when it comes to you. That's not excusing her behavior, only explaining it so you'll understand. She's trying, but it's going to be a long road for her to work through her issues. She'll come around."

"I hope so, Dad. But you're right, her issues are hers to work through. I'm done sacrificing my own happiness for her." If it wouldn't have been highly inappropriate, I would have shouted for joy at the certainty of his words. *Finally,* Tanner realized he couldn't gauge his worth on her appraisal of him. "I'm only sorry that we're leaving right when I realized you're a pretty awesome dad."

"Well, then we'll have to arrange a time to come and visit," he suggested. I appreciated that he wasn't assuming we'd be the ones coming to them all the time. "And from the sounds of it, there will be plenty of work to do arranging the wedding. Whatever the two of you need, you just let me know."

"Thank you, sir, but I've got everything under control," I told him. When we got married, I would be the one footing the bill for everything. I didn't want anyone else thinking they got a say in my boy's dream wedding. And, thanks to Haley, I already had a jumpstart on the plans. "The only thing we'll need is to know you'll be there."

"You give me the date and location, and I'll move heaven and earth to make sure his Nana and I are both there," Pat promised.

Tanner cleared his throat. When I turned to him, his gaze was fixed on my hand.

"Did you want something," I teased. He narrowed his eyes. I leaned in, whispering so only he could hear, "Remember, just because you'll be my husband doesn't mean I'm not still in charge. Do you remember what happens to boys who get greedy and demanding?"

Tanner groaned, sagging against my body, straddling my thigh so I could feel his arousal.

"Not greedy, Daddy," he insisted. "Just excited. Can I at least see it?"

"See what?"

"The ring." He tried prying my fingers loose. "I know you have one in there."

"Oh, I suppose I did forget that." This time, I dropped to one knee, holding out the ring as I proposed all over again. "Tanner, will you accept this ring as a token of my love for you?"

His hand shook as I slipped the ring onto his finger. "I don't need anything tangible to prove you love me. You already show me that every day."

"And I'll keep doing so as long as we live."

Working at DeSires has given Danny a way to serve others without having to put his heart on the line again. Pick up Surrendering Desire to see what happens when Blake's determined to show break down his walls.

If Tanner and Ryan were your introduction to Club DeSires, Start Reading Dressed in Desire to see how Mav found the perfect Daddy for himself in Annandale.

Nothing could derail his season like being forced to spend time with the only man he'd allowed close enough to hurt him...

Read Down by Contact to see the sparks fly when Zach and Griffin come together for a common goal.

WANT MORE OF ANNANDALE?

The fictional town of Annandale currently has four running series. While there is overlap between the different settings, the books can be read in any order!

Marino's - Mama was definitely shocked to learn all of her sons were kinky in one way or another, but she's proud of the men who are running the family restaurant.

Club 83 - Eli's worked hard to build a welcoming bar for the LGBTQ+ community. These daddies and boys will work their way into your kinky little heart.

The Lodge - As Jayden so astutely pointed out, The Lodge is like a mullet: it's innocent (enough) in the front, but the party is most definitely in the rear. So far, we've only seen the sweeter side, but there will definitely be a trip to The Back Deck in the future.

Talbert Hall - Take a trip to the first book set in the kinkiest residence hall on campus. It's a known fact that those who thrive in Talbert don't fit in well other places.

Want More of Annandale?

Club DeSires - Where The Lodge is vanilla-friendly and designed to appeal to those who are curious about the lifestyle as well as the Littles, Club DeSires is for those who aren't scared of heavier kinks. While you'll still get the Daddies you love, you'll also get to meet some hardass Does who want nothing more than to see their boys cry. But only in the best ways...

A NOTE FROM QUINN

If you enjoyed *Understanding Desire*, I would love it if you let your friends know so they can experience the relationship of Tanner and Ryan as well! As with all of my books, I have enabled lending on all platforms in which it is allowed to make it easy to share with a friend. If you leave a review for *Understanding Desire* on the site from which you purchased the book, Goodreads or your own blog, I would love to read it! Email me the link at **quinn@quinnwardwrites.com**

You can stay up-to-date on upcoming releases and sales by joining my newsletter or readers' group.
Sign up for Quinn's newsletter to claim your free bonus scene!
Quinn-tessential Readers on Facebook

ABOUT QUINN WARD

Quinn Ward is a zamboni-driving, hockey-loving parent of two kids who are pretty okay most of the time.

When Quinn was three, their parents received a call from the principal asking them to pick them up from school. Apparently, if you aren't enrolled, you can't attend classes, even in Kindergarten. The next week, they were in preschool and started plotting their first story soon after.

Later in life, their parents needed to do something to help the socially awkward, uncoordinated child come out of their shell and figured there was no better place than a bar on Wednesday nights. It's a good thing they did because this is where Quinn found their love of reading and writing. Who needs socialization when you can sit alone in your bedroom with a good book?

Quinn's been kicked out of the PTA in three school districts and is no longer asked to help with fundraisers because they've been known get lost in a good book and forget they have somewhere to be.

Made in the USA
Coppell, TX
15 June 2021